UNSPOKEN VOW

STEELE BROTHERS BOOK TWO

EDEN FINLEY

UNSPOKEN VOW

Copyright © 2019 by Eden Finley

Cover Illustration Copyright © AngstyG
http://www.angstyg.com

Development edit by Susie Selva
Beta read by Leslie Copeland & Jill Wexler
LesCourt Author Services
https://www.lescourtauthorservices.com/
Email: lcopelandwrites@gmail.com

Copy-edited by One Love Editing
http://oneloveediting.com/

All rights reserved.
This book or any portion thereof may not be reproduced or used in any manner whatsoever without the express written permission of the publisher.
For information regarding permission, write to:
Eden Finley - permissions - edenfinley@gmail.com

DISCLAIMERS/TRIGGERS

Author note:
While this book is heavier and not as fluffy as my other books, it is in no way a dark book.

Trigger warnings:
PTSD, depression, and anxiety.
Mentions of past domestic assault.
Mentions of date rape (non-explicit).
Mentions of animal abuse.
Light bondage.

Disclaimers:
Anders struggles. It might get frustrating at times.
Generalised Anxiety Disorder (GAD) is frustrating. It's important to remember that "generalised" is in the name for a reason: it is never triggered by a single thing each time, and the reactions by the person suffering will never be consistent. Every person is unique, which means how they cope with their mental illness will be unique.

Brody is an associate lawyer. Australian law school is a lot different than in the US. It consists of a three- or four-year degree for high school graduates and then twelve months of practical legal training to gain the right to practice law. The process is a lot shorter than in the US, which is how Brody is in his position at his age.

1

ANDERSON

It's a sight I never thought I'd see. Hell, I'd never even contemplated it. Yet, there it is in front of me in a gay bar, happening as if it's the most natural thing in the world. It's been over six months, but—

"It's still weird," I yell over the loud music.

My brother doesn't stop kissing his boyfriend. Yup, boyfriend.

"So when you said you're not straight, you really meant it, huh?"

Law doesn't pull away from Reed, but he does flip me the bird.

Thanks, bro.

Law's kept a lot of secrets from me lately, but it's not like I can blame him. If I had pretended to be him and slept with one of his dates, I probably wouldn't have told him either. Not that I'd do that. I have some morals.

My conscience laughs at me.

Okay, so I might have a grey moral palette, but it comes from self-preservation instinct, not complete wanker-ism.

"Oh, come on," I complain. "I get this is still new for you guys, but being the third wheel sucks."

Finally, they break apart, but their matching *in love* smiles may be worse than watching them attack each other's mouths.

Eww, happy people.

Law keeps his arm wrapped around Reed as he says to me, "You could always leave us and go pick some rando on the dance floor to fill your next month."

"Funny. So fucking funny."

He knows I haven't dated since I stupidly decided to change my life six months ago.

I realised I'd been too reliant on Law to carry around the burden of my issues, and I couldn't do it anymore.

This is supposed to be the new me.

More independent and put together.

I've had one tentative boyfriend since I decided I needed a *new me*, and my issues were still the same. No connection, no trust, and I ended up needing Reed to break up with the guy for me because I was sweating more than a hooker in church. Nothing's really changed, even though I've been trying.

I've been trying really hard, and I'm getting nowhere.

I'm about to give up and go back to my old ways of using guys and then running away. It's unhealthy and unfair, but it's easier.

A large body appears behind me, and not in the *it's so crowded in here I'm just trying to slip past you* kind of way. I don't have to turn around to know who it is.

"Hey, guys, sorry I'm late." The warm, soothing voice makes me jump. It always does. There's been no progress on trying to change that either.

Fucking Brody Wallace.

In short: he's perfect.

The reality: he scares the shit out of me.

It's not only his size—taller and wider than me. It's everything about him. His charm, his easygoing nature ... He's smooth and too good to be true, which is why I avoid him every chance I get.

At times, his mannerisms and stature remind me of the same man who gave me my issues.

He rubs me the wrong way when my body wants him to rub me in all the right ways.

I hate him.

I hate him because I want him.

Reed actually manages to pry himself away from my brother to give Brody a hug, and I hate that too. But oh, look at that, he springs back to Law like they're attached by a rubber band.

It's not that I don't like Reed. I do. He's great, and he makes Law happy, which my brother deserves after all he's been through with me. But they get to have the life I thought I'd have once upon a time. A long, long time ago. You know, back before I became this shell of the person I used to be.

Law believes everyone's life is divided into two—before some event or defining moment and after—but I call bullshit on the theory.

Absolute bullshit.

My life hasn't been divided into two. You can call me Voldemort with how many times my soul's been split apart.

One: the day I came out. I had the perfect amount of support from my family and friends, but it was still scary as fuck.

Two: the day my boyfriend, Kyle, attacked me.

Three: the day I realized I was no longer able to leave my apartment because of fear.

Four: the day I had to move in with my brother because I couldn't look after myself.

Five: the moment I finally accepted I'll never go back to the person I was before number two and learning to deal with my shortcomings.

Six: the night six months ago when I found out all the things Law had been keeping from me because he knew I'd revert to number three.

Seven: the moment I met Brody Wallace and realised if I didn't do something to get over my issues, I'd never be able to have someone like him.

My soul's been split seven ways, and I'm only twenty-eight.

Fuck that.

"Anders." Brody's usual cocky tone is ever present and ever annoying. So is that damn smile that has the ability to bring me to my knees. Or would, if I didn't know an impending panic attack would follow.

I tip my head in way of greeting because I don't trust my voice.

"We're going to hit the dance floor," Law says, dragging Reed away. Probably from Brody.

Reed and Brody are childhood friends or whatever, but Law says they had something going on at one point and Brody might not be over it.

Friends with an ex. Nope. Sorry. Brain does not compute. *Who does that?*

"You want a drink?" Brody asks.

I clear my throat and hold up my beer. "Got this one. Thanks."

"It's almost empty. I'll be back in a sec." Brody walks away before I can stop him.

Noooooo.

Deep breaths, Anders.

He's just a guy. It's just a drink.

I mentally beg Law and Reed to come back so I'm not

alone with Brody, but that whole twin psychic connection thing is a total myth. Or Law and I just don't have it.

Brody takes all of one minute to buy drinks, and I have no doubt it's because the bartender beelined for his gorgeousness and got his flirt on.

He stalks back towards me from the end of the bar, and I can't help admiring how his long, muscular body moves.

The club is dark, but his baby blue eyes still shine.

His brown hair is as it always is—stylistically messy and framing his chiselled face perfectly.

Old me would've been salivating over being the object of this guy's advances.

This me? I'm torn between running away and trying to find an ugly stick to beat the shit out of him.

Not that I'd ever actually do that, because one, ugly sticks don't exist, and two, I'm not a violent person.

But why does he have to be so hot?

He holds out my new beer, and I tell my mouth to say, "Thank you," but all that comes out is something that sounds like "Ah. Eh."

This is the problem with me. Put me in a group of people, I can generally hold my own. One on one? It's like I need instructions on how to construct a conversation and my manual is in Swedish.

My life is the equivalent of an IKEA flatpack.

As soon as the beer is in my hands, Brody asks, "Gonna go on that date with me yet?"

"Nope." I take the drink and swig a huge gulp.

He's been trying to get me to go out with him ever since the night we met, and every time he asks, a little piece of me dies because I can't bring myself to say yes no matter how much I want to.

"You know, I'm starting to think you don't like me."

"What gave you that impression?" I ask dryly.

"The whole saying *no* thing is a big tip-off." Even in rejection, he's calm and cool.

He has to be a psycho. No matter what Reed says about him being a stand-up guy.

"Yet, you keep asking." I stare out at the dance floor, watching the bodies of different size grind up on one another.

Out of the corner of my eye, I see Brody doing the same, but when I follow his gaze, I notice his is locked on two people. Or maybe just one. Reed.

He must sense me watching because he averts his eyes and trains them on me. "Gotta go with the odds. The more I ask, the more chance of the answer changing, right?"

"That logic is flawed. Majorly."

Brody laughs. "Fair enough. Worth the shot."

Even his persistence is charming. On any other guy, I probably would've filed a pre-emptive restraining order. I think deep down I know Brody's harmless, but that's not the point.

The point is I can't control my trigger symptoms around him, and that's why I say no every time. It's also why I hate being around him.

"How's the apartment hunting going?" he asks. "Reed said you're looking for a place."

I hope my groan isn't out loud. "Fine." *Lie.*

Every time I open the real estate app, my hands shake and my vision blurs, so I close it again and tell future me to deal with it. Then I get hit with my rent due notice and I cringe at spending money I can't afford for a two-bedroom apartment I don't need. But it's a comfort. I don't deal well with change.

I don't deal with much of anything.

Law deciding to move out of our place and in with Reed is the most recent thing I can't let go of. When I found out, I smiled and managed to act cool about it, but in all truth, I hate living by myself. And the idea of getting a roommate terrifies me even more because sharing close space with a stranger? No, thanks.

"Oh, so you got a place?" Brody asks.

"Nope. I'm good where I am." It's my bank account that has the issue with it. "Future me can deal with debt."

"That doesn't always work out well. Putting everything on your future self."

"I know. Past me is a dickhead."

Brody laughs as if I'm joking, but it's totally the truth. "I ... uh ..." He mumbles something I can't hear.

I lean in closer. "What?"

"Never mind."

I frown.

"I was going to say I have a guest room if you get stuck, but—"

"Not a good idea." The worst, actually. I don't even know why he's offering. We barely know each other thanks to me running away from him every chance I get.

"Figured. Can't even get you to agree to a date, so wasn't getting my hopes up at an offer to move in with me." He flashes that grin—the cocky, *I'm so sure of myself* grin that I both hate and am jealous of.

I used to have a grin just like it.

We wouldn't survive five minutes living together. Or, at least, I wouldn't. But there's something, even if it's only a small part of me, that doesn't dismiss the idea immediately. Living with him would still be better than living with a stranger. And living with a stranger would still be better than begging Law and Reed to move in with them.

They're still honeymoon-phasing, and the last thing they need is me hanging around.

Plus, I promised Law I wouldn't rely on him so much anymore.

He's done so much for me. He takes me to my appointments if I need that extra bit of help in going. He checks in with me constantly to make sure I'm still going okay. He used to break up with guys for me because I never had the nerve. The perks of having an identical twin.

I'd been depending on him for five years, and it needed to stop. That's why I decided six months ago to try to stand on my own for once.

Living with Brody would be an anxiety nightmare, but the same could be said about any of my other options. At Law's, I'd be worried about slipping back into old habits. With a stranger moving in ... I shudder. Big bucket of nope on that one.

I find myself saying, "I'll think about it."

Brody's as surprised by my words as I am.

2

BRODY

Anderson Steele is the quirkiest hot guy I know. I've seen the way he acts with his brother; I know he can socialize like a normal human being, but he's different with me, and I can't figure him out.

He's more on edge around me. Colder, maybe.

I don't get it, because I've seen him checking me out, which is confusing as fuck when he keeps saying no. I don't know why, but I kind of like it. He's a challenge, and it's no secret I love those. I'm not one to usually go for the thrill of the chase when it comes to guys, but Anders is different.

He intrigues me.

You'd think after six months of trying and failing to get him to even agree to go on a date with me, I'd know when to admit defeat, but I'm a sucker for punishment. In my professional and personal life it seems.

I guess I have a thing for wanting attention from men who don't want to give it to me.

Can anyone say daddy issues?

"Moving in is one way to ensure I'll stop asking you out." I take a sip of my scotch, which now tastes sour going down. It may stop me from chasing him but won't stop me from wanting him.

Hmm, maybe it's not such a great idea to offer him my spare room.

"That's the secret? Why didn't you tell me six months ago? I would've moved in right away."

"Ha, ha." I nudge him with my elbow, and he flinches. What is with this guy and being jumpy?

At first, I thought it was a mutual attraction thing, but now I'm legitimately wondering if I scare him. Which is the most ridiculous thing in the world. The worst I do to guys is ghost them, and that's usually by accident.

I've only been able to do casual relationships since my career has been my focus. I work at one of the busiest criminal law firms in Brisbane, and I have the added pressure of being the son of a name partner. It's hectic.

I moved to Brisbane to go to uni and follow in my absentee father's footsteps to somehow get his attention. Because that sounds so healthy and all. But my last six years has been filled with law school and then trying to prove myself.

I date, and I've played up the commitment-phobe angle in the past, but the sad truth is nothing ever has the chance to become serious because I'm always busy. I work around the clock, and I'm generally too exhausted to go out. In the past six months, my occasional catch-up with Reed is all the socialising I've done.

I'm not scared of a relationship; I just don't have the time for one. But Anders seems scared of me for entirely different reasons, and I wish I could say it turns me off, but honestly it makes me want to know more.

Again, probably not the healthiest thing to be chasing a man who doesn't have the time of day for me, but I'm looking for breadcrumbs here. Something. *Anything.*

I don't know why ... okay, I have a fairly good idea why, but rejection only makes me want to do better, fight harder, and change that no into a yes. It's why I did so well in law school.

"Wanna dance?" I ask him.

He side-eyes me.

"The way I figure it, your brother and my best friend are now shacking up. We're gonna be seeing each other a lot, so I figure ... friends?"

"Do you ask to grind against all your friends?"

"What can I say, I'm a really friendly guy."

Anders glances out at the dance floor again, and I try to be subtle as I check him out. It really is unfair how good-looking the Steele brothers are. Anders' dark hair is longer now than when I met him, and his beard is thicker. It looks as if he hasn't had the time to get to a barber or he's growing it out and it's in the messy middle stages between neat and long.

The barbell sitting through his eyebrow glints off the flashing lights in the club, and it makes me wonder if the piercing means something, because he can't be wearing it for aesthetic reasons. It's not 1999.

Then again, as I stare down at his acid-wash jeans that are fraying at the heel and his plain black T-shirt, I'm guessing following trends is not on Anders' list of priorities.

I'm thankful Law shaved off his beard. When he stands next to Anders, even with that massive difference, it's hard to tell them apart. Reed knew from the beginning, somehow. Maybe Law's dick is magical and cast a spell on Reed's eyesight, because it's uncanny and kinda creeps me out sometimes how much they look alike. Even their mannerisms.

I'm sure a therapist would love to get a hold of me and dissect why I've been chasing after a guy whose identical twin is with my ex-boyfriend, but I'm not going to dwell on that now. Or ever. Yup, never sounds like a great time to assess my mentality when it comes to Reed.

I feel someone staring, and when my gaze moves from Anders' jeans to his face, he bites his lip and looks as if he wants to say something. Or do something.

"Fine. We'll dance." He stalks off, and I freeze because I can't help wondering if I heard him right.

Still, not gonna say no to that. I down the rest of my drink and follow Anders out onto the dance floor.

Someone cuts us off, but I don't have time to pull myself up. I collide with Anders and grip onto his hips to steady us. When I don't remove my hands right away, Anders cranes his neck and cocks his head at me.

My hands go up like a busted perp, but I don't move away from him. I'm pressed against his back, loving the feel of his toned body against mine. "Not my fault."

"If you're gonna get handsy, deal's off."

"How do you propose we dance without touching?"

I'm not sure if it's from him or me, but whosever heart is beating erratically between us, it's going way too fast. It's very possible it could be mine, because my cock is more than interested in how close we are, so I'm assuming my heart might be all in too.

"If you need to ask that, I worry about your dancing skills."

"Oh, I have skills," I murmur in his ear.

Anders lets out a shuddery breath and breaks away from me, moving farther into the throng of guys on the dance floor.

He finds us a spot, wedged in between sweaty bodies, and he moves to the beat. It's obvious he knows how to use his long and lean frame to get attention as his hips dip and roll. Anders' tight muscles are hypnotic as he moves, and as he lifts his arms, his shirt rises. I get a view of a sliver of abs, and it makes me want more.

Even though he's toned and tall, he's never come across like the dancing type. He gives off more of a hipster vibe—the type who'd stand along the edge of the dance floor claiming to be too cool for it.

I inch closer to the sexy way he moves his body. A confidence I've never seen in Anders comes alive, and it takes all my strength to make sure to keep a few feet of distance between us.

Anders' body heat licks over my skin, though we're not touching. One small step would bring us flush against each other.

A smallish guy squeezes his way into the gap between Anders and me, and at first I think he's trying to make his way through the crowd, but his intention becomes super clear when he stays where he is, grinding against both of us. He comes out of nowhere like a dancing ninja. He's facing me, has his back against Anders, and the look in his eyes is pure hopefulness.

The kid looks barely old enough to shave, and as he leans back and looks up at Anders, a blinding, gorgeous smile I've never seen on Anders' face appears. He's definitely never smiled at me like that.

That's when I notice Anders' hand on the guy's hip. How long has that been there? Did Anders stop him to purposefully dance with us, or is he just humouring the guy?

I've heard Reed and Law mention Anders' penchant for younger guys, but I figured they were joking.

Guess not.

I don't quite understand what's happening, but as Anders moves in closer, I feel a hand on my lower back. The young guy has his hands on my chest, so ... Anders is touching me?

The three of us find a rhythm, moving as one. The music fades in my ears, and all I can hear is our mixed breaths.

Anders' hand moves over the contours of my back, and I risk a glance at him.

My heart skips a beat when my eyes land on Anders nuzzling the smaller guy's neck.

Both of them still have hands on me, but the chemistry between the two of them is explosive. And hot.

The other guy has his head thrown back, his eyes closed, just enjoying the sensation of Anders buried in the crook of his shoulder.

I've never had a threesome, and while the fantasy of it is something I've thought about, the reality is … I kinda feel like the odd one out right now, and all we're doing is dancing. Even if my granite-hard cock is begging for this to continue, I don't know what the fuck is going on.

I can't take my gaze off Anders, wishing it was me he was ravishing, but a hand cups my cheek and my attention is brought to the other guy.

He pulls my head close and brings his lips to my ear. "Must be my lucky night."

What am I supposed to say to that? "Mmm … Must be."

Smooth. Real smooth.

I swear I normally have more game than this, but whether it's the Anders thing or the three of us thing, I can't seem to pull out my usual charm right now.

He turns towards Anders, but I'm still close enough to hear him beg. "Please take me home with you guys."

Anders and I lock eyes on each other, and something happens to the hand on my back. It becomes stiff, Anders' shoulders become rigid, and his face pales.

Plastering on what I know to be a fake smile—because he's thrown so many of them my way the past six months—Anders leans in to kiss the guy's cheek. "As fun as that would be, I've got to go. Sorry. You two have fun though." He leaves with an awkward wink, and his lips are back to being tight but slightly turned up as if he's trying to smile but can't quite do it.

It happens so fast. One minute Anders is with us, and the next he's gone.

"Your wingman doesn't know how to wingman properly. He gets me all worked up for a threesome and then bails."

I rise on my toes to try to find Anders over the crowd. My eyes catch on him right before he walks out the exit.

When I go to follow him, I realise the young guy is still in front of me. "Uh, yeah, sorry about him. I don't know what that was."

"I'm still up for a twosome if you are?" Bright eyes blink up at me. He's cute, I'll give him that, but he's not really my type. Not that I'm normally picky, but I'm just not feeling it. The guy I want walked out the door.

"Thanks, but I should go check on my friend. Have a fun night."

I chase after Anders before the guy can stop me. When I reach outside, I'm pelted by unexpected rain. Standing under the awning of the bar and scanning the street, I realise I'm too late. Anders is gone.

3

ANDERSON

*L*aw and Reed's housewarming party.

Ugh. Kill me now.

The ball of stress tightening my gut has me hesitating as I pull up to their place.

They're gonna ask. All of them are gonna ask about the apartment. Law, Reed, Mum, Dad ...

They all know I can't afford to stay where I am, and Law knows when the lease is up. Which means all of them know that it's soon, and they're all gonna want to know what my plan is.

When I don't have an answer, they'll offer me solutions—none of which I wanna hear.

I check my reflection in the rear-view mirror. The bags under my eyes, my untrimmed beard, and my unruly hair are gonna bring on even more questions.

Yeah, I'm a bit of a mess, but I could be worse. This isn't my usual anxiety-ridden exhaustion but stress from trying to figure out where I'm gonna live. I'm already in debt, and re-signing the lease for another six months will put me further in the hole.

If I could ditch out on today, I would, but that'll raise alarms and I'll never hear the end of it.

It's times like these I wish I did what Karen tells me more often. My therapist is always on me about not putting things off until I have to get them done.

Excuses and rationalising control most of my life, and then when I'm hit in the face with the here and now, where my lease is up and I have nowhere to live for instance, I look back and scold myself for not having the strength to pick up my phone and look at a real estate app.

As far as my family is aware, I'm dealing now. I'm doing great. I really need them to keep thinking that, because I am. I'm doing better. It's just, for whatever reason, I can't bring myself to move out of that damn apartment.

In the last five years, it's the only place I've felt truly safe.

With confidence I'm totally faking, I grab one of the bands I wear around my wrist as a coping mechanism and tie my hair up into a bun on top of my head to try to look somewhat presentable. I'll probably never hear the end of having a man bun either.

When I finally put my emotional walls in place and build the courage to do this, I practically jump out of my skin when I climb out of the car and see Brody leaning against the boot with his arms folded.

"You have to stop jumping out at me," I say.

His laugh is annoyingly inviting.

Last week at the club, I could've stayed on that dance floor with him all night. With someone between us, my hand felt comfortable roaming and exploring Brody's insane body, and if it had lasted longer, I would've explored more than just his back. I had the safety of the other guy against me but could feel every muscle through Brody's shirt.

The music. The crowd. It was the safest I'd felt in Brody's

presence. I thought maybe that little breakthrough would mean I'd be comfortable around him now. Turns out, nope. He still makes me flinch.

Standing here with him, though, I do think something has changed. I don't know what, but I'm not as edgy around him.

I want to know what would've happened had the other guy not ruined it by trying to come home with us. The idea of two on one made me short of breath, and the sickly feeling of wanting to get away kicked in. I had to leave before it turned into something worse like a panic attack.

One year. I had an entire year where I was in control of my episodes and had even stopped going to therapy. For whatever reason, they came back the night I was supposed to go on a blind date with Reed. When I panicked and Law took my place, I thought it was a one-off, but I guess they're back to stay, and I feel like I'm starting over at square one.

Although, it's not quite square one. Instead of being housebound, I can still go out and have fun. Only certain things trigger me. In the big scheme of things, I'm doing better than I was directly after the assault, so that's something.

"Took you long enough," Brody says. "Why were you sitting in there for so long? Steeling yourself to endure this party too? Get it? *Steeling* yourself?"

I ignore his poor attempt at a pun of my last name. "Why didn't you want to be—" Oh. "Your thing with Reed."

"I do not have a thing with Reed." His protest is way too emphatic.

"Okay. Sure. I didn't say you did, but now I'm totally thinking you do."

"I don't. I just ..." Brody runs a hand through his brown hair. I wait for him to elaborate, but he doesn't.

And I don't know how to feel about that. It's not like I have a right to be jealous when I'm the one who keeps rebuffing Brody, but I'm sure he wants me in a different way than the way he looks at Reed.

I'm the guy he'd fuck. Reed's the guy he'd marry.

"Ready to head in?" Knowing someone else isn't going to be having fun in there makes me more at ease.

"About as ready as I'll ever be." His tone is solemn. "Seeing as we're arriving together, can we fuck with them and say we're on a date?"

"Sure. Would you like to meet our parents as my date too? That's their car over there." I point to the red mini-SUV in the driveway.

Brody stutters, and I bark out a laugh.

"On second thought ..." he says.

I clap his shoulder and immediately scold myself for touching him. Rule number one of being friends with Brody—no touching. Touching leads to wanting more touching, which feeds my anxiety.

The old Queenslander home Law and Reed are renting isn't much to look at. The peeling yellow paint on the dilapidated clapboard façade kinda reminds me of the beachfront shack Law and I grew up in, and if I had to guess, I'd say Law chose this place because of how much it feels like home.

"Reed said they'll be out back," Brody says.

"This way's quickest." I lead him down the side of the house and through the gate that leads to the backyard.

"Been here before? Oh, wait, of course, you have. Your weird closeness with your brother."

"Ignoring that."

Law and I hate it when we're called out on our co-dependent relationship, but it's not like people don't have a point when they say it. If they knew the complete details, they'd probably understand, but we're not about to air the darkest part of our lives to everyone.

"What's with that anyway?" Brody asks, and my feet move faster. The sooner we get to the party and around more people, the quicker I'll be able to relax.

"We're identical twins. Voodoo sharing the same brain bonding and all that shit," I say.

I don't think he buys it.

"I'm getting a drink." I stalk away from him and hit the backyard.

There are a million people back here. Brody heads directly for Law and Reed, who are hanging by the barbecue. Some old friends are gathered near the table with food that Mum obviously brought because Law and I can't cook for shit, though I'm trying to get better. Law's still shit. But even with the bustle of partygoers around, Mum seeks me out right away.

Of course.

There's no escaping this woman.

Not that she's a horrible person—definitely the opposite. But if I think Law is bad sometimes with the overprotectiveness, it's triple with our mother.

"Hey, Mum."

"You've lost weight."

I roll my eyes and then smile when I see Dad do the same thing behind her.

"You look great. You been getting some sun?" Deflection is something I've learned over the years, but it rarely works on my family.

"Just my usual daily walks along the beach. Have you been going for your walks?"

Yep. Knew I wasn't getting out of it that easy. As part of my therapy, I need to go for daily walks for at least half an hour. Do I do them? Not every day. But I can't admit that to Mum or she'll worry. The point of the exercise is making sure I get out of the apartment for something other than work, so if

I go to dinner or go out dancing or go see Law and Reed, it counts in my book.

My therapist suggested the walks during a time when I couldn't bring myself to leave Law's and my apartment at all. Not even to go to work. I don't have that problem now.

I lie anyway. "Of course, I am."

"We're staying with Law and Reed for a few days. Maybe I can come with you."

Sounds fun. If fun meant being grilled about every single aspect of my life. But I'm not going to argue with the woman. "Sure."

"We thought you might've had a new place by now too. We could come and help you move."

I rub the back of my neck. "Not yet, but I will soon. I'm looking into a few places."

Lies!

"You could always move home," Mum says.

I could always go jump off a cliff, but that's not gonna happen either.

I shouldn't be so hard on her. She has every right to play overprotective mumma bear on me, especially when I'm not the most forthcoming with my issues.

It's a vicious circle of wanting to protect one another. She wants to protect me from my ghosts, and I don't want her to worry that I'm still haunted.

"Who's the guy you came in with?" Dad asks, eyeing Brody by the barbecue. I'm thankful for the subject change, and I'm certain Dad did it on purpose. He knows how overbearing and worried Mum can get.

"We didn't come together. We just arrived at the same time. That's Brody."

Mum's face lights up. "*The* Brody? Reed talks about him a lot. We should go and say hi."

Ah, my parents, the social butterflies. They'll probably adopt Brody because he's an extension of Reed, and they love Reed already. Pretty sure they've got wedding bells ringing in their heads.

"You do that. I'm gonna go find me a drink."

An alcoholic one. Of any kind.

I'm gonna need it today. Especially when I see Mum and Dad approach Law, the golden child, and Reed, his perfect partner in every way. They were made for each other, I have no doubt about that, but there's one thing about them that grates on me, and it doesn't take a therapist to tell me I'm a lovely shade of green with envy. Not only do they have each other and a promising future, but I'm sure Mum and Dad don't look at them as if they could break at any moment. And I'm sure they're not asking Law about his weight or exercise habits.

I make my way onto the back patio and take a beer from the esky. They'll have something stronger inside, and it's tempting, but a small voice behind me catches my attention.

"Anders?"

When I turn, two smiles from people I haven't seen in years greet me. Dawn and her husband, Nash, went to high school with Law and me. High school sweethearts to the extreme, they got married right after graduation. I haven't seen them since.

"Hey." The sight of two people from my old life—the life I crave to have back again—has my flight instincts kicking in.

Dawn throws her tiny arms around me, and Nash holds out his hand for me to shake.

"It's been a long time," Nash says. "Missed you at the reunion."

Right. Our ten-year reunion. There was no way I was gonna go to that.

Hey, Anders, I'm a doctor now. I'm married, successful, and my life is perfect. What have you been up to?

Oh, you know, I had the mental strength to leave my house today, so that's a win.

"Yeah, you know how it is. Tax season and everything. Barely get time to eat, let alone go out."

They both look at me with confused expressions.

"I'm an accountant," I say, and they both do the whole "Oh" thing and avoid eye contact. Their facial expressions scream *Dear God, don't let him go into the details or I'm gonna need a refill on this wine*. "I'm guessing the reunion's where you ran into Law."

"With his boyfriend." Nash chuckles. "Everyone was surprised. I mean, we always thought you were the gay one."

I can't tell if he's joking or not, but hey, talking about my sexuality is easier than telling them what I've been doing for the past ten years. "I am. Law's bi and only dated girls in high school."

Nash's eyes widen. "Oh shit. We thought ... you guys looked exactly the same and ... ah, fuck."

"What he's trying to say is," Dawn cuts in, "that we thought we had you two mixed up."

"Wouldn't be the first time. Or the one hundredth."

"I guess it makes sense though," Nash says, suddenly thoughtful. "Twins. I mean, you're identical, so ..."

"So being queer is in our DNA?" I quip. Most people would be pissed at Nash's ignorance, but fuck, give me ignorance over curiosity about my scar any day. Not that they could see it with my beard.

"I-I didn't mean that," Nash stutters. "It's just, what are the odds of siblings both ... err, both, you know ..."

"Liking dick?" I feel horrible about putting this guy on the spot, I really do, but it's my way of trying to take focus off me.

A short laugh comes from behind me. Brody ambles up the steps of the patio and joins us. Damn his gorgeous face, his perfectly messy hair that probably took an hour to style, and his tight T-shirt that shows off even tighter muscles that are normally hidden by his business shirts. It's the first time I've truly taken him in today, and I should've known better than to drop my guard because he was talking with Reed.

Remember your rules, Anders. Thou shalt not ogle Brody Wallace.

Brody swipes my beer out of my hand and takes a sip.

"There's the esky right there, you know." I point to the ice bucket.

"Tastes better when it's stolen." Then he turns to Nash and Dawn. "And in relation to your question, it's actually common for more than one sibling to be on the LGBTQ spectrum for a variety of reasons."

"Like what?" Nash asks.

"I wish I had the time and the crayons to explain it to you, but I need to steal Anders away for a second."

I try to hold in my laugh as Brody drags me away. "They meant no harm, you know."

"I know, but you looked like you needed rescuing."

Brody keeps dragging me around the side of the house, away from everyone at the party.

My pulse increases, but I tell myself to breathe through it. "What's up?"

"Law said you still don't have a new place yet."

"How would he know? Maybe I'm getting a roommate instead of moving."

Letting someone I don't know into my space? So not happening. Brody doesn't know that though. Law would, so I guess I have my answer.

"You guys tell each other everything. If you had a new apartment, he'd know."

"Your point?"

"Law also said you're not the type to ask for help when you need it, so here's me offering my apartment again. It's two bedrooms—"

"No. Not a good idea."

Brody keeps going. "I'm hardly ever home, and the offer's there. I know you don't want to have to move in with your brother while he and Reed are still"—he screws up his face—"in the 'we just got a new house and have to christen every single room with nakedness' phase."

"Eww, thanks for that visual."

"I mean it. You can stay with me until you work something out. If you need it."

"Why are you doing this?"

"Oh, for fuck's sake. It's not to get into your pants. We agreed to be friends, right? This is me being friendly. Friends help each other out in a time of need."

Where can I find such friends? Mine all deserted me when I deleted my social media and stopped going out.

When he sees I still don't buy his reasoning, he sighs.

"Okay, how about this. You know what I do for a living, yeah?"

"Lawyer."

"I work at one of the most expensive firms in Brisbane. You know what that means?"

Out of everyone in this fucking world, I know what that means. Kyle had the best lawyers money could buy thanks to his parents.

"It means you get rich people off for doing shitty things."

"Right. My sister is always telling me I need to offset that by doing something good. So think of this as my karmic penance. A good deed for a friend in exchange for my professional sins."

A lawyer with a heart? Didn't realise that was a thing.

Maybe I should take it.

The pressure of finding a new place is getting on top of me, my options are limited, and here's this guy offering me an almost perfect solution.

If it weren't for that part of me that gets all twisted over being near Brody, I wouldn't be hesitating.

"Think about it and get back to me." When Brody walks away, I take another deep breath.

What the fuck is wrong with me?

Maybe deep down, I know I'm gonna end up in Law and Reed's spare room, no matter how much I don't want that to happen, but I can't keep relying on Law.

God, how many times have I said that over the last five years?

"Brody," I call out.

He turns back just before he can disappear back into the yard. "Yeah?"

"I'm in. Only until I can find somewhere else I like."

With a smile, he keeps walking, and I can't help staring after his ass as he does.

I'm so going to regret this, but I'm looking at the bigger picture.

Place to stay.

Independence.

Giving Law a break from being my rock—the person to keep it together when I can't.

It's official. I'm applying for that reality show *Hoarders*.

When did I buy so much crap?

Insomnia and impulse control issues should never mix. I think I own every product they have on the shopping channel.

Moving day is going about as well as I expected. Half the time I'm telling myself I'm an idiot for agreeing to move in with Brody, and the rest of my time is spent warding off panic attacks.

I want to go back and slap past me upside the head. There's no way I can do this.

"Still can't believe you agreed to live with that douche-nozzle," Law says.

And then I remember why I'm doing this.

For Law. Even if he hates Brody.

Brody and Reed's friendship turns Law into a green-eyed monster that he only shows to me. It's not that he's insecure about his relationship with Reed. He just thinks Brody's watching him, waiting for him to fuck up so he can strike.

"He's not a douche-nozzle."

At least, I don't think he is. Even though he might have feelings for Reed, I get the impression he has absolutely no intention of ever acting on them. And he couldn't be a douche if a guy like Reed vouches for him.

"We have a spare room," Law says.

I scoff. "You and Reed got the place to get away from me, remember?"

Law drops a box of my kitchen utensils, slicers, blitzers, and NutriBullets, making a huge clatter as they fall to the floor. "Dude, not even. We wanted a house so we can, you know, be grown-ups and—"

I shudder at the notion. "Eww."

He smirks, and the nakedness of his skin along his jaw still throws me sometimes. For so long, we both had beards, but when I decided to move on, I needed him to shave so I was never tempted to ask him to pretend to be me to get me out of a sticky situation.

He would break up with guys for me so I wouldn't have to, but now there's a noticeable difference in our appearances, and I can't use him as a crutch anymore.

"Right, your allergy to adulthood," he says dryly.

"I don't want you to start the rest of your life by having me in your way. You've looked after me for too long, man."

Way too long.

"So you're gonna let Brody look after you?"

His words grate on me, because while I know how he came to that conclusion, it reiterates my insecurities.

I *hate* being that guy.

"I don't need anyone to look after me."

If we really did have some sort of twin connection, I could totally hear Law saying "Bullshit" in my head.

"And it's not like that with Brody," I say. "He's giving me a place to crash until I find an apartment in my budget. I'm looking after myself."

Law reaches out and pulls on my man bun. "And you're doing a great job of it."

"Man buns are cool."

He laughs so hard he has to hold on to his stomach.

"Oh, fuck off." I grab the box he dumped. His laughter follows me as I leave the apartment and take the stairs leading to the garage in the basement.

I don't want Law to make a point, but I'm scared he does. I've been living alone for a few weeks since Law first started moving his stuff out. Maybe I need to keep living alone to prove I can.

If I could afford somewhere in a safe area, I'd do it, but unfortunately my options are getting a roommate or living in Stab City.

This is my only option.

One level down, I run into Brody coming the other way. He's in tight jeans and another tight T-shirt. Gah, where are his stuffy suits when I need them?

I adjust the box on my hip. "What are you doing here?"

He tips his head behind him. "Reed came to pick me up to help with the moving, *roomie*." He claps my back, and I try to hold in my flinch. Brody doesn't notice. He bounds up the stairs as I continue my way down, but right before hitting the basement, Law's voice travels down the stairwell.

"Hey, Brody, what's your opinion on man buns?"

I love my brother, but sometimes I really fucking hate him.

4

BRODY

I find Anders outside our apartment building, looking up at it with a box in his hands. He doesn't pay attention to everyone on the street bustling by him and doesn't even flinch at a guy on a bicycle who crashes in front of him because a car pushes him out of the bike lane.

Instead of startling my new roommate—I'm learning not to do that—I go and stand next to him, trying to look for whatever he sees up high.

There's nothing out of the ordinary. The building is still gaudy and over-the-top and is situated along the Brisbane River, so it costs a mint.

I didn't find this place. My father did. The outside might be pretentious, but inside my apartment, thanks to a decorator my father also hired, the style is modern and laid-back as per my instructions on how to furnish the place.

Without even acknowledging me or turning to face me, Anders says, "I can't afford to live here."

I glance at him out of the corner of my eye. "I don't remember asking you for rent."

"I can't live here rent-free. How is it only occurring to me now to ask how much it costs?"

"Uh, because you're only here until you find a permanent place?"

His skin pales. "Right. Of course."

My eyes narrow. "I'm guessing you figured that'll be a while."

Anders finally turns to me. "I'm kinda ... particular about things."

Somehow, I think he's understating that a bit.

"Finding somewhere in my price range that I'm comfortable with might take a while."

"Take as long as you want. Like I said the other day, I work seventy, sometimes eighty hours a week. I'm hardly ever home."

"I'm gonna pay you rent."

"If you insist, you can, but you don't have to." I'm trying to explain to him the last thing I need is money but without actually coming out and saying *My dad is rich and I don't even pay rent. Or a mortgage.* I also know how some people can be about money, so I respect his need to pay something—even if it's small. "Anything you can manage will be fine. Whatever you can afford."

Anders adjusts the box he's holding. "Why are you offering this?"

"Like I said when I suggested you move in: we're friends now. Friends do shit for each other."

"Yeaaah, I'm not that type of friend. I'm the type of friend who promises to catch up with you but never sets a date. I say I'll be there and then never turn up. I'm the guy who owes a million different favours with no intention of repaying them."

I laugh. "At least you're honest? Come on, let's get all this moved in." We already dumped most of his stuff off at a storage unit he's renting for his big furniture items, so we've only got a few boxes to haul upstairs. At least this place has an elevator unlike his old one.

And as if on cue, a loud whistle comes from the front entrance. "What are you two doing?" Reed yells.

"On our way," I call back.

Anders takes a deep breath. "I can do this."

I have no idea what he means by that, but it sounds as if he has to convince himself living with me isn't going to be like needing a root canal.

Maybe living with him will give me more insight into his quirky randomness. That's not even coming from a place where I still want a date with him. I've promised myself to behave. In fact, seeing as he's adamant we won't hook up, I won't allow myself to look at him like that anymore.

My eyes obviously haven't gotten the memo because they track his ass the whole way to the elevator, dammit.

We make three trips back and forth between our cars and the apartment until all his stuff is moved in. By the time the last box is hauled up to the twelfth floor, it's well past dinnertime.

"You guys can stay if you want," I say to Reed and Law. "Beer and pizza?"

Reed's lips twitch. "Thanks, but we're adults now and don't accept favour repayment in pizza and beer anymore."

"Fine then, scotch and whatever Videre can send over."

"Videre?" Anders asks. "Isn't that the fancy restaurant no one can ever get into?"

Reed doesn't even hesitate to sell me out. "Oh, Brody can. He's Mr. Fancy Pants."

Before Anders can question me more, I hold up my phone. "I'm calling. You two staying or not?"

"We should get home," Law says, puffing out his chest.

I try not to roll my eyes. Why he thinks I'm a threat when Reed is so obviously under Law's dick spell and in love with him is beyond me. That doesn't stop the tiny bit of pride at being able to drive the man crazy simply by being friends with Reed.

Reed leans into him. "We really should stay. The food is amazing, and we can't afford it."

Law stares down at his boyfriend, and just like that, his expression softens. He relents, and I can understand why. It's impossible to say no to Reed when he looks at you with puppy dog eyes. I know from experience. "Fine."

"Great." I head to my bedroom to call, because now that Reed's pointed out I'm basically a regular and VIP at one of the trendiest restaurants in the city, I don't really want to flaunt how casual my relationship with the owners is. They're my father's best friends and technically my godparents, though I barely knew them growing up. Now they just feed me lots. They're my main source of food these days because my work schedule is so hectic.

I don't have time to cook let alone shop.

When I open the door to my room, Lucky, my sister's demon cat, runs out. I had her locked up so she wouldn't interfere with the moving of all the boxes.

I'm halfway through ordering a massive meal, even for four guys, when I hear a high-pitched squeal come from the other room.

Without hesitation, I rush back out into the living room where Anders is standing on the couch, staring at Lucky with wide eyes and making a squeak-like noise.

Law's trying not to laugh, but Reed looks concerned.

"Y-y-you have a rat," Anders stutters. "A giant one the size of my head."

"Can I call you back?" I say into the phone.

"Tell you what, honey," Marion, the owner of the restaurant, says. "I'll put together what I think you and your friends will like and send it right over, okay?"

"Thanks. You're the best." I hit End on the call and pocket my phone. "Umm, I guess you've met our other roommate, Lucky."

"It's a rodent," Anders says, and Law can't contain it anymore. He loses his shit, laughing.

"It's a cat, bro," Law says, breathing heavy.

"Like fuck it is. What's wrong with it? It's all patchy and, like, has no fur down one side. Or on its tail."

In Anders' defence, he's right. Lucky does kinda look like a grumpy, oversized rat.

"It's my sister's cat, and she's a rescue."

"Your sister's a rescue?" Anders asks.

"The cat, dumbass," Law mumbles.

Anders shakes his head as if scolding himself for not thinking that one through.

"Lucky was a stray, and my sister found her ... uh, well, yeah, let's just say what she went through wasn't pretty, but she survived."

"Why do you have your sister's cat?" Reed asks.

"She's gone off to save the world," I say. "Guatemala for the next year, after that, who knows."

Reed smiles. "Sounds like Rachel."

Lucky jumps up on the couch and circles around Anders' feet. He tenses, and his hands fist at his sides. Law's still laughing, but when Anders starts counting backwards from ten, all humour is gone.

"Shit, Anders, you okay?" Law's by his brother's side in a flash, helping him off the couch.

Seems like a bit of an overreaction to me, and obviously to Anders too, because he shakes him off.

"I'm fine," he grumbles. "It's just a rodent."

Law laughs again. "Cat. Can you say the word?"

"Why do I get the feeling we're not hearing a story?" Reed asks.

"When we were, like, eight..." Law looks at Anders, who scowls.

"Tell this story and die."

Anders getting all threatening and growly is hot.

No! Bad Brody.

"So, we were eight, and this stray cat kept coming to our back door every day. Mum and Dad told us not to feed it, but Anders snuck it food anyway." Law can barely talk, and his words come out all breathy from trying not to laugh. "He fed it for like months, but the cat wouldn't let him anywhere near him. One day, he decides to sneak up behind it to try to pet it while it was eating—"

"It attacked me," Anders says. "The end."

"Aww, man, totally cut me off and make it anticlimactic, why don't you," Law says. "But yeah. He's been scared of cats ever since." He starts laughing again. "But fuck, it was funny. Like, picture a little Anders—"

I don't know why, but I'm picturing an eight-year-old with a full beard.

Law wheezes and he continues. "This little kitten would not stop chasing him all over the yard—"

"It was not little!" Anders yells. "It was the size of a dog."

"A Chihuahua maybe," Law mutters.

"It had huge teeth, and need I remind you domestic cats are related to like lions and shit? They're fierce."

"Mmmhmm."

Law and Anders' brotherly bickering is the most normal I've seen him act in my presence. I've seen it from a distance before, like the other night in the club before he realised I was there. Never up this close.

I pick up Lucky and cuddle her. She hates it but doesn't fight me. "Think you can live with the big bad kitty?"

"I'll be fine. That thing's not a cat."

As if understanding, Lucky lets out a little kitty growl, though I think it's because I'm holding her, not at Anders.

It rattles Anders all the same.

Being roommates is gonna be fun.

Being roommates is gonna be torture. Sweet, wank-inducing torture. Because one dinner down, I'm harder than an iron bar underneath the table. All Anders has done is relax and show this whole different side of him. I've seen him with Law before—their weird bond and brotherhood that seems stronger than any other sibling relationship—but I've never seen him fully relax.

It's even hotter than the nervous twitching. Maybe. Hmm, nah, I love it when he's all awkward too.

I'm so fucked.

"I think she likes you," Law says, looking behind Anders' chair where the cat hasn't left his side.

Lucky meows in response.

"She has … particular tastes usually," I say. "It took a week for her to stop hissing at me every time I fed her."

"I dunno, that sounds like she has great taste," Reed says.

I rub my temple with my middle finger, and Reed laughs.

"I need a smoke," Anders says and stands.

He smokes?

"You're back on that shit?" Law asks.

"Sorry, Mum," Anders says sarcastically and heads out to the balcony. Unsurprisingly, Law follows.

I watch their identical asses as they go.

Reed clears his throat. "You better be checking out Law's ass because the other one is even more off limits than my boyfriend."

"I actually can't tell whose I'm looking at," I say, only half-joking.

"Brody—"

"Yeah, I know," I say, feeling defeated. "You don't have to say it. But why do they have to be so damn pretty?" Pretty's probably not the right word for their rugged appearance, but ... so pretty. Like Jason Momoa pretty.

Reed laughs. "Yeah, it's kinda unfair."

Fucking whatever. Reed is your typical blond, blue-eyed, and gorgeous type. He's traditionally good-looking. Anders is something else.

Which is probably why I've been imagining running my hand over his bearded jaw and gripping that top knot on his head and pulling to the point of pain.

"I'm serious, Brody. Anders is a no-go."

"Wow, you sound just like him."

Reed's blue eyes widen in realisation. "Wait, *he's* the guy you said keeps rejecting you? And you asked him to move in? *What is wrong with you?*"

"Wrong with me? I'm helping the guy out."

"And hoping to fuck him in the process."

I mock gasp. "I object."

Reed gives me his *I call bullshit* face. "Okay, Counsellor."

"He's adamant it's not going to happen, and I do have *some* dignity."

"Do you?"

"Fuck you." I laugh.

Reed stares at the balcony doors even though all we can see of the brothers from here is the occasional red glow of Anders' cigarette. Reed bites his lip, and it's his tell. He's never been good at keeping anything from me. I know him and his tics too well. "Just … be cautious around Anders."

"Spill it already," I say.

Reed's eyes come back to mine and then out to the doors again, and now I'm really starting to get suspicious.

"Fuck, what is it? Is he a recovering addict or something?" I don't know why my brain immediately goes there, but it would explain the twitchy behaviour. "I can't have that shit in my home. If I get charged with a—"

"Calm down. Nothing like that. I wouldn't put your career on the line if it was drugs. I mean, well, if we want to get technical, I don't think that's a cigarette he's smoking out there, but—"

I wave him off. "Weed is practically legal. As long as he's not growing the stuff, it's not ice or heroin or heavy shit, it won't matter."

"I know you need to keep your record clean. Even if it's ironic that lawyers are usually the biggest criminals of them all."

"We just know how to play the law to our advantage."

Reed coughs in between saying "Criminals."

My smile fades as my brain works overtime to try to work out what Reed's trying to tell me. "Whatever Anders' thing is, I'm sure I can handle it."

"That's just it. It's not my story to tell."

I purse my lips. If I thought trying to get Anders to go out with me was going to be a long game, I think it's gonna take even longer to get to know every little piece of him.

At least with him living with me now, we've got nothing but time.

5

ANDERSON

"When did you cave?" Law asks, nodding at the joint in my hand.

Oh, about the minute I realised I'd left it too late to actually find a place of my own and had to move in with the hottest guy in history who makes me break out in hives.

"Last week," I say.

"Why—"

I grunt. "Can we not do this? Smoking works better than any of the fucking meds they tried shoving down my throat." I take it in my mouth and light it.

Law fake coughs, but what-the-fuck-ever. Weed takes the edge off my nerves without making me feel numb.

I tried so many different types of meds in the beginning, and I wish they'd worked because I would've given anything to have a moment of peace, but there's only so many times you can hear "You just have to find the one that suits you."

Cymbalta took away the lows, but it also took away the highs. Ativan made me too drowsy to function, and Xanax made me tired but not sleepy, which made me irritable when I couldn't sleep even though I desperately wanted to. And that's only a handful of the ones I've tried.

Valium works for me in an emergent situation—it takes the edge off—but if I'm at home, I'd rather smoke a joint than pop a pill.

Medication can work for the right people, and I'm jealous of those it does work for, but it's not for me.

I blow out the first breath and instantly relax a little.

"You really think you can do this?" Law asks tentatively.

"Thanks for the faith in me, brother."

"Fuck off. You *know* that's not what I mean. I know Brody intimidates you. He looks like—"

"I'm well aware of who he looks like, and I'm here anyway. I know this is a huge step. I don't need you doubting me."

"I don't."

I say, "Bullshit," which is difficult while also sucking in another drag from my joint at the same time.

"Fine," Law relents. "I'm worried about you, but that doesn't mean I don't think you can do this. I want you to do this. And I get why you chose to move in with Brody over Reed and me, but our spare room will always be there if you need it. Reed will understand."

"I'm done being your dead weight."

Law steps closer. "You're not dead weight. I've looked after you for five fucking years, and you're saying you're fine, but I don't think you are, and what happens if you can't leave the apartment or you start calling in sick to work until they threaten to fire you again, and—"

I grab his shoulder and try to give a reassuring squeeze. "I'm fine. I mean it. Yeah, moving in with Brody is stressing me out, but it's something I need to do, and I'm not hiding anything from you."

Sucky thing number five thousand one hundred and forty-five about being me: no one believes me when I lie to their face. I'm not fine. Not at all. But I'm dealing, and for the first time in years, I'm dealing with it on my own.

"When's your next appointment with Karen?" Law asks.

"Monday."

"What does she think about you living with someone like Brody?"

Nothing, because I haven't told her. "She was encouraging."

"I've got my appointment with her this week," Law says. "She reckons I can start going monthly instead of every two weeks."

I take another hit to hide my surprise and jealousy. Law started getting counselling six months ago after he assaulted his student's abusive father and he realised he'd never dealt with my attack properly. He was the one who found me lying in a pool of my own blood. He's the one who held me as I almost died in his arms. When he wrings his hands together, I know he still feels my warm blood on his skin. He hasn't done that in months now.

Mum, Dad, and Law focused so much of their energy on me back then they stopped looking after themselves, and Law suffered because of it.

Basically, everything shitty in Law's life, I'm responsible for in some way or another.

I'm glad he's doing better and is moving to monthly sessions, but I can't even get my therapist to agree to biweekly appointments for me. And I know if I tell her how much I'm truly struggling these days, she'll add more appointments to our three-day-a-fortnight schedule we've got going on now.

Lying to myself is even more dangerous than lying to Law and everyone around me, because if I want to believe it hard enough, I can convince myself I'm fine and don't need any help.

I might be pushing myself into something I'm not ready for, and I might be freaking out a little, but I can do this.

Then again, am I lying to myself even more by thinking there's a light at the end of this tunnel?

Denial is a powerful thing.

The flat line of my therapist's lips says everything I need to know, but she lectures me anyway. "I'm concerned."

I snort and try to refrain from saying "No shit."

"Have you told Brody about your past?"

"No. Why would he need to know?"

"What happens if you have an episode? What if you have a nightmare? It's important for people in your life to know what to do in such a situation. Especially someone who you live with. Your home needs to feel like a safe environment."

"I haven't had a panic attack in months. Not one I haven't been able to pull myself out of, anyway."

"This is a big step, Anderson."

"It's something I wasn't planning on doing, but my options were limited, and this came up, so I took it. Shouldn't that be a good thing? That instead of depending on my brother, I've done something that scares the shit out of me? Breakthrough, right?" My tone is too upbeat, and I'm sure Karen can see right through it. She has treated me for too long not to know my tells.

"It's fast. And from our past sessions, when you've mentioned Brody, you've expressed conflicting opinions about him. He's intimidating to you, which could be a trigger."

"He's a good guy." I truly believe that in my heart. It's my head that keeps telling me he's dangerous. I'm nervous a switch could flip with him too and he could try to kill me at the drop of a hat. That's part of it. But he's mostly dangerous because he makes me push myself—or, the idea of him makes me push myself.

"You're attracted to him," Karen accuses.

"And?" I shrug nonchalantly. "We both know there's no way I'm going to act on it."

I *can't* act on it. My body won't let me. Meaningless hookups with skinny eighteen-year-olds I can handle, because I could easily overpower them if I had to. Brody is taller and wider than me.

"You're jumping a few steps," Karen says. "We still need to deal with handling your triggers before we can go to exposure therapy, and from what you've told me, Brody is a massive trigger."

"So is being on my own. Which am I supposed to pick? At least this way, I'm taking steps forwards, right? You always tell me I'm too stuck in my comfort zones. I seek out comfort everywhere I go. The one time I step out of it, you tell me I'm going too fast."

"I urge you to take baby steps outside your bubble, not run as far away from it as possible and just hope you can find your way back."

Great metaphoring there, Doc.

"Is Lawson no longer an option for you? You and I both know he'd take you in."

"I don't want him to be an option."

"Then you need to tell Brody about your past."

Like fuck I do. "Okay," I lie.

———

*B*rody doesn't own many shirts, apparently. At least, that's the only reason I can think of as to why he's shirtless most of the time.

He gets home from work wearing his big, fancy, *costs more than my car* suit, and then not two minutes later, bam, shirtless and wearing sweats.

I am not built for that type of agony—having to watch him move about his kitchen shirtless. Watching TV shirtless. Looking so fucking hot. *Shirtless.*

His abs haunt me in my fucking sleep. His beautiful, washboard abs.

But at least it's better to be haunted by abs than my other ghosts.

All my "It's cold in here. Aren't you cold?" hinting gets laughed at. And fuck if that sound doesn't get to me too. His voice is warm and comforting, and his laugh even more so.

The strong part of my brain, the part that forces me to get up every morning and drowns out the doubt and anxiety tempting me to stay in bed all day, tells me I can handle it. The other part—the part that makes me want to dive in, setbacks be damned—forces me to leave the apartment each night as soon as Brody comes home.

I head to the gym on the ground floor of the apartment building just to get away from all his temptation. It's become routine. I get home from work, manage to scrounge up some dinner, change into workout gear, and then watch TV and wait for my roommate to come home so I can hide from him downstairs.

Karen still insists I need to be open and honest with Brody, but I like my plan better. Avoidance is the key to mental health ... said no mental health professional ever, but oh well. It's working.

The last thing I want to do is blurt out "Oh, thought you should know, the reason I'm such a flake is because you kinda remind me of my ex who tried to kill me. And not in the *we fought a lot* sense, but literally in the *charged with attempted murder* kinda way."

When it comes to baggage, airports have nothing on me.

I'll have to tell him eventually. I don't think I can avoid it forever, but for right now, we only see each other in passing, and I'm okay with that.

Obviously, he isn't. Because as I land on the couch at seven, already dressed in workout gear just waiting for Brody to come home, he walks in the door two hours earlier than usual.

While Brody works an insane number of hours, he always manages to walk in at nine o'clock on the dot. He's gone long before I wake up in the morning, and I swear I heard him up and about at four thirty the other day to get into the office.

Fuck that for a job.

He leaves before me and gets home after me, and I've never been more thankful to have a boring nine-to-five job.

Brody looks more dishevelled than usual as he walks through the living room and past me to get to the hall leading to his bedroom. He always looks a little tired when he comes home—goes with the territory of eighty-hour work weeks—but tonight ... tonight it's as if he's not really here. His head's held low, his steps are heavy, and everything about him screams exhaustion.

"You're home early."

He jumps as if I scared him, and his eyes snap to mine. "Shit. I didn't even see you there ... Uh, hey." He breaks his gaze with mine, and his jaw seems tense, like he's mashing his molars together.

"Bad day? You look like shit."

"Bullshit. I always look hot." His false front is completely see-through, and I think he knows it too because he immediately deflates. "But yeah, totally shitty day. I can honestly say today was probably the worst day of my entire career so far."

"What happened?"

He sighs so loud, as if the weight of the world is behind it. "I can't give a lot of details, but today was one of those days where I found out I have to represent someone who doesn't deserve it. The piece-of-shit rapist belongs in prison."

I tense and swallow hard. "He's guilty?"

Hearing Brody represents people like that makes me queasy. Which is stupid, because I've always known he was a defence attorney. I guess knowing it and having to talk about it are two different things.

It makes me sick to my stomach, but I know that's not Brody's issue. It's another one of mine that I have to deal with.

He throws himself on the couch next to me, his presence the butterfly-inducing phenomenon it always is. "I want to recuse myself, but I know that won't happen. I'm not in a position to pick and choose my cases yet."

I swallow thickly, as if my tongue's too big for my mouth, and choke out any rationale I can find. "If every lawyer wanted innocent clients, I don't think they'd get much work."

He breaks into a smile. "Right. And I'm sure my dad's going to say the exact same thing tomorrow."

This is hitting a little too close to home. Kyle didn't rape me, but he stole something from me. He stole my right to feel safe. From the many therapy sessions I've had with Karen, I've learned it's how a lot of rape victims feel.

It brings back memories of Kyle's trial. Although trial isn't really the correct term for it, I guess. Brody would know—he's the lawyer. Kyle had pleaded not guilty by reason of intoxication. Claimed he was high as a kite. The trial preparations had started, his defence team painted me as the instigator of the altercation, and then when I refused to testify because I couldn't face being on the stand and reliving the fear, the hurt, the realisation that the man I once loved could break me so easily, the prosecutor offered Kyle a plea deal for the lesser charge of aggravated assault with a deadly weapon. The physical scar isn't the only thing that lingers from that day. I can no longer trust, no longer relax around people I'm close with. Law and my parents are the only people who I'm still me around, and even then I try to hide my neuroses because I hate when they worry about me.

Six years. Kyle only got six years for slitting my throat and leaving me on the floor of my apartment to bleed to death. Doesn't seem like a fair trade when five and a half years later, I'm still paying for his actions.

The feel of cool steel moves along my skin right now, and I have to reach for my throat. My vision blurs, and shit, my throat constricts. The telltale signs of panic set in, and they've snuck up on me so fast, I don't know what to do.

Recognise it, break it down, challenge it, Karen's voice says. That's what I'm supposed to do when warning signs pop up, but I'm too busy trying to stop the knife that's digging into my throat.

"Anders." Brody snaps his fingers in front of my face, and I flinch.

I'm brought out of the memory and realise where I am. My cheeks are wet, I can feel it, but Brody doesn't call me on it. My heart still pounds, but the panic clears. I don't know if it's from desperation because I don't want Brody to see me like this or because he somehow disrupted my usual descent into panic, but I can breathe again even if it's shaky.

"You okay? You spaced out there for a bit."

"Sorry. Uh, yeah, I'm fine." Ugh, I think I've muttered "I'm fine" about a billion times in the last few weeks that I'm starting to redefine it as "I'm one small step away from losing my shit."

Brody stands. "I'm gonna go get dressed, and then how about I call for takeaway and we can watch a movie or something?"

"Umm ..."

He looks towards the sink and sees my recently washed dishes. "Oh, you already ate? That's cool. I'll order something for myself, and then—"

I reach for my shoes next to my feet and struggle to put them on because I'm trying to rush. "Thanks, but I'm gonna go work out."

Brody runs a hand through his hair. "Can we not do that tonight?"

"What?"

"The whole dancing around us being roommates, avoiding each other because ... well, I don't know why you do it, but you've done it to me since we met. I'm getting used to it now, but tonight ... tonight, can you just be my friend?"

Well, now I'm screwed, because how am I supposed to say no to that?

"Shit, man, it's not like I asked you to fuck. Don't have to look so freaked about hanging out."

"I ..." I can't find words. "I'm not freaking out." *Liar!* "I just ..."

"You ... can't make sentences?"

I nod.

"Why not? I thought we were cool or whatever. We're friends now. Roommates. We should be able to hang out."

But I should also be able to break up with guys on my own and get through one single day without thinking about what Kyle did to me. Those things don't come easily either.

"You're right," I say. "We should be friends who hang out."

Should be being the key phrase there.

I'm terrified because the darkness is trying to sneak back into my head again, but something just happened that never has while I've been mid-PTSD episode. Brody somehow pulled me out of it.

I know my triggers. I know my warning signs. I know when I need to escape and give myself some air.

Yet, tonight, it snuck up on me so fast I didn't have time to register it.

But Brody ... Brody fixed it.

"Good. I'll be back in a second. You pick something to watch."

He goes into his room, and Lucky runs out as soon as the door is open. I put her in there earlier when she was staring me down and plotting my murder.

She runs up to me and sits at my feet, glaring at me. If I were an animal whisperer, I could swear she was calling me a wanker.

I rearrange myself on the couch in a position that makes me look most comfortable, even though I'm not. I rest my arm on the side and lean back against the cushion. It's awkward as fuck.

"Why was Lucky locked away in my room?" he asks as he walks back out.

"She was staring at me," I say, not breaking eye contact with the rodent.

"I love so much that you're scared of a wittle kitty cat." Brody's laugh makes me break my gaze first. Dammit, the cat's winning at this dominance game. Or is that only a dog thing? I don't know, but I think Lucky knows I'm her bitch.

That is, until I raise my eyes to Brody's and realise, nope, I'm his bitch. His ab bitch, because again, he's shirtless, and again, I can't control my reaction to him.

I stand, preparing to leave before my semi becomes a full-on boner. "Okay, if we're doing the friend thing, you need to put on a shirt, or I'm going to go for that workout."

I need to exercise away all this sexual frustration.

Brody tries to hide a smile. "*That's* your issue? You find my skin offensive?" His hand trails down his torso, starting with a slow glide over his pec and then farther down until he reaches the waistband of his sweatpants.

I hate him. I really fucking hate him. "It's like you don't own any shirts."

"You should've said so. Easy fix." He disappears back into his room and comes back out wearing a tight, sleeveless muscle tee. So not better when I can still make out the definition in his abs through the shirt.

It's better than nothing, I lie to myself and take a deep breath.

Brody picks Lucky up on his way back to the couch and plops her on his lap. God, why is the sight of him cuddling this ugly, damaged cat so alluring?

Lucky appears to tolerate it rather than enjoy it, but she stays as if she *wants* to like it. I can't help feeling a pull of solidarity towards her. I sink back down onto the couch and watch them with morbid fascination.

Even with the guys I date, I try to enjoy being touched. I want it, and for the most part, I'm okay with it, but I've yet to find someone who truly makes me enjoy it. I can't get out of my head long enough to appreciate someone's hands on me. Which sucks, because before Kyle, I was a total cuddle whore.

Pillows don't cuddle back, and I miss the real thing.

"Did I end up telling you her story?" Brody says and leans down to kiss Lucky's head.

She lets out a little purr, finally melting under his soft touch.

Okay, now I'm jealous of a fucking cat.

"What happened to her?" I ask.

"A group of teenagers were torturing her." His tone, so casual, makes me pause.

"What the fuck?"

"They burnt her." Brody runs his hand down her hairless side and then down her tail.

"It was recent?" I ask, wondering why it's still patchy.

He shakes his head. "My sister's had her for over a year. Vet says it won't grow back. Too much skin damage."

My breath gets stuck in my throat, and I find it hard to swallow.

"They'd hogtied her so she couldn't get away," Brody continues. He lays the cat down on her back, and I'm surprised she allows it. Then he brushes her fur on her stomach and parts it. "Here she has some hidden stab wounds. Just in case you ever wanted to pick her up. I thought I'd tell you where she's sensitive."

My hand mindlessly rubs over my jaw, unable to feel the thin ridge of my own scar running along my skin because of my beard.

I manage a nod. "I don't see me picking her up anytime soon, but thanks for the heads-up."

"She's been through a lot, and it takes a while for her to trust. She still takes a while each time I pick her up for her to settle in my arms, but she eventually does."

God, this guy is killing me. If a damaged cat can let him in, then I should be able to too.

"How did your sister end up with her?"

"She saw what the boys were doing to the cat in an alley and ran in there to break it up."

My eyes widen. "She fucking what? Did you kick her ass?"

Brody scoffs. "Wait until you meet my sister if she ever comes back from saving the world. She's headstrong, stubborn, and does stupid shit all the time in the name of being a good Samaritan."

Envy laces his voice, and I wonder what that's about but don't want to pry. Prying means he could turn around and do the same to me.

"She sounds like a good person. There aren't many truly good people in the world anymore. I can pretty much only name one that I know."

"Your brother?"

"Yup."

"Lying to Reed and assaulting the father of one of his students aside?" He smirks, but his words hit me in the gut. Because both of those incidents were my fault.

"There were extenuating circumstances surrounding both those things. He's a good guy who did a shitty thing, and hitting that parent ... he still feels guilty about that. Even if the guy was a douche and bashed his gay son. An eye for an eye doesn't work, but in Law's case, it was out of his control, because ... because ..." *Because of me.* I can't say that though.

Brody loses his smugness. "I know. I think it's easier for me to see your brother as a villain, but it's not like I can talk. Tomorrow I get to defend the scum of the earth, so yeah, I'll give you that one."

With one simple conversation that isn't particularly deep and a night of watching mindless movies, hope that being roommates could work burrows its way into the back of my brain.

6

BRODY

When I awake to Anders' moans, at first I think I'm dreaming because the noises he's making are pure sinful. But as I become more aware of my surroundings, his sounds of pleasure quickly escalate to groans of pain.

I bolt out of bed and almost lose my footing as I try to rush to get to him. When I flick on the living room light, I wince from the brightness, but at least I won't trip on any of the furniture.

Considering I could hear Anders through two doors and across the apartment, something has to be seriously wrong.

Lucky paces by Anders' door and gives me a concerned meow when she sees me coming. God, she's a weird cat.

I don't hesitate to barge into his room, but the door is locked, and all I do is make a loud thud as my body slams against it.

The noises from inside the room quieten.

"Anders?" I ask through the door.

"No, stop! Don't hurt me," he wails.

What the fuck?

I push hard and hear the lock snap, to hell with the

damage. The door flies open, making a giant bang against the bedroom wall.

Frantically, I check the room, thinking I need to ward off an intruder or something, but Anders is in bed alone. Long arms and legs thrash, while whimpers fall from Anders' mouth. His eyes are shut, and his face is scrunched. It makes him look not only anguished but downright tortured.

I don't even think before I climb onto his bed and kneel over him. My hands go to his shoulders, trying to get him to snap out of whatever nightmare he's having.

My heart lurches and aches for him, and a weird protectiveness washes over me that I've never felt before. I mean, I've kinda been protective of my sister, Rachel, but she's a force to be reckoned with, and there's no way to keep on top of her. She's her own person even if sometimes I want to lock her away and yell "Stop doing reckless things and I'll let you out!"

Right now, I want to hold Anders and reassure him he's having a nightmare, but he's not waking up. The only light to fill the room comes from the living room, but it's enough for me to make out his features.

After Reed all but confirmed Anders' quirks are more than just a personality trait, I've wondered what that's been about. It's taken all my willpower not to research it. I'm a lawyer—I get paid to dig up the ugly parts of people's pasts.

But I'm trying to be respectful here and get Anders' story the old-fashioned way—by making him trust me enough to tell me himself.

I shake him a little more roughly. "Anders."

He stills. His eyes fly open so fast they startle me, but it's as if he sees right through me. Before I even have the chance to blink, something hits the left side of my face, and my head explodes in pain.

I fall onto my back next to Anders, but then a heavy weight climbs on top of me and another punch is thrown my way. At least I see it coming this time, and I throw my hands up to protect my head.

"Anders," I yell. "It's me. It's Brody."

"B-Brody?" he croaks.

The fight in him stops, but he doesn't move from straddling my waist.

A few hours ago, the idea of being underneath Anders and practically naked would've turned me on. Now, with my head pounding and Anders' whimpers ingrained into my brain, I can't feel anything but fear. Not for me, but for him.

I slowly lower my hands but prepare to throw them up again in case Anders isn't truly awake.

I'm so not prepared for what I find in Anders' eyes.

Absolute horror.

"Hey, hey, it's okay," I whisper and reach for his cheek. I don't know why. It's like a reflex or something. But it's the wrong move, because I barely scrape his beard when Anders flinches. He doesn't move off me though, and I get the feeling he's using his body weight to keep me pinned to the bed so I can't get up.

I quickly withdraw my hand from his face and put them up near my head to show him I'm not going to touch him.

"It's me," I say reassuringly.

"Brody …" It's as if he's trying to convince himself it's the truth. "Fuck," he hisses and scrambles off me.

I remain on the bed, feeling exposed as he eyes me from top to bottom. I'm only in my boxers, and even though he's not checking me out in a sexual way, my skin heats.

"What are you … I mean … did I …" Anders' gaze lands on my swelling eye. "Fuck." He drops to his knees beside the bed, and cool fingertips graze my sore cheekbone. "I'm sorry. Holy shit, I'm so sorry."

My hand covers his. "Don't. I'm okay." I sit up slowly but refuse to let him move his hand from my face. "But, are you all right? You were having a nightmare, and you wouldn't wake up."

Anders' skin flushes bright red, even in the dim lighting. "I ... yeah, it was just a nightmare. I ... umm, get them sometimes. I'm sorry for scaring you. I locked my door and woke up with you on top of me, and—"

"Shh, it's okay." I want to reach for him and bring him against me, but I don't. Something tells me that might make things worse, so I keep holding his hand to my face. It should feel weird, but it doesn't. I'm trying not to lean into his touch and rub up against him like a cat.

And speaking of cats, Lucky is right by our feet, walking in and out around Anders' legs.

I look Anders in the eyes. They always seem to hold darkness behind them. "I'm sorry. I shouldn't have barged in here, but I thought you were in danger. I thought someone was in here with you."

"No one in here but me." He taps the side of his head. "And what's up here is probably worse than what anyone else could do to me. I'm sorry for hitting you. I should get you some ice."

He tries to pull away, but there's something inside me that won't let him go.

I hold his hand tighter and try to grin but wince instead. "Guess it's my fault. I should remember you Steele brothers are like kung fu masters."

Anders scoffs, but I can't tell if it's a laugh or self-deprecating dismissal. "That's Law. Not me."

"Well, you've got a mean right hook. Just sayin'."

One of Anders' rare genuine smiles breaks free.

"So, the nightmares. Did you, you know, wanna talk about it?" God, could I be any more awkward than I am right now?

"I really don't."

"Okay." I don't blame him. Just because I want Anders to trust me, doesn't mean he ever will.

"But we will talk about it, because I should've done it when I moved in."

"You don't have to—"

"Actually, yeah, I do. Especially if this is gonna happen again. I don't want to keep punching you. Well, mostly." Anders smirks and reaches out, a single finger running from my eye along my jaw and down to my chin. "But ice first."

I nod. "Ice."

7

ANDERSON

*F*uck.

Double fuck.

Fuck, fuck, fuck.

I hit Brody. I was in the middle of an episode, and I hit him.

This is why you should've told him before now.

Yeah, thanks, Karen. I don't need your voice in my head right now.

Why is it when I start to feel comfortable, my brain has to go and ruin everything?

I've been here two weeks now. Two weeks where I expected this shit to happen, and it didn't.

I thought, maybe, I was stable enough here.

Good feelings never last.

Never forget that, Anders.

I grab a bag of peas from the freezer and wrap a tea towel around it, but when I turn, Brody is right there at the entryway to the kitchen.

I jump out of my skin. "Fucking hell."

"Sorry. I didn't mean to make you jump. I didn't know if you wanted me out of your room or out here or—"

I hand him the icepack as I pass him on my way to the pantry where Brody keeps his liquor. "Want some?" I pull down an open bottle of scotch. "This conversation might need it."

"Sounds like we're in for a long night." Brody's tone drips with innuendo, but I don't think it's intentional. It's probably my brain reading into it, because words out of Brody's mouth can make anything sound sexual.

"Certainly not of the fun variety."

I pour us both more than two fingers and slide his over to him. Brody sips his slowly, but I can't get mine down my throat fast enough.

His stocky frame leans against the kitchen counter. The abs that like to torture me are out again—shocking—and like always, my eyes betray me by scoping out every inch of bare skin.

"So, is it like a night terror thing from when you were a kid, or …"

Yeah, I'm gonna need more alcohol. After another two-ish fingers of scotch, I put my glass on the counter and gesture to move to the living room. Brody follows, taking a seat on one side of the couch and dragging a blanket onto his lap.

"Boxer situation." He smiles coyly, and I think it's the first time I've ever seen him bashful.

"Sweatpants. Should always go sweatpants." I run a hand down the leg of mine, because my palms are clammy and sweaty and gross.

"I'll remember that for next time."

And reality comes crashing back. "About that. Chances are high it will happen again."

"And why is that?"

"You want the professional diagnosis or the personal recount?"

His hand pauses halfway to his mouth as he goes to take a drink. "Whichever you're comfortable with."

"Well, if you ask my therapist's opinion, she says I have PTSD, GAD, and a whole heap of other acronyms."

I can't look at him. I don't want to see pity or judgement, and I don't want to feel the shame. I've done a lot of things I'm not proud of—a lot of which has been in the last five years. I had guys warming my bed when I've felt nothing. Treated them like shit. Didn't even have the balls to break up with them in person. But the Kyle stuff makes me feel dirty and shameful in ways I never knew were possible.

For being so naïve, for not seeing the warning signs, and because I had no idea I was living with a supposed addict.

That was his defence—that he was high when he attacked me—but I'd never known Kyle to touch drugs.

We thought it was bullshit and he was using it as an excuse for his actions, but the toxicology report showed he was high when he turned himself into police. There's no disputing that.

When we were together, he was possessive but in a way that made me feel treasured. He'd smile, we'd have fun, and fuck, I was so in love with him. The last six months of our relationship, though, the feeling something wasn't right gnawed at me.

He became stressed at his job, and his possessive side became worse. He was constantly on me about what I'd been doing while he was stuck at work. He'd be suspicious if I went out with Law, and he even followed me one night.

When I called him on it, he said he'd finished early and wanted to see me, but I'd never told him where I was, so I didn't know how he found me.

When I found the tracking app he'd hidden on my phone

in the folder labelled "Phone crap" which held all my useless apps, I broke up with him.

He said he was sorry, promised to delete the app, and I stupidly took him back.

I ignored his downward spiral, his increased possessiveness, and his frequent distrust until I couldn't take it anymore.

His attitude was no longer fun. We no longer laughed. We were tense around each other, and the loving, carefree boyfriend I fell in love with over lazy Sunday mornings making breakfast and cuddling on the couch was gone.

And apparently breaking up with him again was the last straw. He turned up at my apartment with nothing but coldness in his eyes.

He asked for another chance. I should've gone with it until he'd calmed down. The smart thing might've been to call the cops right away. But I stupidly believed that no matter how fucked up Kyle was, he'd never hurt me. He loved me.

Boy was I fucking wrong.

Even when he tackled me and held a knife to my throat, I still didn't believe he would really hurt me. It wasn't until I lay dying that I truly comprehended what had happened.

I had been blinded by my feelings for Kyle, and I promised myself I'd never be that dumb again.

"That must be tough." Brody's sincere tone makes the shame worse.

My gaze meets his, and all those things I'm expecting to see aren't there. There's only concern.

"Tough is one word for it."

"What happened? And remember you don't have to tell me anything you don't want to."

"I was attacked." I swallow hard. "About five years ago."

Brody's whoosh of breath is audible even from the other side of the couch. "I'm sorry, man. That's ... I was going to say tough again, but I've already said that. I might need a thesaurus."

I want to smile. I really do. But I just can't do it.

"Was it random?" Brody asks, more serious now. "Please tell me they got the guy?"

Something goes wrong in my gut. My stomach turns sour, and my hand begins shaking. Great. Apparently my body's had enough excitement for one night. There's no way I can tell him about Kyle and survive it.

"They got the guy," I whisper.

"Were you ... uh ..."

I think I know what he's trying to ask, and it's one question I have no trouble answering. "No sexual assault. Umm, he just took a knife to my throat."

Brody's look of relief is short-lived. "Just took a knife to your throat? There's no *just* about that. That's a big fucking deal, Anders."

I take in a shuddery breath. "I know. Believe me, of all people, I know it's a big fucking deal. I have the fucking scar to prove it." I turn my head and part my beard so he can see the rough skin beneath it.

I don't show anyone my scar, and I don't know what possessed me to do it just now.

"Sorry, I didn't mean it like that. You sound dismissive of it. As if what you experienced isn't as bad as someone who was raped, when it's not true. Your whole situation is terrifying. Was it a mugging or ..."

My throat constricts, and I can't find my voice. So for some stupid reason, my brain thinks it's okay to nod.

And I'm back to lying.

Fuck.

"Is the scar painful?"

"No. I'm just self-conscious of it. Hence the beard. It covers it so I don't get questions."

Maybe Brody senses it's getting too much, or maybe he doesn't know how to handle the situation, but he says, "You look wrecked. I should let you get back to bed."

He moves as if he's going to place a hand on my leg but thinks better of it and pulls back.

I quickly realise I want his touch. I want his reassurance. I want him to be able to touch me without me reacting.

"Hey, can you ... uh, not do that?"

His brow furrows. "Do what?"

"Not touch me because you're worried I'll flinch?"

Brody cocks his head, and his unkempt hair which is normally perfect falls into his face. "I thought you might've ... I mean, this whole time whenever I hit on you or tried touching you in a flirty way, I thought you recoiled because you felt ..." He blows out a loud breath. "God, this is embarrassing. I thought it was because you wanted me too and you were playing hard to get. Not because I fucking scare the shit out of you. So, I'm a shithead because I liked getting that response, but now I know the truth—"

"Please, don't stop. It's true I don't like it. Law, my parents, even Reed now, they all treat me like I'm fragile, and fuck"—I huff a humourless laugh—"I totally am, but I don't want you to see me like that."

"Can I hug you?" he asks.

He takes me off guard, and my brain freezes for a second.

"You can say no." His laugh is self-deprecating, and it's what I need to force myself to do this.

Closing the gap between us is harder.

Brody stands and pulls me up off the couch. Then I'm there, against Brody's strong frame. Our arms wrap around each other, his skin on mine creating a burning heat between us.

Even though he's slightly taller, it turns out it's only by an inch or so. It seems like so much more from afar. Brody is a strong, commanding presence, and it makes him appear taller.

I'm stiff against him, but that's not surprising.

My heart races, just like it always does when this guy touches me.

Brody pulls back, his hand finding the rapid pulse beneath my chest. I hold my breath, because I know he can feel it.

"Do you have a heart defect?" he asks with genuine worry.

"What?"

"It's racing like crazy." He rubs my bare chest.

I still haven't taken a breath.

Fingers trail down my pec. "Nipple piercings? Shouldn't be surprised because of your eyebrow."

Our eyes lock, and I'm stuck somewhere in between wrapping myself around him and pushing him off me, so I stay where I am, where I'm both safe and scared.

Brody's close. So freaking close.

Holy shit are his lips moving closer? Is that his hand tightening around me?

I think I'm losing my head because I can't actually be sure if any of this is happening. And I should be bugging out. Normally, I'd be trying to level my breathing, but the closer he gets, the more his presence chases away the fear.

Brody blankets me with an oddly calming haze. My anxiety claws at me, wanting out, but for the first time in a long time, I'm in control of it.

"Thank you for telling me," he whispers, his breath catching my skin. "I won't take it personally when you recoil at my touch anymore."

Lips land on me, but not on my mouth. They skim my

cheek, and my eyes close, taking in the sensation of Brody's softness.

As quickly as they're there, they're gone, and so is the warmth of him against me.

I go to take a step to follow him because I want that feeling back. I want to see how long I can hold on to it. I need ... I don't know what I need, but I want it.

Only, my foot trips over a furball at my feet.

"Fuck, Lucky," I grumble as I try to keep my balance and stop myself from stepping on her.

Brody helps steady me. "I think she knows."

"Knows what?"

"What you've been through." He picks her up, cradling her in those strong arms, and again, I feel jealous of a fucking cat.

"I think that animal-sensing bullshit is just that—bullshit."

"She's never once shown concern for me since she moved in."

The quip is on the tip of my tongue. "Like Reed says. That means she has good taste."

Humour is a defence mechanism I've built. I don't even realise I'm doing it, but it's successful in making the atmosphere lighter.

Brody laughs. "You going to be okay for the rest of the night? I kinda ... broke your door down, so you won't be able to lock it."

Shit. "I'll be fine. I'll work something out."

"Is the lock thing a comfort for you? Because you can take my room, and I'll call someone in the morning to come fix yours."

The thing inside me telling me I'm weak wants to take his room. The man ogling Brody for the billionth time says I've shown my hand enough tonight.

It doesn't matter how many times Karen says I need to

forget what social convention dictates a man should be, because apart from that being complete bullshit, it's conducive to my therapy.

Comparing yourself to what is perceived as normal will always set you up for failure.

Still, the egotistical part of me—whether it be a natural or learned behaviour—doesn't want to put the entirety of my issues on Brody.

"I'm good. It's not a big deal."

I wonder at what point a person can be called a pathological liar.

Because as we part ways and go to opposite ends of the apartment, I'm left alone in an empty room with no lock, crumpled sheets, and the memory of thinking Brody was Kyle.

Yeah, I'm so not getting any more sleep tonight.

Lucky sneaks in before I can close the door and makes herself comfortable on my bed.

"Nuh-uh, rodent. No way. Out." I point.

She doesn't move. All she does is knead my blanket and look at me through narrowed eyes as if to say, "Just try to kick me out."

I allow it, but only because I know I'm not going to get any sleep.

"Stay at the foot of the bed, and I won't make you leave."

She keeps doing her thing, completely ignoring me.

I settle with my back against the headboard and wish social media wasn't a cesspool. It's times like this where my insomnia almost drives me to the cave of the evil that is Facebook and Twitter, but I haven't had an account in years, and I don't plan on going back anytime soon.

Hell, even Instagram is a no.

Snapchat? Fuck that.

During my recovery, all I saw on those sites were people

posting about their happy lives. Granted, it's social media, so chances are the mum who posts a million baby photos of their kid is probably suffering postpartum depression. The couple posting anniversary photos and thanking each other for being their soul mate and claiming happiness is on the brink of divorce. And anyone posting about how happy they are probably has a daily dose of Prozac.

That doesn't stop me from seeing perfect lives that aren't mine all over my screen. I don't need that kind of negativity. It makes my anxiety worse, because not only do I have to worry about my triggers, I have to deal with the self-added pressure of making sure I'm as happy and normal as everyone else pretends to be.

I'd read through the news, but that's just as bad. If the positive of fake happiness is bad, it's even worse seeing the negative reality that is the news.

The news makes me realise how many survivors there are out there like me—that I'm not alone in my battle. I should take comfort in that, but I don't, because I wouldn't wish my experiences on anyone.

It seems domestic violence is all over the news these days.

Then there are the ones who don't survive their ordeals. Whether their partners were more successful than Kyle or the aftermath is just too much for them to handle.

The ones who end their pain themselves are always the worst for me. Because I don't need those suggestions put in my head.

Depression is a side effect of my anxiety. If I have an episode, the feeling of complete worthlessness seeps in. I believe I'm a waste of space and the world would be better off without me.

If it weren't for Law, my rock, I could definitely see myself going down that path.

News articles are definitely out tonight. I'm not in the right headspace to be reading that shit. So I play some game apps, and when I get over that, I put on a relaxing playlist and lie back. For some reason, Lucky takes that as an invitation to climb onto my stomach.

"Hey, no, wait ..."

The rumble of her purr vibrates against me, and it melts my cold, dead heart.

"You're still a rodent," I mumble and pat her head.

She seems cool with my assessment.

The sun will start coming up soon, and then Brody will be up and about.

I don't want to face him. If I thought living together was going to be weird before, it's amplified now. I know deep down this was inevitable, but now it's here, I want anything to take last night back.

It's five thirty when I hear Brody moving around the apartment. Maybe I'll get some sleep once he's gone to work.

I hate myself for not being able to blindly trust him, and I also hate that a stupid, useless lock has made me feel safe the last few weeks staying here. When I get the lock replaced, I already know I won't have the security again knowing Brody can break the new lock just as easily as the first.

My bedroom door clicks open, and I sit upright, scaring Lucky. She jumps off me and makes a break for the exit.

"Shit, sorry," Brody whispers. "I thought you'd be asleep. I wanted to check on you."

I'm both touched by his gesture and uneasy. I like that he cares, but him letting himself into my room so quietly I wouldn't hear it if I was actually asleep is not cool.

"I'm fine."

Oops, there's that *fine* word again.

"Did you get any sleep? Wait, why was Lucky in here, and were you ... cuddling her?" Brody's face lights up.

"We weren't cuddling," I grumble. "She was using me as a pillow."

"You were cuddling."

"We weren't ..." I grunt. "Shouldn't you be getting to work?"

"I should, but I can stay if you want? Call in sick?"

"Any excuse to get out of that case, huh?"

"God, don't remind me. And no, daddy dearest will kick my ass if I call in sick, but I'll do it if you need me to."

"Daddy issues?"

"Understatement. He's my boss, and one of the many partners at the firm."

"Yikes. Pressure."

"Pretty much."

"I don't need you to stay. You should go."

Yet, even as I say the words, I can't help thinking that I'm lying. Or, if I don't need him to stay, I at least want him to.

I want to see if last night was a fluke or if it's possible to replicate that new level of calmness Brody gave me, even if it was only small. No, smaller than small. It was a blip. But it's a hopeful blip.

No one outside of my family has given me that. It makes me think all the work I've been putting in these last six months might be working.

I'm so close to taking it back—asking him to stay—but I don't get the balls to do it in time.

"I'll see you tonight." Brody leaves, and disappointment about his absence gives me even more hope.

8

BRODY

I stare at my phone at the text I sent Anders at lunchtime. That was five hours ago now. He doesn't have that function where it tells you if it's been read or not, so I have no idea if he's ignoring me or hasn't seen it.

I feel for him. Hell, I'm scared, heartbroken, and angry for him.

I want to protect him and save him from the torment he has to endure every day.

Going through something like that ... what does it say about me that it makes my pull towards him deeper?

Maybe I have a hero complex. Or maybe I really do see him as my karmic good-doing after having to endure today—the shittiest day in the history of my career. The whole time I've been reading about what my client did to his victim, I can't help thinking about Anders and his situation. It sickens me.

It's days like today where I lose confidence in being able to be a criminal attorney. I'm supposed to be impartial, and for the most part, I look at the law like a game. It's not about innocence and guilt. It's about bending the law to make it go my way. And this case, for it to go our way, we're pitching the young, dumb, and incapacitated state of inebriation defence on why this shithead had sex with a passed-out girl at a party.

I can't fuck it up, and I can't throw the case. Everyone has a right to legal representation, and as a lawyer, I have to vow to work to the best of my ability in getting this guy the least amount of justice our stupid system will allow.

There's a knock at my office door, and Dad steps through.

I'm not quick enough to put my phone away, and I curse myself.

The people in this office think I get preferential treatment because I'm John Davenport's son, but the opposite's the truth. When I started here, Dad sat me down in his office and told me exactly what he expects of me—to set a good example for the other grads.

"Break time, is it?"

Condescending time, is it?

Dad pulls back when he notices my face. "What happened to your eye?"

"Oh." I press against the bruise. It didn't come up too swollen this morning, but it's still noticeable. "Rachel's stupid cat tripped me, and then I got into a fight with the coffee table."

No way am I telling him I have a roommate who thought I was attacking him, so he punched me. Nope. Actually, no way I'm telling him I have a roommate, period.

Dad paid for my apartment, but the deed is in my name. No joke, it was a graduation present for me. My brother and sister think he was trying to buy me, but I actually think it's to keep tabs on me.

Then again, I sometimes get the feeling he doesn't even care enough to want to keep tabs.

He's a confusing man.

Dad doesn't question my tale of how I got the black eye. "Thought I'd check in on the Steinfeld case."

"Just catching myself up on it."

"Do you think you're ready for it?" His question sounds supportive, but it's a trap.

If I say no, he'll crack a joke about going into environmental law.

"The associate in charge of it picked me for a reason."

"I know why Annabelle picked you. I'm wondering if you think you're ready. It's a big case. It'll have media presence, and you'll need to hold yourself in a certain way. Come across strong. Not get affected by the nature of the trial."

It's not only a big case. This is my *first* big case. I've only recently reached associate level after doing my practical training and then working as a solicitor. That basically means I've spent most of the last three years writing reports and assisting on cases, and while I'm still not the main lawyer on this case, it's the most responsibility I've had since getting my law degree. It makes sense for Dad to check up on me, but it annoys me all the same.

"I know what I need to do."

"But you don't like it." How can this man read me so well? It's annoying.

"Of course, I don't like it. I didn't realise we were supposed to enjoy defending rapists."

Dad points to me. "And that, right there, is what you have to watch. Your client isn't a rapist. He's a young, messed-up kid who made a teeny, tiny mistake. That's what you have to defend."

Hmm, no, I'm pretty sure he's a rapist.

"If you can't do that, you might as well have become a divorce lawyer or something."

Ooh, family law comparison this time instead of environmental. I silently wonder if that's a step up or step down.

"Got it."

"Okay, I'm out of here for the day. Are you staying back awhile?"

"Yep."

"Good man. See you tomorrow."

As soon as he leaves, I let out a relieved breath.

I try to concentrate on the words in front of me. Reading over and over what this kid did to his victim, and I can't help thinking about Anders.

He said he wasn't sexually assaulted, but I also got the feeling he didn't tell me the whole truth.

When I finally call it a day and head home, I expect him to go back to his usual hiding routine where he disappears to the gym downstairs.

Only, when I walk in the door, my nose becomes intoxicated by the aroma of Anders' dinner. It's garlicy and tomato-y, and I don't even care what it is, I want it. My stomach rumbles, and I probably should've picked up takeaway on the way home.

I find Anders in my kitchen, plating up two meals. He's wearing a T-shirt and short exercise shorts that are so fucking hot. I pause a moment to admire his ass that I wish I could forget about. I'm brought out of my daze when the two-plates thing registers in my tiny, ass-obsessed brain.

"You expecting company?"

He turns to me. "Are you considered company or like ... not really because you're my roommate?"

"You cooked for me?"

Anders shrugs as if it's no big deal.

"I could kiss you. I'm starving."

Tension stiffens his shoulders, but he tries to play it off like I don't affect him.

"I mean, I won't," I reassure him. "I understand why you're so reluctant to go out with me now. I knew it couldn't have possibly been my personality."

My joke does the trick, and Anders appears to relax again.

"Of course," he says dryly.

I lean against the bench while he scoops meatballs onto a bed of spaghetti. He looks good all domesticated. I'm not going to say that though.

"Hey, question? You don't have to answer if you don't want to though."

"Mmhmm?" He sounds suspicious, and I guess he has a right to be.

"Is all that stuff last night the reason you only date smaller guys?"

This time, Anders doesn't freeze. No, he drops the fucking hot pan. I see the moment it touches his thigh, right before the loud crash of the pan hitting the tile echoes through the apartment.

"Shit!"

Anders stumbles back and grunts in pain.

The floor is completely covered in marinara sauce and meatballs, and my foot lands right in the middle of it to get to the freezer.

It's squishy and slippery beneath my shoe.

I grab the same bag of peas that nursed my eye last night and rush back over to him. My knees hit the floor, yep, in the sauce, but I don't care. "We're a pair, aren't we?" I wrap the peas in a tea towel and press it to Anders' thigh just under the hemline of his running shorts. "Maybe we should invest in some icepacks."

Anders winces and speaks through gritted teeth. "Maybe I should wear pants."

"Pants are overrated. Especially when you look like you do."

And just like that, I make things awkward, because Anders doesn't stiffen this time. Well ... correction, a certain body part I'm eye level with right now does.

I shouldn't look at his cock. I'm not going to look.

A moan tries to escape when my eyes don't listen. I can practically make out every vein, the thick head, and long length through the thin material of his shorts.

A choked sound gets stuck in the back of my throat, so I force myself to pull my gaze away.

But then it lands on Anders' flushed face and his chest rising and falling with rapid breaths. Yesterday I would've said it's because he's as turned on as I am, and while it's evident he's hard, that doesn't mean his harsh breathing is because of that. I don't know how far his night terrors and list of diagnosed acronyms extend, but with how twitchy he is most of the time, I can assume it doesn't only affect his sleep patterns.

Anders clears his throat. "I ... uh, I can take it from here."

Right. I'm still touching his thigh. I remove the peas and grimace at the large red welt beneath.

I stand, not realising how close we really are, and come within an inch of him. Yet, I'm unable to step back. He pins me with heat in his eyes. Eyes that are locked on my mouth.

"Here." I hold out the peas.

Anders blinks but doesn't move.

My breath hitches.

Anders' hand reaches for the peas. Or, I think it does, but I'm so wrong. The peas drop into the pile of marinara as Anders cups the back of my head and pulls my mouth to his.

It takes more than a second to get my bearings.

Yes, his mouth is definitely on mine, his beard soft against my skin.

The groan that comes from Anders goes straight to my cock, and any other guy I'd think it was a sound of encouragement. With Anders and everything I learned last night …

I try to pull away, but Anders doesn't let me. If anything, he holds me closer and kisses me harder. His tongue seeks entrance, and I open for him, letting Anders take the lead, because I'm way out of my league.

My thread of control frays with every second Anders continues exploring my mouth.

Even though I've wanted this for months, I now have two voices in the back of my head telling me I should stop. One voice says he's my roommate, and the second tells me that with Anders' PTSD and his admission that he's not completely comfortable around me, this might be taking advantage or something.

Anders pulls back, but his lips still ghost mine as he says, "Stop overthinking and kiss me properly."

And apparently that's all it takes for me to tell my two inner voices to shut the fuck up.

I dive back in, kissing Anders with more enthusiasm and focus than before.

His beard, so much softer than it looks, feels amazing against my skin.

Our feet stumble back as I push into him, trying to close an already impossibly tight gap between us. Anders' back hits the kitchen counter, my thigh finds its way between his legs, and the slight friction of my cock against his is almost too much.

The grunt that comes from Anders this time is definitely not one of pleasure. That much I'm sure of.

I back off. "Sorry."

"Don't be sorry. It's my leg." He reaches behind him, gripping the counter tight.

I move quickly and get back down on my knees. One look and I know it's not good. "It's blistering already. We should go to the hospital."

"Hospital? It's not that bad. I'll be fine." His panicked tone sounds a hell of a lot similar to his shaky voice from last night, and I'm reminded of his vulnerability.

I pick up the bag of peas again, but the tea towel is covered in sauce. I reach for another one hanging on the oven and lightly touch the coldness to Anders' leg again. "Don't like hospitals?"

He shakes his head. "Not since waking up in one thinking I was dead."

"Oh, shit." I can't look at him, so my eyes go back to my hand pressed against his leg. "Can we at least get you to the after-hours doctor? It looks really bad. Like, might not need a skin graft bad, but bad enough for maybe prescription ointment or something. It'd kinda suck for you to die of infection after that kiss."

Yeah, his leg is severely burnt, and I'm wanting to talk about that kiss. Priorities.

"I'll go to a doctor," Anders says.

"You hold this, and I'll run and get changed out of my marinara pants."

I'm quick to move and already halfway to my bedroom when I hear him say he's fine to get there on his own. That only makes me move faster. I'm going with him. End of story.

It's lucky walking while holding ice to his leg slows him down, because I catch up to Anders at the elevators.

"I'm driving," I say.

"Fine," he grumbles.

9

ANDERSON

I hate myself, but what else is new?

I hate that I kissed him. I hate that he drives me to the clinic, stays by my side the whole time, except when he goes to a vending machine to make sure I eat something, and even goes in to see the doctor with me. Who the fuck does that?

But even worse, I hate that I like it. A lot.

While he was kissing me, it was the closest to *normal* I've felt in years. That safe feeling surrounded me, covering me like a fire blanket during an inferno.

The thing about that though is just like covering yourself in a blanket, you still need to get the fuck out. I wanted to stay where I was, in the false safety of his arms, but I knew I'd get burnt if I didn't escape.

The night I met him, my brother had been arrested on assault charges, and while Brody sat there as Law's lawyer, telling me about everything that happened, all I could do was watch his mouth. His lips. I was mesmerized from the minute I met him. But I've always known if I got too close, it'd be a disaster.

And look at us. Brody has a shiner because he tried to wake me from a nightmare. I'm sporting a burnt leg.

Yet, I can't stop thinking about him kissing me. Or rather ... me kissing him. Because it was definitely me.

I couldn't not kiss him. One minute he's on his knees, and I'm imagining other things he could've been doing while he was down there, and then the next, his face was right in front of me. Only an inch away. I had the opportunity, and I didn't hesitate to take it.

I don't know if this is a breakthrough or a huge mistake, but considering we're entering the one apartment building, riding the same elevator to the twelfth floor, and going into the same flat, I'm gonna go with mistake. I'm roommates with the guy, so there's no easy escape when I ultimately want to bug out.

Being honest with myself is important according to my therapist, but right now the truth looks like a whole lot of ugly.

Kissing could lead to more which could cause my one-month timeline to kick in. It's always a month. I don't know why, and I don't know how, but it takes thirty days for the unbearable *I need to run away* mode to take over.

I have no lock on my bedroom door, Brody and I haven't said a word about mauling each other in the kitchen before going to the late-night clinic, and now everything is awkward and even more strained than before.

Way to fuck things up, Anders.

We hit the living room and pause while the silence drags on.

"Uh, thanks for taking me," I say.

"Even if it was a waste of time?" Brody chuckles.

"I told you I was fine."

"In my defence, it looked really bad."

I nod. "Well, thanks. For caring about me enough to be sure." I turn on my heel, but Brody stops me.

"Wait, you thought I wouldn't care? After I give you a place to stay when you didn't have anywhere, and after—"

"It's not that. It's ..." I don't know how to explain it. If something like that had happened when I was with Kyle, he would've told me to shake it off. It's like being gay meant he had to overcompensate his masculinity. He'd always tell me to "man up" even though I'm almost the furthest thing from effeminate. "I figured you'd think I should just deal with it."

"Well, that's a stupid way to think. If you're hurt, you get help. Pretty simple, right?"

"Right."

My head wants to believe in the things he's saying—my head wants a lot of things—but there's still that voice, no matter how small it may be now, telling me that Brody's words are a trick. A trick to get me to trust him to the point it'll be hard for me to walk away when red flags start popping up.

Brody steps forward, crossing into personal-space territory. "Are we going to talk about that kiss?"

"Kiss?" I play dumb. "What kiss?"

Brody huffs. "Guess I have my answer. We can forget about it. No worries."

Dammit. Why does he have to be understanding? And simple. And easygoing.

I look at the ceiling as if asking a higher deity to send me some red flags so I can at least justify my hesitance. There are obvious reasons I'm hesitating: he's my roommate, I haven't dated someone like him in over five years, I still feel the need to lock my bedroom door, and I'm a fucking mess, but clearly these reasons aren't working if I'm shoving my tongue down his throat.

I need to make a therapy appointment.

"I'm gonna go to bed," I say.

"I'll clean up the kitchen."

Fuck. The mess in the kitchen. "I'll help."

"No, it's okay. You look wrecked. Did you sleep at all last night after …?"

I shake my head.

"Then go. I've got this. And you did cook me dinner even if we didn't get to eat it."

"Thanks."

I should stay up and help, but I'm exhausted. Even my bones are tired. Yet, I have no expectation of sleep.

This becomes more evident when I hit my room.

"What the ever-loving fuck!" I yell.

Red. Everywhere. All over my bed, by my feet, and a trail leading out the door I'm only now noticing. Looks like a fucking bloodbath. In the middle of it? A cat licking her paws like she's cleaning herself after a job well done.

Brody's heavy footsteps pound, and he skids to a stop when he reaches me. "What's wrong?" He's breathing heavy, and I've probably knocked five years off his life. "Whoa."

Lucky stops grooming herself to look at us. Her expression is one hundred percent angelic and innocent-looking. What little fur she has is all matted and caked with marinara sauce.

"So that's why the kitchen seemed messier than when we left it," Brody says. "I thought I just wasn't paying attention earlier. Too … distracted."

I side-eye him.

"With your leg."

"Right. My leg."

"Not mentioning the kiss that didn't happen." Brody tries to hide his smile, but it's not convincing.

"So glad we're already joking about this."

"I'm trying to think about how to get marinara sauce out of

the carpet and your bedding. If we can't laugh, we're gonna cry."

I take a deep breath and let it out with resignation. "Okay, game plan. You bathe your cat, and I'll change my sheets."

"Whoa, whoa, whoa, slow down there. First of all, Lucky is my sister's cat, not mine, and since you've moved in, I think it's become pretty clear she loves *you*." Brody gestures to my bed. "She made this for you! So, I'm thinking you bathe the cat, and I'll swap out your sheets. Like a good roommate."

Something else occurs to me. "Fuck, I don't have any other sheets."

"Hold up. How do you not have any other sheets? Eww, do you not change them … ever?" He screws up his face.

"Of course, I change my sheets. I wash them and put them in the dryer. But that's gonna take two hours, and I'm fucking dead tired."

"How about this," Brody says. "Team effort. We both bathe the demon cat while your sheets are in the wash. If they're not done by the time Lucky is clean, then you can use my sheets."

"What about the kitchen?"

"I'll do that later. Priorities, Anders."

"I've never been good at those," I admit.

"I'll teach you. Now, who's picking up the demon cat?" Brody blinks at me.

I stare at him right back.

Lucky, the traitor, jumps off the bed and starts rubbing herself against my leg.

"Looks like she's chosen."

I flip him the bird as I pick up the blissfully unaware cat who has no idea what's about to happen. "Bath tub or laundry sink? How the fuck do you wash a cat?"

"I imagine it'd be much like washing a dog?"

Brody strips my bed, and I follow him into my bathroom which doubles as the laundry.

"A dog who's afraid of water?" I ask as I close the bathroom door, shutting us in here. This is gonna go bad. I just know it.

"Who knows, maybe Lucky is one of those weird cats who likes water?"

Spoiler: she isn't.

I put her down while we fill the bathtub, but as soon as it's full of water and we corner her, she becomes Houdini, the wonder cat. Escape artist extraordinaire.

Every time I go to pick her up, she bolts as if she knows what I'm doing. Someone's a perceptive little kitty.

Brody finds our game hilarious.

"A little help, maybe?" I ask.

"Fine. You need to approach more casually. You're trying to catch her which lets her know there's a reason you need to hold her." Brody steps closer to Lucky with soft feet. He says to be casual, but he looks like a caricature of an evil villain in movies where he tiptoes his way across the room to make himself less obvious.

All it does is cause Lucky to freak out more. Only, this time when she runs away, she runs right to me as if I can save her.

And instead of saving her, I'm gonna put her in the tub of death. I mean, I'm not gonna drown her, but I assume that's what cats think when they come into contact with water.

I pull her close to my chest and hug her tight—like a silent apology. When I move her towards the water, she claws at my arms and lets out a heartbreaking meow.

We get nowhere close to getting her in the tub. Her tail touches the warm water, and the wail she cries makes it sound like I'm trying to kill a flock of galahs.

"Come on, baby." I hush her with soothing tones.

It doesn't work.

Next thing I know, she leaps out of my arms and makes a break for the door, which is thankfully still closed, but I guess she thinks she can make a Lucky-shaped hole in it and escape.

The loud thunk as she hits it makes me wince.

Brody dives for her, but she shakes off her possible concussion ... wait, can cats get concussions? Either way, she slips from his grasp and runs behind the toilet.

And now she's stuck and wailing for a different reason.

"Fucking stupid cat." I'm exhausted, I want to go to bed even if I know I won't actually sleep, and I'm at that point of tiredness where I don't know what's gonna fly from my mouth. I just want to get this over with.

I get on my knees and try to get her free from between the back of the toilet and the wall where's she's lodged herself.

There's no room down here unless I squish myself, and even then, I can barely reach her.

"Here, I'll get her." Brody moves forward, but as I try to get myself out of the small space, I bump into his leg.

He reaches for the vanity to steady himself, and then the hand soap from the sink lands on my head.

"Shit, sorry." Brody reaches for me to see if I'm okay but then trips on my fucking leg or something, because next thing I know, a ninety-kilogram lawyer has a knee in my back and I'm straining to not let my face hit the tiled floor or the vanity.

"Fuck!" I hiss.

"Shit, shit, shit, shit, shit," Brody chants.

He's fast to get off me, but I'm done. I'm so fucking done.

When I finally manage to move, I land my ass next to the bath and rub the top of my head. "We're a disaster pair, I swear to God."

Brody laughs. "At least we're disasters together."

"Because that's so much better."

"I'd rather be a disaster with someone else than be one alone."

"Ah. See, that's where we differ. Give me solitude with my craziness any day."

So not true, but I'm not getting into it right now. Or ever. Yeah, let's go with never.

"Whose idea was it to bathe the demon cat?" Brody asks.

"Yours."

"Oh. Right. Well, I'm a dumbass."

"No arguments here."

Brody looks defeated. "What are we gonna do?"

I'm ready to give up too. "Leave her like that and change her name to Meatball?"

Brody laughs so hard he has to catch his breath. When he eventually calms down, he stands with determination. "Okay, I'm going in. Wish me luck."

"This'll be fun to watch."

"That wasn't really wishing me luck, but I'll take it." Brody's wider than me, so that small space is even harder to get into for him, but his arms are longer.

Meows of protest fill the bathroom, but at least she isn't screaming anymore.

Brody pulls Lucky out and holds her close to his chest. She tries to squirm out of his grasp, but he holds her stronger than I did.

He takes her over to the bath, but she stares at me with wide, begging eyes that ask me to not put her in there.

It's like one of those moments where I meet someone and feel that tiny spark of *maybe I can trust this person*. Only, this time, she's looking at me like that, and I'm about to do to her what every guy does to me eventually—give her an excuse to distrust me.

Bloody hell, when did I start caring about the fucking cat and her so-called feelings? Can cats even feel anything?

"Wait," I blurt.

Brody pauses. "What?"

"This is mean. She was like, tortured. What if she's having flashbacks or thinks we're gonna do to her what those stupid boys did?"

"Can cats suffer from PTSD?" Brody asks.

"I don't know, but what if they can?" It'd be like someone shoving me in a room with Kyle and telling me everything is okay. "Here, give her to me."

Brody smiles but doesn't move.

"What?"

"You do like her."

"Oh, shut up and hand her over."

Lucky is trembling as he gives her to me. Meatball sauce is all over the bathroom now, as well as our clothes.

"Now what?" Brody asks.

"Get a wet cloth. I'll try to get as much off with her in my lap."

"I'll help." Brody grabs one of my towels off the rack and dips it in the bathwater.

Lucky flinches and lets out a little angry growl when the towel first touches her skin, but when Brody massages all over her and I murmur calming words, she settles.

"I think it's working," I whisper, not wanting to scare her again.

Every time we have to stop for Brody to wet a clean part of the towel and start again, she tries to stop him with her long claws as if to say, "No, keep going." Either that or she's a cat and is playing. It's most likely the latter, but I like to think Lucky is smarter than that.

Oh God, I really am beginning to like the rodent.

"I'm coming back," Brody assures her when she swipes at the towel again. When he starts cleaning her again, I feel his stare on me, but I don't dare lift my head. "We may be a disaster together, but we do make a great team."

I nod, still refusing to look up. I keep my eyes on Lucky.

We get most of the gunk off her, and by the time she's as clean as we can get her, she's purring in my lap and enjoying all the attention.

"Turns out you're an attention whore, huh?" I coo.

"I think she's just smitten with you," Brody says. "And I can't say I blame her."

I keep trying not to look at him, but after words like that, it's impossible not to. His blue eyes shine bright while that intoxicating charm rolls off him.

I used to be smooth like him once upon a time. Mostly, I can fake it now, but it doesn't feel the same as when it came naturally. It always feels like I'm putting on a show, pretending to be someone else—someone who's not broken.

Brody knows the darkest part of my soul and he's still flirting with me.

His lips turn up at the edges. "Sorry. I keep promising to stop saying that shit and then I—"

I lean forward and capture his mouth with mine again. It's the second time tonight I've found myself kissing him with no hesitation. Only seizing the moment.

Lucky protests in my lap, squirming to try to get away from us crushing her. I let her go, because right now all I can concentrate on is the man on his knees next to me, taking my mouth as if it's something to not only treasure but protect.

The weird safeness I get with him churns in my gut again, and like the last few days, the internal debate of letting it happen and backing off has me on edge.

Brody's tongue takes over like it did earlier, and I want to let it happen. I want to let him do whatever he wants to me right here on my dirty bathroom floor. I want to get him off. I want him to get me off.

I'm on that cliff—the one where I want to jump off and freefall. I want to let all my control go, bask in Brody's touch, his mouth, his big hands. But my knees buckle, my heart stutters, and my head screams at me to back away.

Stupid brain.

Brody groans and cups the back of my head. He pulls me closer, and we shift around until Brody throws one of his legs over mine. We go from next to each other to him straddling me in the blink of an eye, and with my back pushed against the cold tile of the side of the bathtub and the heavy weight on top of me and no escape behind me, my body protests.

I'm trapped now.

Cue freak-out.

The whirring of the washing machine sounds like the storm clouds in my head.

I try to breathe, but with Brody's tongue in my mouth, I can't get air.

My body seizes up, trying for oxygen it can't get. I need out, I need to breathe, I need—

As if sensing it, Brody pulls back. "Anders?"

His voice is soothing and actually helps. It sounds nothing like Kyle's and calms me back to that safeness only Brody has the ability to give.

Even though I'm on the brink of a panic attack, my name on his lips has the ability to almost pull me out of it.

"Say it again," I croak. I haven't opened my eyes, but I know he's right there.

"Your name?" he whispers.

I nod.

"Anders."

I even manage a smile. "Kiss me again."

Where I expect his lips, all I can feel is his weight shift as he climbs off me.

"Yeah, as much as I am dying to do that, I don't think it's a good idea."

Now my eyes fly open. "Why not?"

He can't do this to me. I'm having a therapeutic breakthrough here. Never since Kyle has someone been able to get me so keyed up and on the verge of letting go. I want to let go.

I'm so sick of being this way. Always in my head.

"You're not telling me something."

Oh, shit. "What do you mean?"

"Are you … did you … I mean … are you sure nothing sexual happened to you?"

"What?" My voice is shaky and does this high-pitched thing.

"I could feel you tense up just now. Like you weren't into it or you were scared of me."

"I am scared of you," I admit.

Brody looks hurt, and fuck, I'd do anything to take that expression on his face away.

"I'm scared of everyone," I continue. "When it happened … when I was attacked …" My throat starts to close up. "It literally came out of nowhere. I was taken off guard, and it all happened so fast … It's not sex that scares me. It's putting myself in a vulnerable position where if the situation turns, I'll be helpless. I don't trust anyone except for my brother. So, yeah, when you straddled me, I realised I was trapped, and my panic tried to take over."

"Anders, I'm so sorry. If I'd known—"

I shake my head. "Don't be sorry. I'm not. For the first time since it happened, I want to kiss someone and try to push through that haze of panic."

Brody's brows shoot up as if he's surprised, but he schools his features quickly.

"That probably scares you. Hell, it'd scare me if I were you. It's a lot of pressure. Forget I said anything."

"It doesn't scare me. What does scare me is doing something that might make you terrified of me. I can tell you until I'm blue in the face that I will never, ever hurt you, but I'm guessing words don't change shit in that brain of yours."

"I hate that they don't."

Brody huffs. "God, I hate myself for being a good guy right now."

I laugh. "Funnily enough, so do I."

"How so?"

"Sometimes, I want to put myself in the scariest situation possible so I can get it over with, you know?"

"I'm no therapist, but that sounds like a horrible idea."

"That's what my actual therapist says. It's all about gradual steps. But it's so frustrating when I want something and can't go for it."

Brody breaks out into a small smile. "Am I that something you want?"

I grunt. "Only you could turn that into an ego boost."

Now that we've stopped pawing at each other, a different set of paws circles our legs.

"I guess we should get to the rest of the cleaning," I say.

"I'd say we could leave it until tomorrow, but if we let Lucky—"

"Meatball. I've officially changed her name."

"We're not calling her Meatball."

"Yes, we are." I'm proud I'm not freaking out over a "we" label—even if it's only in terms of being roommates and friends.

For the first time in five years, I've made an actual friend.

"Demon cat will just go back out there and get sauced again if we don't clean up the kitchen. And your bedroom."

I pull *Meatball* into my lap. "She's not a demon cat."

"No, but it seems she is yours now."

"What can I say, she adopted me."

Make that two friends.

10

BRODY

Who's the biggest moron on the planet? That would be me. For sure. One hundred percent dumbass.

Kissing my roommate? Dumb.

Doing it again? Super dumb.

Stopping it from going any further? Dumbest dumb to ever fucking dumb.

So dumb that I've got no other word to use than dumb.

Anders makes me not smart.

Clearly.

After the bathroom incident, I send Anders to bed while I clean the apartment because being around him is too much temptation. I want to kiss him again.

I want to do a whole lot more than kiss him.

Anderson Steele is burrowing under my skin without even meaning to, and my heart hasn't been knocked on its ass by a guy since ... well, Reed.

What Reed and I had was puppy love. Not in the puppy kink sort of way, but *boys discovering they're into other boys* type of way. The truth is, I did fall hard for him back in high school. I had all those forever thoughts and thought he'd move to Brisbane for me when we started university. Instead, he stayed on the Sunshine Coast and never came to visit.

We talked about doing long distance, but Reed was adamant it wouldn't work. So, we broke up, but I always wondered. It was so easy being with him.

When he told me he was moving to Brisbane for work, I stupidly thought we'd pick up where we left off, but he'd only been here a few weeks when I first caught up with him and he told me all about this great but weird guy he was seeing.

I know Law thinks I still have a thing for Reed, and maybe I do, I don't know. There are definite feelings there, but when I look at Anders, it doesn't compare.

When I look at Reed, I think, yeah, it'd be easy and convenient to be with him. I see Anders and want to make things right in his world. I want to protect him and hold him and just ... make the scary go away.

With Anders, it's about what I want to do for him, not how convenient he'd make my life. I don't want anything from him but for him to be happy.

I've always had a pull towards him—ever since I met him. I thought it was the thrill of the chase, but I'm starting to think it's this deep-seated need to help him heal.

Last night, after finding out the horrible thing he went through, I made the silent vow to make sure he never experiences that type of pain again.

If only he'll let me.

By the time I fall into bed, it's early morning. My alarm's set to go off in two hours, and I'm going to be dead on my feet tomorrow at work.

The sound of Lucky knocking shit over with her catty—pun totally intended—attitude makes me groan. I don't have the energy to get up and check on what she's doing now. I have no idea what she gets up to at night, but she can get loud. I learned fast that photo frames belong on shelves she can't reach, and books need to be stacked upright on the bookcase. Any edges she can get her mouth around, she chews on.

Weird cat. Weird cat who's as obsessive as I am about our gorgeous roommate who showed her so much compassion even though he claims to not like cats.

I fall asleep with Anders' image in my head and a smile on my face.

Inevitably, though, two short hours later, I'm wishing I were dead. Or at least that my phone battery was dead, because the noise it's making makes me want to cry.

I'm melodramatic in the mornings. Always am.

The only reason I'm able to drag myself out of bed every day is because I'm the boss's son, and if I'm late, it reflects poorly on my dad, and if I reflect poorly on him, my father has no qualms making an example of my bad behaviour.

Welcome to the world of law firm politics. Where who you know gets you in and you spend the rest of the time trying to separate yourself from said person.

It took a while, because my dad and I don't share the same last name thanks to my mother's doing, but everyone knows I'm a name-partner's son. The only people who are nice to me are the ones who think I could put in a good word for them. When they find out I have even less pull than a first-year work placement trainee, they're suddenly less interested in water cooler talk.

Like I have time for sucking up anyway.

Nope, I'm too busy trying to prove I'm worthy of being there without the use of my father's name.

When I manage to get my butt out of bed and amble out to the kitchen, it takes a minute for the sound of the TV to register.

I turn and blink away the sleep to find Anders on our couch. He looks like a zombie with his long, in-need-of-a-wash hair in his face and the prominent bags under his eyes. He stares at the TV, which is on the shopping channel, for crying out loud.

"You're up early," I mumble.

"Mm," he grunts.

I ignore Lucky on Anders' lap. I'm too tired to tease him about it. "Coffee?"

He holds up a mug.

"That's the instant crap, right? I have an espresso machine—you should use it."

"Didn't want to wake you." Anders' voice is groggy with a definite croak. If he didn't look like he was about to keel over, I'd think it was sexy.

"You okay? You look sick."

His gaze goes from the TV to mine and back again. "Just tired."

"Did you sleep at all?"

No answer.

"Is it because your lock isn't fixed? I forgot to call someone yesterday. I'll do it today."

"It's okay, I'll do it. I'm gonna—" Anders slams his mouth shut.

"Going to what?"

He shakes his head. "Nothing."

I purse my lips. Anders has gone back to being the quirky, nervous guy, and I take back what I thought the other night. I like him much more relaxed than nervous. Nervous means he's not comfortable around me, and I was kind of hoping after last night ...

Stupid brain. Two kisses don't take away years of anxiety.

Two kisses clearly haven't knocked him for six like they have me. Two kisses aren't going to magically fix everything.

No matter how much I want them to.

Any progress I thought I made last night has been obliterated.

At least, that's my impression until I feel a presence behind me. Oh, how I want to lean back against Anders' chest. I close my eyes imagining it, when his voice cuts through the din.

"Are we cool?"

I clear my throat. "Of course."

"The last two nights have been kinda heavy, so I'll understand if you want me to go or whatever."

I spin and bring us face to face. "What? Why would I kick you out?"

"For kissing you and then pretending I didn't? Then trying to make you kiss me again because I felt an ounce of my old self coming back when your lips were on mine?"

I don't know what to do with that. Part of me is happy dancing on the inside because everything in me wants to help Anders any way I can. It's instinct. But at the same time, it's a lot of pressure to be the one to "fix" him.

"I'm sorry if I made it uncomfortable." Anders' voice is small, like he's ashamed of the things that are out of his control.

I can't help myself. My hand moves, cupping his jaw. "The only uncomfortable part was trying to get to sleep when all I could think about was ..." Instead of mentioning those mind-blowing kisses and risk freaking him out again, my thumb traces over his lips.

Anders pulls away anyway.

"Sorry," I say.

"Don't be," he whispers.

We stand there, staring at each other, a few feet of space between us.

"How do we make it not awkward now?" I ask. All I want to do is kiss him again. And again, and again, and again.

"Being awkward for the majority of the day? Welcome to my entire life." With a smile, Anders goes to his bedroom and softly closes the door while I remain in the kitchen, both turned on and confused.

Apparently, Anders thinks to make our situation unawkward, he should go back to working out whenever I walk in the door. Only now when he leaves, I'm no longer offended but relieved. It's not that I don't want to see him. I want to see him too much.

With work shit weighing me down, though, I don't want to bring Anders down with me.

When I was assigned to this rape case and I confided in Anders, it triggered his nightmares. It makes me think Anders could still be lying to me about what truly happened to him.

He says his issues aren't with sex, but the lack of control connected with sex. I guess PTSD presents itself in different ways, but I'm still suspicious.

If I had to face Anders after sitting through the countless depositions for the case, I don't think I could hold it together.

There are countless jokes about lawyers being heartless. After today, where I had to ask a sixteen-year-old girl about her sexual habits and imply she's *easy*, I don't find the jokes funny anymore. I am heartless. Or, at least, I feel it right now.

I asked the associate in charge of the case if she ever wonders if she's on the wrong side of the law—especially on a case like this—and all she did was say "That's why we make the big bucks."

Like money is supposed to clear my conscience.

There's not enough money in the world to make my humanity disappear.

At least, I don't think there is. I hope there isn't.

Being desensitised to stuff like this is probably the only way to deal with it, but who wants to be an emotional desert?

When my father offered me this job, I figured I'd be getting corporate A-holes off for tax evasion or, I don't know, crimes that are wrong but don't make me feel sick to my stomach.

I'm beginning to realise why my father's as cold as he is. He needs thick armour to do what he does every day.

Anders isn't even in the apartment when I get home, and I'm so emotionally wrecked, I don't bother changing out of my suit. I faceplant onto the couch on my way to my bedroom.

My phone pings with the work email alert, and I try to find any fucks to give.

Nope. All out. Sorry.

I don't know how long I lie on the couch for. It's very possible I pass out, because I wake to the sound of the shower running in Anders' bathroom.

To get up and hide in my bedroom or to stay where I am?

I try to move and come up with the answer.

Where I am. Definitely stay where I am.

The shower turns off. This is my small chance to make a break for it.

"Rough day again?"

Too late.

I sit up and turn to Anders. Who's only wearing a towel.

Holy shit.

Holy fucking shit.

He usually comes out of the bathroom fully dressed.

I didn't know a torso could be so long. Do the Steele brothers have stumps for legs? I check. Nope. Definitely normal-sized legs. They're toned too.

My gaze travels back upwards, over the perfect V sticking out from the towel, toned abs ... pierced nipples.

"Umm, was it so bad you've forgotten how to talk?"

Nope. I'm just admiring the amazing view.

Don't say that, you creep.

"It was a long day," I say.

He looks confused. "You're home at the usual time."

"Mentally, it was a long day."

"You working this weekend?"

"It's Friday already?" I don't have to go into work on most weekends, but I can't remember the last time I had a full Saturday off. Things at work have been crazy busy since Anders moved in.

Anders laughs. "Yeah. It is. That charity thing at Law's dojo is this weekend. You going?"

"Charity thing?"

"I assumed Reed would've told you. Law's giving free self-defence lessons and trying to find donations to upgrade his dojo. His LGBTQ student program is exploding, so he wants to look for a bigger space."

"Oh cool. Uh, when is it?"

"Tomorrow afternoon."

I nod and use all my effort to stand. I need to get away from a half-naked Anders ASAP. "I'll be there. But right now, I need to go pass the fuck out in my bed."

When I do eventually collapse onto my bed, I can't help wondering if I make a big donation at this thing tomorrow, if my conscience will be clean.

My inability to go to sleep tells me no. That bitch wants

me to toss and turn all night and deal with the implications of my actions.

Great, now my conscience has taken on the voice of my mother. There's no coming back from *that*.

When I hear the TV turn on around two in the morning, I'm thankful for the distraction and hopefully some company.

If Anders is okay with that. And dressed this time.

I find him in the dark; the only thing lighting the room is the blue hue from the television. He's got a blanket over the top of his head and wrapped around him, and he sits cross-legged on the couch.

Anticipating the jump scare I tend to do to him, I alert him of my presence before he can flip out.

"It's only me." I enter the room with my hands up.

He doesn't flinch. That's progress.

"Sorry, did I wake you?" He sounds genuinely concerned.

"I couldn't sleep either. What are we watching?"

"Shopping network. It's the only thing on at this time of night that isn't sucky."

I throw myself down next to him. Anders is kind of in the middle of the couch, so he tries to scoot over a bit without being obvious, but it's so obvious.

It's tempting to lean into him to piss him off, but I think better of it.

Being around Anders isn't like being around any other guy. Wanting him because of that probably makes me a cliché, but my casual charm doesn't work on him. Every move I make around him has to be calculated, and I don't know why I love that so much when the reason for it is so tragic.

I want to say he's like a puzzle, but that would be even more cliché. He's like one of those logic games where you need to be two steps ahead the whole time to defeat it.

Not that I want to defeat Anders. I just want to break

down his walls so he'll let me in. I want to be the one he leans on. Confides in.

Ignoring the tension in his body as he tries to shuffle away from me, I lift my head in the direction of the TV. "Surely, there has to be something better than this."

"Not anything that'll keep me awake."

"Wait ... you're trying to stay awake? Why? Didn't the locksmith come?" I called and organised one.

Anders glances towards his bedroom and then back at me. "There's a new lock. I just ... I haven't been sleeping well, and there's no point in trying when I get like this. If I force myself to stay awake, I generally get to a point where my body does all the work for me by passing out."

My teeth dig into my bottom lip to stop me from telling him how unhealthy that is. He has to know that already.

"It's not ... is it because of me? Because of—"

"No." He forces one of his smiles. I'm a little insulted he doesn't realise I know when he's faking it. "This happens sometimes. It's got nothing to do with you. I promise. We agreed we were cool, remember?"

"Can I please look for something semi-decent if we're not going to go to sleep?"

Anders hands over the remote as if challenging me to find something better, but he's right. There is nothing decent on TV at two a.m.

"You should get Netflix or something," I suggest to him.

"Why me?"

"I never get a chance to watch TV. It'd be a waste of money."

Anders holds out his hands. "Because you're struggling so much."

I frown. "My father is rich. Not me. I'm on an associate's

starting salary. I'd never be able to afford this place on my income."

He must sense he's hit a nerve. "Sorry. I just figured ..."

"This is Dad's place. Well, technically, it's mine, but he bought it for me. I know that should probably make me feel guilty or privileged or whatever, but it's not like I don't work hard."

"I'm not saying you don't. I ... I'm sorry if I said something wrong. I thought you came from a lot of money and it's something you don't have to worry about."

Dammit. I slump in defeat. "No, you're right in a way. It's something I don't have to worry about. But it gets to me when people imply I'm living off my father. It happens at work, so it's a touchy subject."

Anders smiles. "Consider it dropped."

"How about we rent a movie from Google Play—something actiony and brainless."

Anders pauses briefly but nods.

And that's how I end up on a couch in the middle of the night, watching *Die Hard* for the billionth time.

11

ANDERSON

My first reaction when I wake up on top of Brody should be to panic. My body tenses, and my brain tells me I should be freaking out, but no trigger warnings are present. Just the ever-loving need to get the fuck up.

How did this happen?

More importantly, how did I let it happen?

He's using the armrest as a pillow, and his legs hang off the side of the couch. With my head on his chest, I'm practically curled into his side while his arm is draped around me.

Brody is as still as can be, his breathing long and laboured like he's asleep. But when I lift my head, he's not asleep at all. "Are you freaking out?" he whispers.

Yes. "Not as much as I thought I would be."

"I can feel your heartbeat against my rib cage. You're freaking out."

"I'm not moving though. I don't have the need to run out of here right now." Just the want, but there's a big difference between need and want. Anyone in therapy will tell you that.

"We're great at this not-making-things-awkward thing, huh?" Brody jokes, and I manage to huff a laugh.

"How ... uh, did this happen?" I have a feeling all the non-sleeping I've been doing might've caused me to perhaps black out, but I can't for the life of me imagine a world in which I'd let myself do that in front of someone else other than Law.

Brody wiggles beneath me, and oh, yeah, I'm still on top of him. I sit up, and he follows, stretching his impressive muscles as he does.

"You looked pretty wrecked. I asked you a few times if you wanted to go back to bed and you said no."

I must've been more out of it than I thought. Since the other night where Brody broke the lock on my door, I've been waiting until he slips out for work so I can relax enough to drift off. By the time I do fall asleep, it's not long until my alarm goes off and I have to drag myself out of bed to get to work.

Which is why falling asleep on him doesn't make any sense.

It's been about a week of hardly enough sleep, so granted, I was tired, but the reason for the lack of sleep somehow became the cure? I don't understand.

At all.

Maybe I've reached that point where it's all getting on top of me. I got called out at work yesterday for inverting some numbers, which happens sometimes in general, but never with me.

I have a meticulous eye for detail when it comes to numbers, and I think the only reason my accounting firm didn't fire me a few years ago when all the major shit went down is because I'm good at my job ... when I turn up.

I could see the concern in my boss's eyes when I told her I hadn't gotten much sleep and would catch up this weekend. Like a few years ago when I needed a heap of time off, excuses of little sleep, personal issues, and sickness were the norm. I think she was a second away from asking if everything was all right, but I hightailed it out of her office, because I'd have no idea how to answer that.

"When you fell asleep, you kind of slumped over and used my shoulder as a pillow," Brody says. "I again asked if you wanted to go to bed, but instead ... you, uh ... you asked me to stay."

"I did?"

Brody's face pales. "Shit, did I do something wrong? Like, was I supposed to not let that happen or—"

"No, it's fine. I ... I guess I'm surprised. I didn't think I'd be comfortable enough around anyone to ..."

"It was just sleep, Anders. It's okay."

But it's not okay. This has to mean something, right? That maybe not all hope is lost?

"Anders?"

My gaze flicks to Brody's. The striking contrast between the brown hair and light eyes is usually the thing that takes me off guard. Not this time.

This time it's the deep worry in his eyes. The fear he did something wrong. Brody doesn't understand that he's somehow done something right. I just don't know what it is.

I want to know so I can get him or anyone else to replicate it. "I want to try something."

"What?"

Ignoring morning breath, the crick in my neck from using Brody as a pillow the last few hours, and all the rest of the bullshit, I lean forward and capture his mouth with mine.

It only lasts a second or two before Brody pushes me back. "Wait, wait, wait. Anders, we've already done this."

I shake my head. "I don't want to stop this time."

"I don't want to hurt you or do something that makes you tense up in the way you do."

"You won't." I wince. "Okay, I know you won't intentionally. I can step out of my issues long enough to know that if I'm being rational, you're someone I should be able to trust. But that's just it—I haven't been with anyone since the attack where rationality has outweighed the anxiety. And you're ... I don't know what you are, but I have to know."

Brody blinks up at me as he contemplates what I've said. Apparently it's good enough for him. He moves closer, and this time—for the first time ever—he's the one who closes the gap between us.

It's almost an immediate switch. From thinking I can do this to knowing I'm screwed. Literally two seconds ago, I was begging for more.

Now that it's happening, my body's protesting and my brain's screaming that I fucked up.

Instead of enjoying the sensations of his dominating kiss, I can't let go. All those insecurities, my past demons, my inability to relinquish control ... they don't allow me.

I thought—no, I hoped—it would be different with him. I've had glimpses of what it would be like to do this with Brody, and the level of comfort I have with him confuses me.

But in this moment, when Brody's hand cups my jaw, I cringe. He mistakes it as a shudder of pleasure and moans into my mouth.

Breathe through it, Anders. It's just a hand.

I told him I want this, and now I'm scared I'll have to take it back.

He pushes his tongue into my mouth. His lips are soft, and the kiss sends all the blood south to my groin. It's enough to make my brain switch off, if only for a second.

I want more. I want it to stop. Want to breathe and pass out at the same time.

That damn hand is ruining everything. It moves from the side of my face to the back of my hair, and that's when I know for sure this isn't going to work. The move is too controlling, and that it's on my left side makes it worse. I'm self-conscious of my scar, and it reminds me of why I can't have this.

I pull back, probably a little too fast to be considered normal.

"What's wrong?" he asks, his voice barely above a breath. His brow scrunches in concern, and I hate that look. I don't need pity. I just need to do this. I need to prove to myself I *can* do it.

Instead of stopping this like I should, I try to come up with ways to make it happen.

"Sit on your hands," I say.

"Huh?"

"Sit. On. Your. Hands."

He doesn't move, waiting for me to elaborate. So not gonna.

When he gives in, he does as I say, and my fingers travel down and skim the outline of his impressively large, and incredibly hard, cock through his expensive Calvin Klein boxer briefs. My own cock twitches.

I only get harder with how hot he looks, sitting on his hands, his eyelids hooded and mouth slightly parted.

Okay, I can do this. *This*, I can handle.

My hands work to free his cock through the small hole in his boxers, and I drop to my knees on the carpet. In fear of panicking any second, I don't have time to tease him like I normally would, so I take him as far as I can in my mouth. Everything about him is bigger than the guys I'm used to dating, and when I gag, I'm brought back to a time where I dated only bigger guys. That makes me think of Kyle, and I don't want to go down that path right now.

Push him out of your head. He doesn't belong there anymore. Breathe through your nose and think about the here and now.

Brody.

His smile.

His kindness.

I force myself to slow down and drown everything out, even though I want fast and messy just to get it over with.

I'm in a conflicted state of constant want for more and the urge to run away, but the noises falling from his lips root me in place.

His cock is thick in my mouth, and the heady flavour of precum hits my tastebuds. I hum around him, and for a brief moment the rest of the world finally fades away.

My mind clears.

It's as if time slows down, and all I can do is hold on and savour the moment. I hope it never stops.

Then I feel him shift, and I'm brought back into the present. My heart rate kicks into overdrive. I glance up, my lips still around his cock, but I prepare to pull away the second he removes his hands from underneath him. But he doesn't. He's only trying to get closer to the edge of the couch so he can control his thrusts as he fucks my mouth.

I let him do it, because as long as he's sitting on his hands, I can take it. As long as those hands don't move, I can let go the most my brain has ever allowed me to.

The need to rush this is long gone, and I close my eyes, experiencing. It's like I'm having sex for the first time. Brody's moans, and the way his cock pulses in my mouth, he has an all-consuming need I can feel from him as he trembles beneath me.

My hand cups his balls, squeezing lightly.

"Anders," he says breathlessly.

Even my name on his lips does something to my insides.

"I want to touch you."

I freeze. My shoulders tense, and my throat constricts. The

throat that currently has a cock occupying it. That makes me choke and splutter.

Dammit. So close.

"Not part of the deal," I say. "If you want to come, don't touch."

He opens his mouth but pauses as if choosing to say something else instead. "That kinda sounds like something a hooker would say. You're not gonna charge me after this, right?" He smiles, and I'm so fucking relieved he went for the joke instead of making this a thing.

I scoff. "Like you could afford me."

Brody laughs, but when I lower my head and go back to sucking and licking him, something's changed. The mere suggestion of him touching me means I'm back in my head, overthinking and overanalysing. I think he senses the moment's gone too.

That connection we had is replaced with awkwardness, and while he's still hard in my mouth, he's not urgent and needy like he was before my minor freak-out.

I pull off him, trying to fight the urge to avert my gaze from him, and look him in the eyes as if asking a silent question.

"I'm sorry," he says.

"It's okay. It's my fault." It's always my fault that I can't do something normal people can every day.

"No, I shouldn't have pushed."

"You didn't."

Brody's lips form into a thin line. "I want you to know that if I ask to do something and you're not comfortable, you don't have to do it. You're free to say no to anything. I'm not going to get mad or frustrated. Ever. Okay?"

I manage a nod.

"Can you come up here?"

I stare at the cock in front of my face. Still hard, swollen, and needy-looking. My stupid issues ruined the mood, but apparently not for Brody's little guy ... or not-so-little guy. Thick and veiny, it's impressive to say the least. "I don't want to let you down."

"Am I allowed to move my hands from under me yet?"

Oops. "Uh, yeah. That's okay."

When Brody cups my head this time, it's less controlling. It's more like he's trying to reassure me. "Stand up and straddle me."

I hesitate.

"You're still in control here, Anders. You'll have me pinned to the couch. You can get away anytime you want. I just ... I want you close. I want to take care of you, not the other way around."

Part of me loves that he wants to work through this with me. The other part of me hates it. I hate he even has to think about things like that.

In the past few years, I've had countless men warm my bed ... or technically, I've warmed theirs. I never brought guys back to my apartment if I could help it, but there were a few of the less intimidating guys—guys who appeared even more awkward than me—who I brought back to mine, mainly because they still lived with their parents and there was nowhere else to go.

None of the countless men knew about my issues. Actually, none of them even got a glimpse of the real me. If I ever tensed or started feeling uncomfortable during sex, I'd make sure they got off, and then I would lie and say I'd had too much to drink to come even though I never drank enough to get tipsy, let alone drunk.

I can't lie to Brody.

He already knows me better than any other guy, but he still

doesn't know every corner of my darkness. He's only aware of the abstract part of me that was once hurt and now wears the scars of his past.

Yet, he still stares at me with softness, not judgement. Worry, but not pity. Okay, there's a little bit of pity, but the biggest thing I see in his eyes is protectiveness.

I want to trust it. I'm close to tears because I want it so much, and I'm not sure I can do it.

The push-pull I have towards Brody drives me to the edge of crazy because I'm not in control.

There's a part of my brain that doesn't trust and a part of my heart that revolts at the thought of letting someone else in.

But then there are the parts that are so desperate to chase a high I haven't felt in so long. So, so long.

"Anders."

Brody saying my name breaks me.

It breaks every single part of me.

I climb into his lap. His cock, which had begun softening, twitches against mine, only separated by my boxer shorts.

When I lower my mouth to his, our tongues meet, but it's not enough.

I need something ... need more.

Brody's hands stay by his sides.

"Touch me," I whisper against his lips.

He pulls back. "Are you sure?"

No.

I'd give anything to be certain of sex again.

"Complete honesty," Brody says. "That's the only way this is going to work. I can be patient, and I can back off if you need it, but you have to tell me."

"I want to try." I'm so quiet, I don't know if he hears me until he cracks a smile.

This time when he kisses me, his warmth and comfort

outweigh the hesitance. When his fingers dip inside my boxers, his softness outweighs his scary hard lines. And when his hand fists around my cock, I shudder from a sensation I haven't felt in so long. Ripples of pleasure travel over my skin.

My hips rut against him.

"That's so good, baby," Brody says. "You're doing so good."

His encouragement should trigger something inside me, but his voice is actually one of the few things that sets him apart from my memories of Kyle. He sounds nothing like my ex.

It makes me let go that little bit more.

Precum makes Brody's strokes more fluid, more rhythmic.

I'm still in control, I chant in my head as I get closer to release.

Brody's hips push forward while his free hand pulls me closer.

Our cocks meet between us, and Brody uses his hands to jerk us together.

"You should come," Brody says.

I laugh, but it comes out breathy. "You should."

"Trust me. I'm struggling to hold out here. You feel amazing against me."

Leaning closer, I bite down gently on his neck to prevent myself from saying stupid shit that's stupid. Like, he's the only guy in forever who's turned me on this much. His are the only pair of hands I've truly enjoyed on me. His words are the only comfort I've felt, and his presence is still the only thing that makes me antsy and needy at the same time.

Brody's breathing quickens, his body tenses, but I beat him to the punch.

"Fuck, Brody." I come on a loud grunt and lose myself in the orgasm.

My muscles ache, but I keep convulsing, coming all over our shirts which we didn't even think to remove.

Only when I catch my breath and lean back do I realise I don't know if Brody finished. At the end there, I was too distracted by my own orgasm slamming into me to notice if he came, but if the amount of cum between us and the satisfied look on his face is anything to go by, I'd say he enjoyed it as much as I did.

So, of course, *that's* when the panic sets in.

When my brain isn't clouded by lust, it reminds me that he could've done anything to me while I was distracted, and I would've been taken off guard.

For the second time in my life, I could've been the guy who froze.

There have been studies about the natural fight-or-flight reaction. Humans and animals will only fight if they have to—most choosing to flee where they can. Unless they're like bears or some shit. And not the fun gay type of bear.

In the most pivotal moment in my life, I chose neither and fucking froze. By the time I'd snapped out of it, I was already pinned to the floor with a blade at my neck, staring into the dead eyes of someone who told me they loved me.

The memory tries to take over. Even when I clutch at my throat and my fingers sink into my thick beard, all I feel is the knife piercing my neck. I shut my eyes and try to shake the sensation away, but it doesn't work.

No, this can't happen. Not now. Not right now. Not after that.

"Hey," Brody says, his tone soothing. But it's not soothing enough. "What happened just now?"

I keep my eyes closed and start counting to ten silently, though I feel my lips move.

"Anders, it's okay. It's me."

I shake my head, because before Brody sounded nothing like Kyle, but now all I can hear is the gruff, deep voice of my ex-boyfriend.

God, I'm a mess.

I'm on top of my roommate, our cocks still out, cum everywhere, and I can't fucking breathe.

On wobbly legs, I pull away and stand. "I have to shower."

"Uh, I think we both do."

"Right. I'll ... uh, go first."

I need to get away from him so I can get some oxygen.

12

BRODY

I've fucked up.
Reed's going to kill me.
Anders is off limits.
Apparently, my dick heard *"Maul him."*

It wouldn't be so bad if he wasn't in the shower right now, clearly panicking.

Everything was fine—it was slow and a little awkward watching Anders try to relax, and the blowjob was great until I pushed and fucked it all up, but when Anders let go? It was fucking perfect. Right up until he ran away.

I can't pretend to understand what he's going through, which is exactly why I shouldn't have crossed the line with him.

When the shower shuts off, I snap out of the doubt and try to put on a confident face. I need to act like his reaction isn't affecting me, because he doesn't need the added pressure of that on top of what he's dealing with.

I've never regretted something while not actually regretting it. What we did ... I've wanted that for months. But not at the cost of Anders' mental health.

Anders appears wearing a towel, just like he did last night. My brain short-circuits again, forgetting all the reasons why it's a bad idea to mess around with him.

Until I see his face. Guilt is back with a vengeance.

"So, umm …" he says at the same time I say, "My turn to shower."

Anders grips his towel tighter. "I'll probably be gone when you get out. Law asked me to help him and Reed set up the dojo for today, and I kinda lost track of time."

"If you wait for me to shower, I can come with if you need more hands on deck."

"Uh, thanks for the offer, but I'm already late."

I want to cock my eyebrow in challenge, because a few extra minutes won't kill him or the dojo or Law. I want to call him on his skittish behaviour, but I'm so out of my depth, I don't know if that will push him away more.

"I'm sure you've got work to do anyway, right?" Anders' hopeful tone tells me all I need to know.

And I mean, he is right. I always have stuff I could work on. I brought my work laptop home with me last night so I could go over some case files, but I don't want Anders to walk out that door without resolving anything.

I nod. "I do have work to do, but it can wait. If you can—"

"I'll just see you there this afternoon. It's fine. I'll save you a spot in Law's class."

Great, I'm back to getting fake smiles.

―――

When I turn up to Law's dojo a few hours later, Anders is nowhere to be seen.

Shocking.

Part of me wants to slip out of here before I'm spotted, but no dice.

The second I turn my back to walk out the door, Law's voice hits my ears. It sends a shiver through me, because it sounds exactly like the voice I hoped would be here.

"Chickening out?"

Ugh. I cannot deal with Law's smugness right now. From the way Anders talks about his brother, I get the feeling Law doesn't mean to be smug, but it still pisses me off. It makes me want to yell, *I want your brother not your boyfriend, Mr. Egotistical.*

Still, I plaster on my mocking smirk because I'm me, and I actually kind of enjoy the tension between Law and me. He's fun to piss off, and it's only fair to make him as mad as he makes me.

I turn to him. "Chickening out of what?"

"The free class." He frowns. "Did Reed tell you about it?"

Tempting to say yes, but I'm not *that* mean. "Anders, actually."

Oh, hello. Law's jaw hardens, and he glares at me. I haven't had that big a reaction since he first found out I used to date Reed.

"Living with him going well, then?"

"Wouldn't you know? You guys talk about everything."

"He says it's going fine."

"*Fine?*" I mockingly exclaim. "All I get is *fine?* I need to up my roommate game."

Law loses the tension in his shoulders and finally relaxes a little. I find it interesting his mood reacts off mine. We'll probably have to clear our bad blood one day, but not today.

"Where is Anders, anyway? He said he'd meet me here."

Law opens his mouth, but nothing comes out.

That can't be good.

"Uh, he, uh ... he should be back later. He had to step out for a bit."

Shit. "Did he have a panic attack?"

Law's eyes widen. "How ... I mean, he ..."

"He told me what happened to him. He kind of had to when he punched me for trying to wake him from a nightmare."

More surprise on Law's face until he smiles to cover it. "Is that what happened there?" He points to my eye which isn't so much bruised now but yellowish.

"Okay, I'm starting to think you guys don't talk as much as I thought. This happened last week."

"We don't talk as much as we used to," he mutters.

Aw, dammit. I don't want to feel sorry for the guy.

"Maybe that's a good thing."

When he scowls, I continue.

"Anders has relied on you for so long. Maybe it's good he's doing something on his own."

"Do you and Reed talk about Anders and me often? You sound just like him."

Again, I want to say yes, because it's like a reflex to drive Law crazy. I think it's because I'm protective of Reed, and Law messed with him when they first got together. But if I want whatever is happening with Anders and me to work out, I have to play nice with his brother.

"I haven't spoken to Reed for a while, but Anders told me."

"How close are you guys?"

Mutual orgasms this morning is probably the wrong answer here.

"Nothing forces two people to get to know each other faster than living together."

"Guess that's true."

Reed appears from the back office. "Hey! I didn't realise you were coming."

"Anders invited me. And then disappeared, it seems."

Reed smiles.

Aw fuck no. I know that look. Reed wants something from me. "Whatever you're thinking, the answer is no."

"I was thinking Law needs an inexperienced assistant to demonstrate moves for the class."

"No," both Law and I say at the same time.

Reed pouts, and he looks utterly ridiculous, but one glance at Law and I know we're doing this. Guess one thing we have in common is being unable to say no to Reed.

"Fine," I mumble.

"Can't wait." Law's voice has an edge to it.

The place is mostly set up for the afternoon festivities, and people start arriving. Reed greets everyone at the door, while Law does the finishing touches.

Every time the bell over the door chimes, I can't help myself. I lock eyes with every single person who enters, and none of them are the brown eyes I'm looking for.

Where is Anders, and why was Law being weird about it? Well, more weird than usual. I know he's overprotective of his brother—even as an outsider I could see that the very first night we met.

Law and I are similar in that way. We're protective of those closest to us even when they don't want us to be.

My sister hates how overbearing I can be, but in my defence, she does stupid shit.

Speak of the devil, my phone vibrates in my pocket, and when I take it out to look, a Guatemalan number pops up.

I go to answer, when Reed's voice stops me.

"If Law sees you with a phone in his dojo, you'll be in trouble," he sings.

"It's Rachel."

He smiles. "Worth the punishment, then."

I hit Answer. "Let me guess, you're all out of money."

"Miss you too, big brother." She sounds all sweet and innocent, but this girl can spit venom and snark with the best of them. "And no, I don't need money. Under obligation, I'm calling to check in."

"Where was my call last week?"

"Get off my back. We've got no technology where we are, and you're lucky I found a place with a phone today."

See, reckless. "You being safe?"

"Yes, Dad."

"Sarcasm isn't a good look for you."

"How would you know? I happen to look fucking gorgeous. I'm all tan, and I'm getting muscles from all the heavy lifting—"

"Too much information for your brother. But speaking of dads, have you spoken to ours?"

"Of course not."

"He worries too, you know."

"Worries I'm pissing away his money."

"You're the one who left uni to go save the world."

"No, I left uni because I didn't want to follow the plan Dad set out for me. There's a difference, and you'd know that if you did the same. You can't let that man dictate your life."

I wince. "I don't want to fight."

"Oh, honey, if you think this is a fight, you haven't seen anything. You're always so blasé. It wouldn't kill you to have a little *fight* every once and a while."

Rachel always says I've never lived, always doing the right thing, following the rules, and doing everything everyone else wants of me without complaint.

"You're mistaking blasé for control. I'm in control of my emotions."

"You did not just call me an emotional woman."

"Uh, I don't recall bringing up gender at all. It's a prerequisite to not lose your head when you're in court. That's all I'm saying."

My sister sighs. She hates that I became a defence attorney almost as much as Mum does. "Just don't become an emotional robot, Brody."

"I'm starting to think you only called to lecture me, but that can't be right. You're the one in a third-world country doing God knows what with God knows who."

"I'm saving the world, bitch."

The usual pang of jealousy I have towards my sister hits full force. "I know you are. And I'm proud of you. But that doesn't change the fact I should be worried about you, not the other way around."

"Don't become like Dad. Find your passion and just do it."

Anders and what we got up to this morning pops into my head. I'd love to do him, but I'm not sure where we stand now.

"I'll check in again in a week. If I can," Rachel says.

"You know the point of weekly phone calls is so I don't worry that you've been kidnapped and held for ransom."

"You don't need to worry about that." She pauses. "I'm more likely to be murdered."

I grit my teeth. "Not helping. I knew I shouldn't have let you go."

I can practically hear her eye roll.

"Like you had a say over my life. Stop being a dick. I'm fine. I don't stray from my group, I don't go out alone, and never at night, so you don't have to worry, okay?"

"Telling me not to worry about you is like telling me to stop wanting Dad's approval. Not gonna happen."

"Give Lucky a kiss for me."

"Umm, nice abrupt subject change. But, uh, about Lucky."

"What happened? Is she okay? I didn't save her just for you to forget to feed her because you're never home—"

"No, no, nothing like that. It's my roommate. He might've, sort of, adopted her as his own and renamed her."

"Wait, wait, wait … you have a roommate?"

Someone yells in the background. "Rach, we're rolling out."

"Have to go. Love you."

The phone cuts out.

That girl is going to age me, I swear to God.

When I look up, Law is standing in front of me with his arms crossed.

He holds out a hand for my phone.

"I bet the kids love you," I grumble and hand it over.

"Actually, they weirdly do," Reed says. "I still haven't been able to work out why. He's a hardass, yet they still hang on his every word."

"I'm telling ya, it's magic," Law says.

Right. Magic. Perhaps the same spell Reed's under.

While I was on the phone, the dojo has filled up, so Law gestures to the front of the room.

"You still okay with being my guinea pig?"

I narrow my eyes. "Just so you know, legally you're classed as a deadly weapon. You hurt me, I'll know it's not an accident."

"Why would I want to hurt my boyfriend's best friend?" he taunts.

"Have no idea. I'm delightful, dammit."

He should have no reason to still hate me, but maybe it's like me. We get under each other's skin for the mere reason that first impressions last.

We take our spots in the front of the class while Reed waits by the door to greet latecomers.

Law thanks everyone and explains a little about what his objective is going forwards and how he wants to expand his dojo for the increasing need.

I have to admit, I admire the fuck out of him for what he does.

It reminds me once again that I chased a career that pays a lot to impress a man I've been told is unimpressible.

People like Law and my sister do what they do to help other people, and it doesn't cease to amaze me that the backbone of society relies on selfless people doing good deeds for little return.

And here I am, representing the scum of the earth. Go me!

Law snaps me out of the existential crisis that's been filling my head for days if not weeks. "Attack me," he says.

"Uh, you want me to do what now?"

Everyone in the room breaks into small laughter.

"Come at me." Law lowers his voice. "I know you want to."

I do. I really do. But I'm not stupid. He's a however many black belt kung fu master. He almost went to the Olympics for judo.

"I won't hurt you," he promises.

With a defeated sigh, I reach for his throat as if to choke him. Law swats my hand away as if shooing a fly.

"Try harder than that," Law says, and everyone laughs again.

This time, I grip tight. It only takes him a few extra seconds to get out of my hold. He explains how he does it to the class and then turns back to me.

"Tackle me."

I roll my eyes but do it.

The next thing I know, I'm flat on my back after being

flipped over Law's body. I land on the mats, so it doesn't hurt, but it's still a shock to the system.

Law grins above me. "You okay?"

Smartass.

I grit my teeth. "Fine."

After the fifth time of landing on the ground, I've had about enough. But no matter how hard I try, Law keeps evading me. Which, logically, I expect. It's just so freaking frustrating.

It does distract me from one thing though—and that's watching the door for Anders to come back. Which he doesn't.

At the end of the class, when I realise he's not going to show, disappointment and worry are replaced by anger.

I understand he has issues, but if this is the game he's going to play, I'm out. I refuse to play it.

13

ANDERSON

"Sometimes you meet someone and your souls connect. Your heart and mind identify familiarity, comfort, and safety. That's something you haven't had for a long time, Anders."

"Yeah, and sometimes I think you're full of shit, Karen."

My therapist laughs, because she knows I'm joking ... mostly.

"I don't see how I can feel safe with a man who reminds me of the guy who hurt me. Like, isn't that fucked up? Isn't that like rape victims who then seek out rough sex? It's ... wrong somehow."

"As a therapist who sees this psychological conditioning often, I can tell you that behaviour is perfectly healthy and normal. Your brain is trying to replace a negative experience with a positive one, which is probably why it's attached to the idea of being intimate with Brody."

"But once it was over, I freaked out. Like ... broke down in the shower and cried type of freak out. I could barely face him, and well"—I wave my hand between us—"hence annoying you on a Saturday."

"And how was the intimacy?"

"Why, Dr. Fletcher, are you asking me if my roommate is a terrific lay? That's mighty pervy of you."

"And *that's* mighty deflective."

"Yup." I wink and shoot a finger gun at her, because that's how I deal with shit I don't want to face—I become awkward.

"That good, huh? You had no … issues in that department? I know in the past—"

"I assure you, my dick was fully on board. More so than any other part of my body that tried to protest."

"So there was hesitance and some anxiety there."

I nod. "I worked through it like you told me though. Challenged the thought process."

"And it helped?"

"Until it was over, yeah."

"What happened when it was over?"

Karen's questions don't throw me like they used to. It took a long while for me to open up to her, but now it's second nature. Plus, there's no point trying to hold back. She'll get it out of me one way or another. Generally by asking the same thing with softer words or with a leading question.

"I lost myself in him. By the end, I wasn't even aware of my surroundings. After the fog cleared, I realised he could've done anything to me and I wouldn't have been prepared."

Karen does that judgy thing where she tries to hide her reaction by practically swallowing her lips. "In some big ways, you've made progress, and that can't be dismissed. But if you're not comfortable with the intimate parts, you really need to talk to him about that. Did you talk to him about it?"

I look away, sheepish. "No. I might've run away."

"Of course, you did. Okay, your homework for today is to go home and tell him why you ran away. Then, I suggest you take a step back and assess what you both want. Because even though Brody could be a good thing for you, it could also be detrimental if you don't work through your problems together. You can't hold on to the hope that he can read your mind and automatically know what you're dealing with."

"I was afraid you were going to say that."

"I'll see you back here on Monday to see how things go."

"There you are being pervy again."

"I'm suggesting you don't go there again. Not until you communicate first. But if you think you're truly ready for this step, I could always refer you to a sex therapist. I've studied some units in that field, but someone who specialises could really help you."

I look up at the roof. "Just what you want to tell a guy you've hooked up with once. 'Hey, wanna go to sex therapy?'"

"Think about it."

Thanks to her, I don't think I'll be able to stop thinking about it.

When the key sounds in the lock of the front door, I tense.

I have Meatball in my lap, and we're on my bed, but I've left my bedroom door open a crack as an invitation for Brody.

I've been scrolling through news articles on my phone, making sure to not click on trigger headlines, but I haven't been able to focus. I haven't focused on anything but the thought of telling Brody the truth once he comes home.

I was expecting Karen to tell me what I have with Brody is wrong—that I'm being self-destructive and co-dependent again. I never expected her to say it could be a good way for my mind to heal and forget the horror Kyle left me with.

But I can't come out and say that to him. That'd be way too much pressure. I can't put my recovery on his shoulders.

Karen's right in saying we need to communicate, but I wish she'd give me the words I have to say, because right now I've got nothing, and his footsteps are getting closer.

There's a tentative knock, and I let out a raspy "All good."

Whether time slows down or Brody's unsure, the door moves so fucking slowly it might take a year before it opens.

Brody stands there, his fists clenched by his sides and his intimidating figure taking up most of the doorway.

"Is everything okay?" I ask.

His jaw moves side to side as if he's gritting his teeth.

I should be scared, because he hasn't uttered a word. He hasn't even blinked.

He's showing huge signs of aggressive behaviour, but for some reason, it's not triggering me.

"I'm trying really hard not to lose my shit right now," Brody says, "because I don't want to scare you, but this morning? Not okay."

"I'm sor—"

"No, let me get this out."

Again, I should be scared, but I'm not.

Something about today's therapy session clicked. When Karen said I'm trying to replace the bad memories with happy ones, I realised I was also replacing Kyle's bad behaviour with Brody's possible bad behaviour, thinking they were one and the same.

Kyle broke me in more ways than I ever knew it possible for someone to break. In my mind, men like him in physical appearance and demeanour immediately became homicidal crazies—or at least, all of them had the potential to become one. Lumping them all together is exactly what racists and bigots do with minority groups. One bad apple doesn't turn the whole group sour.

I'm under no delusion that this revelation means I'm cured or even that this feeling will last, but it's keeping me calm in the moment, so I'm going to hold on to it.

If Brody were to raise his hand or make a fast movement, I might lose it, but he's allowed to be upset with me. I deserve it. What I did this morning was shitty, I know that, and I want to make it right.

Brody takes a deep breath. "I know it's hard for you to believe that I will never, ever hurt you, but it's difficult to know where your head is at when you run away from me. I don't know if I've fucked up. I don't know if you're okay. Reed and Law were acting weird—not telling me where you were—and I've been worried sick about you. Yet, here you are, seemingly uncaring about how I've fucking been all day."

"That's not—"

"Stop interrupting," he booms and then calms down. "Please."

"Okay."

His nostrils flare. "I want more of what happened this morning, but not if you're going to run away afterwards. That's not part of the deal. I don't care if you have a breakdown or a panic attack or even if you yell and scream at me. This is only going to work if you tell me what's going on in your head."

"I know."

He doesn't hear me. Or ignores me. "So if you can't do that, then we should forget this morning ever happened and go back to being roommates."

"I can do it."

He keeps rambling. "I like you, Anders. You're adorably awkward and funny, and yeah, you're a little messed up, but in this day and age, I think everyone is to some degree. As much as I want to explore you and the possibility of you, I'm not going to do it if you can't handle it. Because I refuse to be the guy who takes advantage or hurts you."

"Brody," I say loudly.

His gaze finally snaps to mine.

"I know."

"Know what?"

"That everything you just said is true and right, and ..." It's my turn to take in a deep breath. "Law and Reed didn't tell you where I was because they don't know shit about us. I told them I had a bad night and needed an emergency therapy session. That's where I was. I might've run away this morning, but I ran to somewhere that could help me understand why I reacted the way I did. I thought ..."

I stare down at the cat and run my hand over her, being careful to be gentle with the patchy parts. I can't find the words I need and sure as shit don't have the guts to say them while looking Brody in the eye.

Meatball must sense me staring at her the same way Brody is staring at me, and she jumps off my lap to run away.

Lucky bitch. She gets to escape the scrutiny.

I don't have that luxury. "I thought if we hooked up and I got through it, that maybe it'd mean that was it. I didn't know I'd panic after it, and I wasn't prepared to handle it. I fucked up. I know that. And it's completely unfair to you that I ran out of here without telling you that you did nothing wrong."

"You ..." Brody stumbles back. "You went to therapy?"

"Not many therapists have emergency appointments on a weekend, but I'm a special case. Clearly."

"What did your therapist say?"

I crack a smile. "That you might be good for me."

He seems surprised.

"But that we shouldn't hook up again until I deal with what happened this morning."

"Can you tell me what did happen this morning?" He goes to take a step towards the bed but thinks better of it. "Can I ..." He points to the spot next to me.

I lift the covers, and Brody comes to sit next to me, resting against the headboard like I am.

Having him close, in my bed, my cock forgets everything Karen told me this afternoon and is up for a repeat already.

I turn to him. "What happened this morning was ..."

Brody leans in closer and lowers his voice. "I think the words you're looking for are amazing, wonderful, and orgasmic."

"So sure of yourself."

"Let's start from the moment you freaked out." His blue eyes are sympathetic and soft, but this is hard.

"It was easy to get lost in you, and I haven't had that for a really long time."

"So that's what scared you? That you enjoyed it?"

I grunt. "Okay, this is embarrassing as fuck, so I'm just going to blurt it out and hope for the best. I can't ... sometimes ... Farrrrrk." I throw my head back.

A hand lands on my thigh above the covers. "Anders, it's okay. Take your time."

"The reason my last few years have been filled with younger, smaller guys I picked up from bars is because sometimes I get too in my head and I can't ... perform. It's easier to blame it on the alcohol than get into the whole 'Hey, I can't get it up because I'm afraid you might stab me' thing."

"Oh." His hand squeezes my leg tighter, but I have to hand it to him. He doesn't look horrified.

"It's not like I always had that problem, but I needed my hook-ups to go a certain way. I had to be the one in control, and it had to be a comfortable environment. When a guy met all the criteria, I'd try to make a relationship work with him—I'd try to convince myself it'd be different this time—but around the one-month mark, I'd flip out and get Law to break it off with him for me, because I couldn't face it. Not after …"

Shit. I still haven't told him it was my ex who actually hurt me. I can't … that's … just no. I can't go there when I'm already so exposed.

My skin feels raw under his gaze as if I'm naked in front of a live audience.

A deep blush warms my cheeks.

"Anders," he whispers.

I lift my eyes again.

Instead of talking, he cups my face—not in the controlling way that made me freak out this morning, but in that caressing way that reminds me of who Brody is.

He leans in, his soft lips meeting mine and reassuring me that he's still here. It's not a sexual, needy kiss, but one that makes promises I'm not even sure Brody's in a position to make.

He pulls back. "Thank you for telling me."

We stay staring into each other's eyes, his hand still on my beard, my confession and Brody's acceptance thick in the air.

"Where do we go from here?" I ask.

"That's entirely up to you. I have to admit that I suck at the relationship thing."

"*You* suck at it? Hello, did you hear what I just said?"

Brody chuckles. "Right. I want to keep doing … whatever it is that we're doing. I like kissing you. But I probably have to warn you of some stuff too. Like—"

"That it might be too much? I get it. I totally understand. It'd be too much for me too if I were you."

His big hand covers my mouth. "You have a terrible habit of interrupting me today."

"Sorry," I say, muffled against his hand.

"I was going to warn you that I'm so sucky at relationships, I didn't even realise my last boyfriend had broken up with me." He removes his hand.

"What?"

"Okay, 'boyfriend' might be a bit of a stretch of a title, but I was seeing this guy, and things were going great. Work got busy, so granted, I wasn't around as much as usual. When I messaged him to say I finally had a weekend where I didn't have to work, he informed me we'd broken up a month ago after I'd ghosted him for *two weeks*."

My eyes narrow. "You accidentally ghosted someone?"

Brody runs a hand through his thick brown hair. "I knew it had been a while since we'd seen each other, but with my schedule, I hadn't realised it had been six weeks since I'd last contacted him. I didn't mean to be so absent, but when work is super busy, I guess it's easy for me to tune out the real world. I'm worried if we start something, I might not be able to be what you need."

I huff. "Trust me. Clinginess is not what I need. I need someone who knows what I went through and can be patient with me."

"I promise I have the patience of a saint." His words are reassuring, but his demeanour is not.

I take in Brody's sombre expression. "What's wrong?"

His arm wraps around my shoulders, and I willingly scoot closer. It feels weird—this new level of intimacy of just ... touching. I keep waiting for the panic to start, but the rhythmic beating of my heart isn't the same as the jackhammering it usually does when Brody's this close. My increased heart rate has nothing to do with fear and everything to do with anticipation.

"I feel like the biggest dickwad for continuing to taunt you about going out with me. I've never thought of myself as a pushy guy, you know? But something about you—"

"I'm interrupting again, but I need to know. What made you think of this now?"

"It suddenly all makes sense, and I feel like a jerk. Since you moved in, I've seen glimpses of this happy guy. You never laughed or threw a genuine smile my way the whole time I kept asking you out. It makes me no better than the kid I'm representing who wouldn't take no for an answer."

I try not to scoff at that, because it's obvious he's one hundred percent serious. "Comparing yourself to a rapist is a bit of a stretch. And if I'm honest … I both loved and hated the attention you were giving me. The reason I never smiled was because I hated myself. I hated that I *couldn't* say yes. But I wanted to. I really, really wanted to."

Brody still looks tortured.

"You never pushed. You said things, sure, you asked me out, and if I had a problem with it, trust me, Law would've set you straight because I would've tattled on you like a kindergartener whose toy was stolen. But you were never invasive or … *predatory*."

"Still doesn't make it right."

"Lesson learned, then?"

He nods. "Next time a guy says no, I'll leave him alone."

I know I shouldn't trip over the words *next time*, but something inside me doesn't like the thought of Brody moving on after I fuck this up once and for all.

Because let's face it—it's inevitable.

He says he can be patient now, but what if this morning is

only a glimpse of what's to come? What if it takes too long for me to get comfortable enough to truly be with him?

What happens if I'm only interested in him because of the feeling he gives me—the illusion of safety—and I like him by default?

I glance at Brody out the corner of my eye, and I immediately know that's not true. I've been attracted to him from the beginning but never thought it would be possible to be with him.

That doesn't change the many what-ifs and uncertainties. It's hard for me to believe everything's going to be roses just because we agreed to communicate better.

So instead, I go for the oldest trick in the book. "Imagine how much time you'll have if you stopped chasing after every guy who says no to you?"

Brody's lips quirk. "I might need some aloe for that burn, but I'll have you know, you're the only guy who's ever turned me down."

"Bullshit."

A blinding grin takes over Brody's immaculate face, and yeah, I guess I can see how no one would ever say no to him.

"True story."

"Not gonna lie, that makes me hate you a little bit."

He kisses the top of my head. "I'm all right with that."

14

BRODY

Anders' therapist advised refraining from anything physical until he can handle it, and I guess it's up to him and her to come to that conclusion.

Which means, essentially, we've been put back into roommate mode.

When I arrive home from work on Monday, I find him in the kitchen.

"Hey," I say, and I'm greeted with a smile—no flinching.

Yes. I mentally high-five myself.

"Hi." Anders' voice is breathy and sexy. Damn him.

I need to let Anders lead this, so it's hard to stop myself from greeting him how I want to—with our bodies pressed together and him gasping for breath ... but in the good way, not the panicky way.

"I made you dinner."

"No burns this time?" I ask.

"Do I get a gold star if there isn't?"

"An imaginary one, sure."

Anders pouts and holds up his finger. "The oven bit me."

I eye the angry red mark on his index finger. "You're hopeless, you know that?"

"I do know."

I approach and take his hand in mine, inspecting the burn. "Maybe you shouldn't cook."

The urge to kiss his finger better almost has me lifting his hand to my mouth, but I have to remind myself that Anders needs to make the first move.

"I really shouldn't. I kinda suck at it. Both Law and I do."

I cock my head. "How did you never learn to cook?"

"Our mother is the worst. She's the type of mum who doesn't want her babies to leave the nest, so she never taught us to fend for ourselves."

A laugh escapes, and I drop his hand. "You'll live."

"No emergency trip to the doctor this time?"

"No, you're good."

"Okay, but if I die overnight from infection, it'll be on your head."

Maybe I'll have to stay with you all night is on the tip of my tongue, but fuck, I can't.

Yep. Abstinence is going to be even harder than I thought.

"Tomorrow I can bring home food for us if you're going to continue to eat late."

Anders purses his lips. "A decent meal might be a nice change, but I actually don't mind cooking. I want to learn how to do it properly. Law and my parents treat me as if I can't look after myself because of my issues, and even if cooking is an insignificant thing, it makes me feel like I'm sticking it to them and their perceptions of me in my own way."

"I understand." I understand proving myself more than anyone. "Maybe I could teach you on the weekends. I mean, if you want."

"You never cook though."

"I don't have the time. My mum is the opposite of yours. Taught us how to live on our own so we could do it as soon as possible."

"That sounds a bit cold."

I shake my head. "No, trust me. Out of my parents, Mum is as warm as the sun compared to my father."

"Your father who you work for?"

"It's a long story that's full of insecurity about not living up to my father's expectations. It's super boring."

"Give me boring any day."

"Right. Sorry."

Anders shrugs. "We all have our hang-ups. Mine just happen to be bigger than most. I wouldn't mind hearing about yours sometime. A nice dose of normal-people problems is usually good at reminding me that we all have issues."

I smile. "I'll tell you over dinner."

We sit down to eat, and I tell him for a father who was rarely there growing up, he still liked to have a say in his kids' futures. Advised us on what to study, what to do, and what he thought the best path would be for us.

But of course, it always included law of some type.

I was the only one who went through with it.

Anders seems fascinated by a family dynamic that is the complete opposite to his free-thinking and loving parents who only want what's best for their children.

So, the following night when I come home to another home-cooked meal, he asks me to tell him about my mum.

The next night, the topic is my brother, Parker, who I rarely ever see, because after uni he was offered a job overseas. Like our sister, he doesn't care about Dad's approval.

How I got that gene, I don't know, but my siblings sure as shit don't have it.

We spend the rest of the week basically talking all about

me and my pretty boring existence. Though, if I got a choice between my trouble-free life and something like what Anders went through, I would take boring any day.

Because I arrive home so late from work, immediately after dinner we go to our separate bedrooms to sleep alone.

Numerous times while eating dinner and talking, I get lost in what I'm saying as I eye Anders over the dining table.

He lets me talk, rarely interrupts unless it's to ask a question, and he smiles and frowns in all the right places, letting me know he's actually listening.

It's casual and almost feels like dating but with no follow-through at the end.

On Friday, he brings up my dad again.

"So what's the deep-seated reason you want to impress your father?"

I huff. Isn't that a loaded question. "Getting into the hard questions already?"

Anders laughs.

I place my cutlery beside my plate. "Well, if you ask my mum, she'll probably tell you I have abandonment issues. They broke up when I was five. Rachel was two, and Parker was seven. She moved us away from Brisbane and up to the Sunshine Coast to be closer to her family, so we rarely saw him. And when we did, he'd hire a nanny to actually look after us. He was always in his study or at the office. He didn't really make time for us."

"So you decided to become just like him? Doesn't make a whole lot of sense."

I shrug. "I guess it's my way of trying to bond with him and have that father-son relationship we never had. My brother and sister think I'm nuts to even try, but there are these moments with him, where I can see some semblance of a good father, and I think *yes! This is it. This is where I get his approval and acceptance.* Then he'll give the same praise to another associate at work, and I want to bang my head on my desk."

"Why put yourself through that?"

"Masochism is fun," I say sarcastically.

Anders purses his lips. "Can I ask something that may be overstepping?"

"After what you've told me about your life, pretty sure I'm an open book."

"Does it have to do with you being gay?"

I frown.

"I only ask because like you said, your brother and sister don't really care to get to know the man because he didn't seem to ever make the effort to know you. I'm wondering if maybe you're trying to overcompensate. It's not uncommon for queer kids to fight extra hard for acceptance from parents. Does ... does he know you're gay?"

I nod. "He knows. But we don't talk about it. Like, at all. He isn't what I'd call homophobic, but I don't think he likes that I'm gay. He tries to stay out of it as much as possible and kind of pretends my sexuality doesn't exist. And if I'm honest, I'm okay with that. One hundred percent. I don't want to get into it with him either."

"What did he say when you came out to him?"

"'Okay.'" I use air quotes.

"*Okay?* That's it?"

"Yup. Then he told me I should enrol in some online classes at uni over the school break so I could do the three-year degree instead of four."

Anders smiles. "And you ran off and did as you were told?"

"Well ... yeah."

"I guess I should be congratulating you, then."

I cock my head.

"With daddy issues like those, I'm surprised you're not a

rent boy. Or one of those go-go dancers at that fuck bar on Queen Street."

I scoff. "That was my backup plan if uni didn't work out."

"What do you think you'll do if you ever get your dad's approval?"

Well, fuck. There's a question I've never actually asked myself.

What will I do the day my dad says he's proud of me?

Uh, quit working at a job I don't even like?

I mean, I like it enough. I love finding loopholes and studying the law, but it certainly doesn't fulfil me. And trying cases like this latest one has me up at night.

Anders starts singing the thinking song from *Jeopardy*.

"Honestly?" I say. "I don't know. Is it bad that even though I want a good relationship with the man, I don't think it'll ever happen?"

"Do you want an honest answer to that?"

"Probably not."

Anders laughs. "He doesn't sound like he's worth the effort. Anyone can be a father. Not everyone can be a dad."

So true. "What's your dad like?"

He doesn't hesitate. "Awesome."

"Way to rub it in."

"You're welcome."

The way he stares at me over the dining table drives me crazy. Like he's hungry but the food isn't cutting it.

I want to tease him about asking me so many questions and say it's almost date-like with his sudden fascination with getting to know me, but I need to wait for him to do that kind of thing.

A week doesn't seem like enough time for him to deal with his crap, but also a week ago it sounded like he wanted to work on it. Anytime I try to flirt, he turns the convo back to very unsexy things. Like my father. These dinners with all talk feel like I'm being friend-zoned.

Which, I wouldn't have a problem with if he was straight up about it and let me know.

This in-between thing doesn't work for me.

So as I get up to do the dishes, I pause as I reach for his. "Still up for that cooking lesson tomorrow?"

Anders' face falls. "Is my food really that bad?"

"No." I laugh. "I'm looking for an excuse to spend more time with you."

I hold my breath, wondering if that crosses a line, and maybe it does because Anders' demeanour shifts.

He nods, but it's shaky. "Okay, yeah. Sounds good." He stands. "I'm, uh, gonna go brush my teeth and go to bed."

"You don't want dessert—"

He rushes off before I can stop him.

I think I fucked up again.

As I wash the dishes, my gaze keeps going to Anders' closed bedroom door and my brain replays every conversation we've had this week, every meal.

My feet carry me across the apartment to Anders' door, and I knock gently. "Anders?"

There's a moan and then a curse.

I have no idea what I'm doing or what I'm going to say. Demanding answers isn't an option, and neither is laying it all out there that I want more.

He still hasn't opened the door.

I knock louder. "Anders? Are you okay?"

Maybe he fell asleep already and he's having another nightmare.

"Uh, hang on," he calls out.

He sounds awake, but there's something in his voice that sounds strained.

His footsteps get closer but then stop, and the door doesn't budge. I lean in closer to try to hear more, which is when Anders, of course, opens it. I jump back but not fast enough.

He's bare-chested. Breathing hard. His face flushed.

"Bad dream?"

His mouth opens. Then closes.

That's when I notice how poor a job his boxers are doing at hiding the giant erection trying to get free.

"Oh." My gaze flies to his. "Oh. Umm, right. Okay. I ... you know what, it's not important." I practically fall over myself trying to turn and get away as fast as I can, because oops. Interrupting a wank session is poor form.

A chuckle comes from behind me. "It's your fault, you know."

I spin to face him. "Mine? How?"

Anders closes the gap between us with torturously slow steps. "All I've been thinking about is kissing you again."

I feel his voice all the way to my toes, making them curl into the carpet.

He's a breath away now, so close I can smell sex on him as if he's wearing it like cologne.

I want to close the gap. I want to kiss him. My gaze lands on his lips, and I feel my tongue run along my own.

"But we can't," he whispers. There's absolutely no conviction behind it. It sounds more like resigned defeat.

"Why not?" My voice mimics his, low and sexy with a tiny hint of a growl.

Anders takes a step back as if needing space. "My therapist. She said we shouldn't. Not until ..."

"Until?"

"Until I'm ready."

"I'm guessing you're not going to be ready in say the next ten seconds?" I ask hopefully.

Anders laughs. "Goddammit." He rushes me, almost knocking me off my feet as he claims my mouth.

I groan as his tongue meets mine and his hands embrace and cling to me. He pulls me close, and while I'm still so bloody confused, I can't stop myself from taking it.

Anders murmurs words I can't understand against my lips, but when he pulls back a tiny bit, no longer assaulting my mouth but still kissing me, I hear, "Why do you have to be so ... you?"

He kisses my cheek, the side of my jaw, and my neck, while his impressive cock digs into my side. His lower half rubs against me, and my own cock wants friction, but my head gets stuck on his words.

"What do you mean, why do I have to be me? What's wrong with being me?"

"I've tried everything to make you unsexy in my head. Asked you about your mother, your brother and sister, hell, I contemplated asking you about your damn cousins tonight, because I figure if you're thinking about your family, you won't be all cute and hot and ... you. But no, apparently talking about your family lights you up inside and makes you more attractive. Unless it's your dad. He appears to be the cure for your ever-present glow."

"Ah. Hence all the extra dad talk tonight."

Anders nods. "Only, it's not working. I still go to bed with you on my mind and my hand on my dick." His breath is hot on my skin. "I've been trying to be good. Trying not to touch you. Trying to forget how good it felt to have your cock in my mouth. I've been trying to avoid this. I don't want to freak out again. But you feel so damn amazing, Brody."

He's moving into rambling territory as he ruts against me, and I throw my head back when our cocks line up. Even through my sweatpants and his boxers, I can feel how hard he is.

If we keep going like this, we're no doubt going to fall over.

"Couch," I croak.

His head snaps back, and he looks me in the eyes. "Couch?"

"Pin me again. Make it so I can't move from beneath you, and take what you need."

"Brody," he whines but pushes me towards the couch.

I fall onto my back, but I get a chance to whip my shirt over my head before Anders' hard body lands on top of me.

Last time he made me sit on my hands, but that's not going to work in this position, so instead I lift my hands above my head, joining them at the wrists.

"Hold me in place," I encourage. If this is what he needs to get off, I'm more than willing to give it to him.

As much as I'm dying to touch him and hope one day I'll be able to, this, what we have right here, is more than enough for me.

I want to make him forget. I want to hold him until he tells me to fuck off.

I realise what that probably means for me—that I see this as more than some casual thing—but with where his head's at, I doubt he's looking or even ready for more.

The appreciative smile Anders gives me before locking one strong hand around my wrists is nothing compared to the face he makes when our bodies press against each other. His eyes roll back, his lips part, and the image of him above me like this is immediately saved into the spank bank folder in my brain.

His lean body drags along mine, and a hot, eager hand makes its way into my sweatpants, pulling the front down just enough for my warm skin to meet his lube-slippery cock which has slipped through the hole in his boxers.

"Were you jerking off to the thought of me just now?" I rasp.

He buries his head in my neck, and I arch up.

"Every. Fucking. Night." Anders grunts. "I can't get you out of my mind."

"Same."

Anders moves his free hand between us, wrapping it around both of us and thrusting harder.

I'm semi-conscious of needing to make sure he's doing okay. The way his cock pulses next to mine and how hard he is, I know he's at least enjoying himself a little. But I need to know.

"Is this okay?" I ask. I really hope it doesn't bring down the mood, but it's my responsibility to check.

"More than okay."

"Can you kiss me?"

He buries his head deeper, his hips rocking harder. "Only if you want this all to be over."

"I want you to come on me."

Anders' grip on my wrists tightens to the point of pain, but it's forgotten when our mouths meet.

I'm chasing the end, getting closer with every thrust, every lick as he explores my mouth, and every tiny whimper he makes at the back of his throat.

"Come, Anders. Come all over me."

He falls apart, and I follow him, both of us tensing as cum spills between us. Anders melts against me, his grip on my wrists slacking, but he keeps his hand where it is.

We breathe hard, and Anders crushes me under his weight, but I can take it.

"This couch just officially became my favourite place in the entire apartment," I say. "I suspected it last week, but this seals the deal."

"Mine too," Anders says.

He finally lets my wrists go, but I keep my hands where they are, unsure if I'm allowed to touch him yet or not.

"You're not freaking out on me?"

"Not yet."

"Can I move my arms? I might need to do more weight training because it's killing me holding them above my head."

Anders laughs, but it's quick and the air between us goes stale immediately after.

"You okay?" I ask.

"I appreciate you asking, and I know you're worried, but … can we try, umm … like …"

"If you want round two, I'm so not ready for that. Give me at least half an hour."

Anders laughs again. This is already better than the last time we hooked up.

"I was going to ask if you'd hold me."

I can't help smiling. "I find it adorable you can tell me how good my cock feels in your mouth, but asking to cuddle is too much." My arms wrap around his back as I hold him to me.

"I just don't know if it'll trigger me," he says, and I still.

It's so easy to forget that sex might not be the only intimacy he struggles with. I'm reminded of all the times in the past few months where I've seen him pale or twitchy. I thought it was him being awkward, but it's been him trying to control his anxiety.

My heart lurches, and for a brief moment I wonder again if he's holding back something important from me.

The way he says it, he can't ever let his guard down in fear of being in a vulnerable position, but the trust issue he has with me doesn't make a whole lot of sense, unless his attack was worse than he let on.

The thought of sexual assault fills my head, not for the first time, and I want to ask him again, but I've already asked him twice and he's said no each time.

I won't push, but I can't shake the feeling that he's not telling me everything.

Which makes me worry this could be too much for him. Too much for *me*. It could be so easy and unintentional to hurt him, and that would kill me.

Anders smiles down at me. "So far so good." His face makes the doubt almost go away.

"Let me know if it gets too much."

He lowers his head and nods against my neck.

We relax into a pile of limbs and unwashed stomachs, and just before I think I might drift off, Anders shifts against me.

"We should get cleaned up."

"Did I cross the line?" I ask.

He shakes his head. "No. I was kinda thinking … could we try sleeping in the same bed tonight?"

There's nothing I want more than taking Anders to bed and holding him all night. Ever since finding out his deal, it's taken everything in me not to do it, but I'm hesitant.

"I don't want to push you too fast."

"Neither do I, but lying here right now, I think I could go to sleep. And I slept on you the other night. I have to know … like, if we can do this, then maybe I'm getting better."

No pressure. "Then we'll try."

"Thank you."

"We'll go into my bed so you can leave the minute you feel uncomfortable, okay?"

In response, Anders kisses me softly.

15

ANDERSON

I don't sleep. I can't. Apparently, that's still a too-vulnerable position for me. But I also don't find myself getting up.

I like lying next to Brody. I like his body pressed against mine, the way his messy hair gets even messier as he sleeps, and I even find his tiny little snore cute.

It's not until a sliver of sunlight cracks through the blinds in Brody's room that I realise I've stayed with him the whole night without sleeping a wink.

Hours of staring at him, learning every curve of his jaw and perfectly symmetrical nose, and memorising his model good looks.

I can do the sleep-deprived thing. I've done it a million times over and then some. It's not good for my condition because lack of sleep can make me edgy, but right this second, I can't bring myself to pull away from him.

I don't know where he gets his muscular physique from considering he works all the time. My fingers run over his shoulder and down his arm. He's well-built but not veiny big. He's strong in an effortless way, like it's a natural trait for him.

I'd kill to hold on to this moment where I'm completely relaxed around him for the first time possibly ever.

We hooked up, I didn't have a panic attack, and now I'm lying in his arms with no warning signs in sight. Well, apart from the not sleeping thing, but it was probably asking too much to begin with.

He's hard against me, his dick awake before he is, but it doesn't take long for the rest of him to catch up.

"Mmm." Brody moves his hips, digging his morning erection into my hip, but then it's as if he remembers who he's with. He slumps and rolls onto his back. "Dammit. We're not supposed to do stuff, are we?"

"Not supposed to, no, but that didn't stop us last night."

A long sigh comes out of Brody's mouth. "It should have. I don't want to mess this up."

"You're not messing anything up. You're helping me."

Brody frowns. "Helping. Is that what this ... whole thing is?"

"What do you mean?"

Brody yawns and stretches before rolling to face me again. "Looking for clarification, I guess. I don't really feel comfortable being the guy you test your limits on."

"What do you mean?"

"I want to see where this can go. Like properly."

I want that too is on the tip of my tongue, but I can't bring myself to say it. "I ... I don't know if I can promise that, but I can promise to try." How can someone be in a relationship if they can't even sleep next to them?

There's not really much further it can go without bigger freak-outs, and who wants to deal with that?

As if reading my mind, Brody assesses me. "Did you sleep okay?"

I don't answer him.

"Did you sleep at all?"

"Well, no, but I didn't have a panic attack. That's something."

"But you didn't sleep."

"Did I mention insomnia is one of my many diagnoses on a long list of ailments? This isn't unusual for me."

"You weren't sleeping well last week either."

"That was because of my door. I'll nap later. I promise I'll be fine."

The concern on Brody's face is adorable and annoying at the same time. I love that he's concerned but pissed off he even needs to be.

"Why didn't you go to your own room after I was asleep?"

"I liked being in here with you and didn't realise how much time had passed until I noticed the sun coming up."

"Anders …"

"Brody," I mimic.

"You have to look after yourself first. I'll understand if I wake up alone."

"Why are you so good about this? I don't understand."

Brody stretches again and climbs out of bed. "You have to know by now that I care about you. If I was after a random lay, I would've gone for the easy target, not you."

"But why me?" I practically whisper.

Brody smirks.

"No, I'm not trying to fish for compliments here or have my ego stroked—"

"I'm going to say it like it is. Are you ready? Because it's a bit of a mind-fuck. A completely left-field notion that will explode your brain and make you see the world differently."

I expect him to ramble something about maybe being sent from God or it being fate or what-the-fuck-ever.

Instead, he looks me in the eye and says, "I like you."

I roll my eyes. "Completely mind-blowing."

Brody stares at me like he wants to say more, but he doesn't. All he does is find some sweatpants on the floor and pull them up his thick thighs. "I'm going to make us breakfast, and then you can sleep until lunch. Then I was thinking we could do something this afternoon."

"Do something? Like what?"

"I'm guessing you hate surprises."

"Duh."

"Usually on my rare days off I go indoor rock climbing to let off steam."

Ah, that explains the muscular arms.

I've come a long way from the guy who didn't want to leave his apartment. Outings are good for my psyche, and an indoor rock-climbing place will have a lot of people there. Blending in with the crowd is something I thrive at, and it'll show Brody that side of me for once instead of, well, this version of me.

"Sounds good."

"Stay here," Brody says. "I'll make us breakfast, then you can sleep, and then this afternoon, I'll spot you."

"You just wanna see how my ass looks in a harness."

"Hell yes."

"Spoiler alert: it looks awesome."

A warm smile breaks across Brody's face.

"What's that look for?" I ask.

"I think that's the first time you've actually *flirted* with me."

I smile back. "Progress." It's small, and might not mean much to anyone, but it's progress.

$\mathcal{A}$pparently it doesn't take a lot for my flirting switch to be turned on, and even less for me to enjoy it.

Flirting, I can do. I've mastered it over the last few years of dating superficial guys who want superficial banter. I thought it'd be different with Brody, because while he can be light and easygoing, he's completely different from the guys I've dated since Kyle. He's mature, he's got his shit together, and there's an air of seriousness about him.

And it turns out he's one competitive motherfucker on the rock wall.

He scales the bloody thing like a spider monkey in heat ... if spider monkey horniness is a thing. I don't actually know.

Bonus points for the harness though. I joked about Brody using this an excuse to check me out, but I totally forgot it'd be the same for me. And damn, his bubble butt. I'd legit bite it if I was close enough, which I'm not, so it's probably a good thing I can't reach it.

Near the top, Brody reaches for a climbing hold and pulls himself up, moving swiftly with an air of grace. I could watch his muscles work all day.

At one point he turns his head and stares down at me over his shoulder. His eyes smoulder, and those lips turn up. "A little slack, maybe?"

Oh. Right. I loosen the rope enough for him to be able to keep going without me giving him a giant wedgie. Tightening that harness to make his butt pop even more is tempting, but that'll probably leave us both uncomfortable. Not exactly in a position to rearrange my dick so it's not tenting for everyone to see.

The climbing centre has an awesome and laid-back atmosphere. There are easier climbs for kids and more advanced ones for experienced climbers. Brody chose one in the middle, though by the way everyone knows him by name and how fast he is, I assume he could tackle the huge wall with the almost ninety-degree overhang.

Being here with Brody is probably the calmest I've ever been around him.

Here, our focus is just on climbing. Okay, and checking each other out. But it's as if I know that's all it is, and my nerves are nowhere to be seen.

"Anders?" a voice says from behind me.

It's deep, kind of familiar, and when I turn, my nerves appear with a vengeance.

"Chris," I shriek.

Yup, shriek. Chris is a guy I dated almost a year ago now. Funnily enough, he's probably the only guy in the last five years to be the one to break up with me, because he doesn't like drama.

I never told him about my past, but maybe he could sense that shit or perhaps it was another one of my hook-ups interrupting our date and throwing a hissy fit that did it.

Either way, it was never going to last with Chris and me. He was my typical kind of target—the kind who's smaller and meeker. He's a pretty boy with dark, neat hair and bright eyes. I liked him, but not enough. It's never enough.

No one has even come close until ... My gaze turns back to Brody, and we lock eyes.

He leaps off the damn wall to come down, and I'm not ready.

Shit, I must've missed his command that he was about to descend. I scramble to hold on to the rope and almost get pulled off my feet.

Motherfucker.

Chris and the guy he's with are quick to step in and help, and I'm thankful we don't have to add broken neck to the list of injuries Brody and I have unintentionally caused each other.

When his feet hit solid ground and he makes his way over to us, I don't miss the knowing smile on his face.

"Didn't hear me?"

"Shit. Sorry, no. I was ..." I look at Chris. "Distracted. Brody, this is Chris. Chris, Brody."

"I've seen you around here before," Chris says.

Brody's cool demeanour never changes, even as he shakes Chris's hand and asks, "You two used to date or something?"

How'd he know?

"Briefly." Chris laughs as if the memory of it is a joke. In his defence, my dating life is a bit of a joke. Just not a very funny one. "Very briefly."

"He kissed Law if I remember correctly," I point out. Yes, let's put all the focus on Chris's faults and not my own. Please.

Chris gasps and backhands my chest. "I was drunk, and you didn't tell me you had an identical twin."

"Ah, Steele brother antics," Brody says. "Wish I'd known you guys while you were pulling all the switcheroo shit."

My eyes widen and so do Chris's.

"Never did it with you," I say quickly. "Promise." Mainly because he broke up with me before I had a chance to ask Law to end it for me, but that goes unsaid.

Chris eyes me suspiciously but lets it go when he pulls the guy he's with closer. "This is Rhett."

Rhett lifts his chin instead of saying hi, and Brody and I mimic his gesture.

"Were you guys finishing up, or do you mind maybe spotting us so we can do a climb together?" Chris asks.

"Return the favour, and we've got a deal," Brody says before I can stop him.

Guess we're playing nice with my ex.

Does Brody not understand the concept of *exes*? I mean, he's friends with Reed, he's all friendly with mine even though he and I are … well, Brody and I are couch buddies right now. Amazing sex couch buddies.

It's official. I'm never going to look at our couch the same way again.

But that's not the point. If Kyle had run into one of my exes in a place like this? He'd put on a macho display of ownership and tell my ex to fuck off.

Brody's his usual warm self, as if this is all somehow normal for people to do.

I don't know what that says about him. A few months ago, I would've said he was psycho. Now? I think he's just that genuine.

So, of course, my brain's immediate thought after that is he doesn't deserve to be stuck with someone like me.

I shake those thoughts free before they can take root.

One thing I've learned about myself throughout therapy is that nearly all my negative thoughts tie into my anxiety. It sucks to be hyper self-aware when I'm trying to throw myself a pity party, but it can be helpful in times like this where even though I believe my thoughts are valid, deep down I know it's anxiety and pressure disguised as irrationality.

Karen would be so proud.

After we get hooked up to the other guys and they take their positions side by side at the bottom of the climbing wall, Brody leans in closer to me.

"Sorry, was it a mistake saying yes?"

"No, it's fine," I say. "I'm just … confused."

"About what?"

"I don't know how you do it. Hang out with an ex. It's weird."

Brody rubs his chin. "I never really thought about it. Reed

and I were friends first, so it feels like I'm with a friend not an ex. We can leave after their climb if you're uncomfortable."

"No, no. I'm interested to see if the panic will happen. It's weird right now, but I'm not as edgy as I thought I'd be."

I've always been cautious of my triggers, trying to get home before anything bad happens. If I'm outside the house and I have a panic attack, my head immediately starts telling me this is why I shouldn't go out. So when I have a good day and I come across something that challenges me, I always want to go home before it can get bad.

I've never pushed or tested my boundaries, but Brody makes me want to.

Perhaps it's because he gives me a sliver of the kind of future I want.

"Let me know if it gets too much and we'll go home," Brody says. "We can use Lucky—"

"Meatball," I sing.

He rolls his eyes. "If you want to get out of here, just say we have to get home to feed the cat."

"I knew I should've gotten a pet sooner. I could have used it as an excuse to get out of stuff."

"It's a known fact it's the main reason people reproduce."

I can't help laughing. "Right. Because I'm sure love and parental instincts have nothing to do with it."

"None at all. Kids are like your very own little minions who can fetch you the TV remote and you get to blame them for shit. *Oh, sorry I didn't make your lame-ass party. My kidlet was vomiting everywhere.*" Brody's eyes light up as he talks about kids, which scares me.

"You sound like you can't wait." And that doesn't work for me. At all. Kids are not in my future.

Brody looks horrified. "God no. The negatives completely outweigh the benefits. Like, you have to feed them and stuff, and as you're aware, Videre and you are pretty much solely responsible for feeding me lately. Plus, tantrums, neediness, no sleep—"

"Agreed. I couldn't handle that. I'm just gonna wait for Law to have kids so I can spoil them, play with them, and then hand them back when they whine."

"I'm the same with my siblings. Once they start popping out kids, I'm gonna give you a run for your money at the best-uncle-ever award."

The doubt about the validity of that scenario tries to flit through my head, but I'm not gonna let it. I want to hold on to the perfect image where Brody and I try to out-uncle each other in the future.

Chris and Rhett eventually come down off the wall, and then Brody and I get our turn.

"Race you to the top?" Brody taunts.

"Oh, sure, because you won't kick my ass or anything."

Brody covers his hands in the chalk stuff and grins. "I'll give you a head start."

Even with the head start, he beats me to the top. At one point, he gets close enough to slap my ass as he passes me.

"I better not have a chalk handprint on my shorts," I grumble.

He looks down at me and winks.

God, he can be a cocky son of a bitch. But silently, I'm loving it in this environment. Surrounded by other people, I'm not overthinking it. I'm not questioning his motives or thinking there's something sinister behind it.

We spend nearly the whole afternoon and evening climbing, and by the time we're finished, my legs and arms ache.

"There's a bar next door that serves food," Chris says after we hand in our equipment. "You guys up for some dinner and drinks?"

Brody and I glance at each other.

"I don't know," Brody says. "Did you remember to feed the cat before we left?"

He's putting the decision in my hands, and damn if it doesn't make me like him more.

"I'm pretty sure I fed her."

Brody turns to Chris. "Then we're in."

The climbing centre is in the middle of an industrial area in the West End, and right next door is a storage shed that's been converted into the hipster capital of Brisbane.

Rustic furniture, low lighting, fake grass, a vibe that says they're too cool to care but really spent a fortune to appear that way.

"You fit right in," Brody says, pulling on my man bun. Damn him.

I think I've kept it this long to prove some kind of point that it's a purposefully grown hairstyle instead of it being a sign of my laziness, but maybe I've forgotten who the joke's really on, because it gives Law, Reed, and Brody endless mocking fodder.

I shove him, and he laughs.

We find a picnic table to sit at, because picnic tables indoors are totally normal, and Rhett and Brody offer to go get us drinks.

His hand brushes my lower back, and I'm surprised by how easy it is for me to enjoy the sensation. "What do you want?"

"Whatever you're having."

He nods. "Be right back."

"How long have you two been together?" Chris asks, breaking my focus away from Brody's ass as he walks away. I've been staring at it all day but still can't get enough.

"What? Oh, we aren't ... like ... that."

"Really? Huh. I thought for sure. You live together,

though?"

"Yeah. Roommates."

"Wow. Was not getting that vibe. You're relaxed around him, and"—Chris shrugs—"I figured, you were so uptight when we dated."

I want to argue, but I can't. "Okay, we might be slightly more than roommates, but it's not serious or anything."

Chris snorts. "Yeah, I remember that about you. You're not serious about anyone."

Okay, who wants a subject change? "What about you and Rhett?"

"Oh. This is our first date, and it was a disaster up until you guys saved it."

"We saved it? How?"

"I was trying to impress him with the rock-climbing date. Only, when you don't get a chance to talk because you're separated for most of the time, it's hard to really get to know the other person. So, not such a great idea. Once we could climb together or talk while you two were on the wall, then I could actually learn about him."

"Then you're welcome." I smile.

"It's how I knew there was more between you and Brody. I could tell you were familiar with each other. Even when you weren't talking, you were comfortable being near him."

"Really? Interesting."

I watch as Brody and Rhett make their way back over to us, and it suddenly occurs to me that I no longer view him as the intimidating, confident guy I was scared of even talking to.

Today proves that.

He smiles that Brody trademark smile, and I sigh at how good-looking he is.

"How you holding up?" he asks. "The first few times I rock climbed, I couldn't lift my arms for days."

"Oh, muscles I didn't even know I had are killing me." If I wasn't so sore, I'd be taking him home and hooking up with him again when I'm not supposed to.

I have hope that with a little work, Brody and I could have more. Do more.

I really need to make that appointment with the sex therapist.

―――

Sex therapy is a lot less exciting than I could ever imagine. Granted this is my first time seeing Dr. Shearon, and the only reason I got into him earlier than planned was because he had a last-minute cancellation.

My original appointment wasn't supposed to be for another month. Apparently, sex therapists are busy. Who knew?

Brody's been respectful in not asking when I'll be ready, which I'm thankful for, because the last thing I want to do is tell him I'm seeing a sex therapist.

I jumped at the chance for an earlier appointment with this guy so I could get the ball rolling. I left work so fast I'm sure cartoon smoke followed me.

Torture isn't quite strong enough a word to describe what Brody and I have been doing to each other, and the worst part is we don't even mean to do it.

Starting something has awoken a need inside me I thought was long dead, but we need to do this the right way.

Each night when Brody comes home from work, I feed him, and then instead of going to bed or watching TV, where we sit so close to each other it drives us crazy, we both hit the gym in the basement. We work out until we both feel like passing out and then go to our respective rooms alone. I'm not sure about him, but I've spent every night with my fist wrapped around my cock until I come with Brody's name on my lips.

That's why I accepted this therapy appointment before I had a real chance to process what it would entail. Which is a whole heap of talking about my sexual hang-ups, exploits, and the poor way in which I've treated men these past few years.

It doesn't help that the sex guy is hot. He's intellectual sexy—glasses, perfectly shaven face, and light brown hair with golden highlights styled with so much gel I could probably give the guy a noogie and I wouldn't mess it up. He's put together in a grown-up sort of way, even though he looks to be my age.

I have to remind myself it took a long time to become comfortable with Karen, and it'll take time with this guy too, but my dick was really hoping I could come in, talk through some stuff, and then go home and have sex with Brody.

It doesn't look like that'll happen.

"A need for control in the bedroom isn't necessarily a *bad* thing," Dr. Shearon says. His first name, no joke, is Edward. It's hard for me to take a guy seriously when his name is Ed Shearon. Spelled differently than the singer or not, it's still weird. "You just need to be given the right tools to make sure you're doing it in a safe environment that's beneficial to you and your partner."

Tools. I'm really hoping that's a code word for sex toys.

"The thing is, Doc …" Not calling him Ed. No way, no how. "Before my attack, I liked *not* being in control. I liked being cared for and—" I stop abruptly. Talking about sex with anyone is hard enough. Telling a complete stranger how much you love a dick in your ass is a whole other ballgame.

"And?" he prompts.

"I used to like bottoming and being dominated. Okay, maybe dominated isn't the right word. I'm not, like, into kink, but—"

"There wouldn't be a problem if you were."

I get the sense he's fishing for me to tell the truth, but I really am. It's not a dominant versus submissive thing. "I want to let go and let my partner take care of my needs without me freaking out on him."

He writes something on his notepad, and like when Karen does it, I find myself wanting to ask what's written there.

Batshit crazy man is batshit crazy is most likely not what it is, but my mind always goes there.

"And what are your needs?"

Being dicked out until I can't walk ... Yeah, I'm not comfortable saying that.

When I don't answer, he smiles.

"If you can't discuss it with me, you have to at least be able to discuss it with your partner. I know it's awkward having to lay all this out to someone you met twenty minutes ago, but I can help you if you want to move forwards with a few more appointments."

The thing is, I've gotten used to talking about my issues with Karen, but like she said, we've barely touched on the sex stuff. I want this help. I came here for a reason. But that doesn't make it any easier to talk openly about problems society may deem ... unmanly or emasculating. If a man is impotent, which I'm not but have had those kinds of issues since Kyle in certain situations, he's seen as less of a man.

"Would your partner be willing to come to a couple of sessions?"

I rub the back of my neck. "Well, I mean ... he's not really my partner. He's my roommate, and the whole fooling around thing only started a few weeks ago. He ... uh, he doesn't know I'm here."

Ed Shearon's disapproving stare is the same as Karen's. It makes me wonder if they're related. "You need to tell him."

"Why?" I croak.

"I know it's difficult, but if you want to have something real with this guy—"

"His name is Brody."

The doc nods. "If you're going to explore a sexual relationship with Brody, then you need to do it in a healthy way. There needs to be an open dialogue, and you need to feel safe. He won't be able to provide you that if you're only giving him half of the truth."

He makes sense, but that doesn't make it any easier.

"What's your biggest fear about telling him?" he asks.

I want to roll my eyes. "You mean apart from the obvious? That talking about your shortcomings in bed isn't exactly a turn-on? That he'll put me in the too-hard basket and move on? Then we'd be stuck living with each other."

"You say you fool around. Could you go into a bit more depth?"

Ooh yeah, pervy Karen will so love me relaying this conversation to her.

"It's not much of fooling around. I gave him a sloppy blowjob because I couldn't get out of my head, and he finished us off with his hand, and then another time we rubbed off on each other ... or I rubbed off on him while I pinned him to the couch. Same diff, right?"

"For someone with your past issues, I wouldn't say that's not much. That's promising. Is there a reason it's only been those two times?"

"He doesn't want to overstep. Each time we hooked up, I restrained him in some way because if I didn't know where his hands were at all times, I'd start to panic that the switch might flip."

Dr. Shearon cocks his head. "Switch?"

"My ex-boyfriend, Kyle, he had red-flag behaviour, but

never, ever, not once—not even while he was hovering over me with a knife to my neck—did I believe he'd ever hurt me. Brody doesn't have any warning signs, but I still can't trust that he won't flip out one day."

The doc doesn't write anything down or say anything. He thinks for a few moments before asking, "Are you able to let go when Brody is restrained?"

"As much as I've been able to since the attack, yeah."

"Well, it's a good starting point. If you want to keep working with me, I don't see why we shouldn't be able to eventually get you to a place where you could bottom for your partner without any anxiety."

"Really?" I hate that I sound so damn hopeful.

Another warm smile. Normally, I'd be edgy, because being with a hot guy who has brains, one on one … this would've been my worst nightmare a year ago. Whether it's because I've laid all my sexual issues out for this guy or that I'm actually getting better, I don't know. Maybe it's that even though he's good-looking, I have no attraction to him whatsoever. All I know is I want to keep working with him. I want to so I can be with Brody, and maybe, just *maybe*, have some sort of semblance of a real relationship again.

"We can work through the bigger issues during our next sessions, but for the rest of today, I'm going to give you ways to enjoy your partner now through methods you're already using."

"Methods?"

He leans back in his seat. "How do you feel about bondage?" He must see the look of horror on my face, because he clarifies, "Tying your partner up, not the other way around."

It occurs to me that sex therapist Ed Shearon might be a genius.

16

BRODY

My body's almost as exhausted as my mind. I can't remember the last time I was this sexually frustrated. I can go months without the touch of another man, but spending every night with Anders, whether it's in the gym or on the couch we've hooked up on twice, is driving me crazy. Not figuratively either. I found my car keys in the freezer this morning. I was lucky it didn't fuck up the electronics in the key fob, and I still can't understand why I put them in the freezer.

The more I'm around him, the more I want to touch him.

I try to find excuses to give him affection here and there, even the smallest of touches, like squeezing by him in the kitchen to reach for some water I don't need. Or handing him something and lingering when our fingers brush.

They're tiny gestures, but it's getting to the point where my dick gets hard before I even step into our apartment.

He's got me wound tight, and my hand is no replacement for the real thing. It barely scratches the surface of my growing need. I can come while whispering Anders' name, but it feels nothing like coming while pressed against him.

Arriving home from yet another gruelling day, I'm thankful to be going to trial soon. Although with any luck, the client will go for a plea deal. I don't know if I can sit through a trial and listen to every aspect of this rape again.

Burning out on my first official case won't win me any brownie points with the partners or my father, so I've been trying to suck it up.

It's like the doubt in my head has taken on my dad's voice, telling me I'm not cut out for this type of law. Before, that voice urged me to do better. Now, knowing what Anders went through, all I can see is what I'm doing to the victim of my client. What she's going to go through for the rest of her life.

Will she ever trust a man not to hurt her? Will she not be able to have sex with someone because it will make her feel out of control?

I push through the door to our apartment to find Anders where he's been every night these past two weeks—cooking me dinner. He's moved his usual dinner back to fit my schedule so we can eat together. I want to hate him for it because it makes my need for him deeper, but honestly, it's the only part of my day that I'm enjoying lately.

I just wish I could have more.

Call me greedy, I don't care. Restraining myself around him sucks, and it's harder than my cock. Which is painful at this point.

Anders turns to me with a smile. It's fucking blinding. I've never seen the man so ... happy.

I want to crack a joke about what meds he's on, but I guess that would be in poor taste. I assume he's on meds for his long list of diagnoses. "What are you so smiley about?"

Instead of answering me, he saunters ... yeah, saunters over to me. That's also something I've never seen him do.

"What are you—"

I'm cut off by his mouth on mine, his hands cupping my face, and his tongue demanding mine come out to play. We stumble back because I'm so not prepared for it, but it's easy to regain balance when I lean forward so there's no space between us.

That little voice in my head telling me I shouldn't be doing this is drowned out by the blood rushing south to my already hard cock.

I let myself enjoy it a lot longer than a good man would. Not that I'm a bad man, I know that, but I definitely could stand to be less selfish right now.

It's Anders who finally breaks the kiss.

"What was that?" I rasp.

We've still got our arms around each other, hard body against hard body.

"I, uh … so …" His skin pinkens at his cheekbones, the rest of his cheeks hidden by his beard.

"Spit it out," I mock.

"Bet you say that to all the boys."

"Never," I say coyly. "Seems like you've had a better day than me."

"Uh, yeah. I have something … to, uh, discuss with you?" It comes out like a question, and I don't know whether to be scared or excited. "Over dinner?"

"'Kay." I don't know if I pull off the casual tone I'm going for.

"Go change out of your suit, because I know you hate them. Then we'll talk."

I tilt my head. "How do you know I hate my suits?"

"The first thing you do when you get home every night is strip down to the least amount of clothes possible."

"Maybe I just hate clothes."

Anders turns to face me. "Can you please put clothes on tonight so I can at least get out what I need to say?"

"So this isn't a clothing-optional event?"

"If you're still with me after everything I have to tell you, then we can get to the clothing-optional part."

Anders' laughter fades as I bolt for my room. Even though my heavy feet go nowhere near Meatball, she still meows at me from where she's lying in the middle of the floor as if to say, "I'm here, don't step on me!"

I'm tempted to forget my shirt but decide I'm too interested in what Anders has to say to taunt him.

Once dressed in jeans and a T-shirt, I head back out to find the cat still staring at me. She's changed so much since Anders moved in—more cat and less demon—and when I approach, she looks up at me as if she wants me to pick her up.

I give her a quick cuddle and take her over to her food bowl where there's biscuits for her to eat.

"If she's telling you I didn't feed her, she's a lying whore," Anders calls out from the kitchen.

I laugh. "She still has food there."

Anders and I meet in the dining room and sit across from each other.

"This is new," I say at the plate in front of me. Looks like sweet potato mash, chicken, and— "Is that fennel?"

"Yup," Anders says proudly. "I had to call my mum and ask what the fuck it was, but I think I cooked it right."

He's learning, though I thought fennel was one of those vegetables you don't cook. But I'm not going to bring that up.

"Well ..." I eye him expectantly.

Anders takes a deep breath. "Okay ... so ... when I told my therapist that something happened between you and me and she advised me to stop, she also suggested something else I didn't tell you about."

"Okay ..."

"This is another one of those things where I kinda have to blurt it? Because it's embarrassing."

I put my cutlery down as I prepare myself to hear him out fully.

"She suggested I go to sex therapy." Anders' words are so fast, I'm not entirely sure I hear him correctly.

"Sex therapy. What exactly is that?"

"Where you go talk to someone about any sex issues. Like my need to be in control in the bedroom and my inability to let go."

"Oh, okay. Sounds less kinky than I was thinking. I thought it was a fancy word for 'hooker' or something."

Anders laughs. "You wish."

Actually, I don't. I don't even know how I feel about Anders talking to some other guy about sex even though I have no right to him in that way.

"Is he hot?" falls out of my mouth.

Anders smirks. "His name is Ed Shearon."

"Get the fuck out. Please tell me he's a ginger like the singer?"

"Nah, looks nothing like him. Last name's spelled differently too. But it's still weird saying my sex therapist is Ed Shearon."

My eyes narrow. "You deflected the question, so he is totally hot."

"He's also married according to the ring on his finger, and it's probably to a woman. Though, he was quite knowledgeable about gay lingo."

"Would probably have to be in his line of work."

"True." Anders shakes off the thought. "But you have nothing to worry about. Nothing turns you off someone more than having them psychoanalyse your sexual habits."

"Did I say I was worried?"

Anders eyes me. "Are you worried?"

Time to downplay the interest I have in Anders by avoiding the question. "What did he say?"

Anders swallows hard and looks away. "Finish dinner first?"

I agree but can't help wondering if it wasn't bad, then why he'd want to put the conversation off. Then again, he kissed me when I walked in, so I really have no idea what he needs to say. "Are you sure we can't talk about it now?"

"Umm ... I don't think that's a good idea."

"Why not?"

Anders averts his gaze as he says, "Because if you're okay with what he had to say, then I assume we won't even finish dinner."

I groan. "Why'd you have to go and say something like that?"

"Don't get too excited, because we do kinda have to discuss some shit."

"Like what?"

"Well, today with him was mostly giving him my history and setting goals, so it was pretty boring."

"Ah." I take a giant bite of chicken.

"Until the end anyway," Anders adds.

"The end?" I ask, my mouth full.

"Yeah. When he suggested I tie you up and fuck you."

The food gets stuck in the back of my throat, and I choke.

Anders tries to hide his amusement while I can't breathe and beat on my chest.

"Need a hand?" he asks.

I wave him off and swallow the chunk of food because spitting it out would be gross, and the last thing I want to do is turn Anders off after that proposition.

Reaching for my water, I wince as it washes the last of my choking fiasco down.

"Did your therapist really say that?" I ask.

"Okay, well, not in those *exact* words."

"What exact words did he use?"

"Well, he started by saying that we're fine to continue what we've been doing so long as I'm comfortable with it and it doesn't bring on any anxiety."

I put my knife and fork down. "And dinner is done. Let's go."

Anders laughs and puts his hand up. "Wait. That's not all. I said there's quite a bit to go through." That adorable blush of his that's mostly hidden by his beard sneaks in.

"Like?"

"If we're gonna do the whole ... bondage thing, we're supposed to set up limits and guidelines. Come up with a safe word."

I purse my lips. "Isn't that a bit extreme? I mean, we're not talking hardcore BDSM here, right? Just a little ... restraint?" Okay, now it's my turn for my cheeks to heat.

What the fuck? I don't blush over sex. Granted I've never done the whole being-tied-up thing before, but I'm definitely open to it. If it means I get to be with Anders, I'd be willing to try anything. Might draw the line at kissing his feet though. Feet are gross.

Oh, so you can lick someone's butthole, but feet are gross?

I don't know why that thought was in Anders' voice, but it makes a point. Still, I stand by my opinion of feet. Most unsexy body part ever.

"Ed Shearon"—he snickers—"says you need to feel safe. Being tied up is putting you in a vulnerable position."

"It'll be a level playing field, then, right?"

"Exactly. I'll need a safe word too so it's easier for me to tell you if I'm struggling. And you should have one so if it gets to be too much, you can be untied fast. It's the best way to do it. Clear and hard lines. The sex guy was pretty adamant on that. He was also adamant about me telling you all this even though I wanted to wing it and hope for the best."

I want to lecture him about that, but he's told me and that's the main thing. "I think it's probably best we leave it to the *professional*."

"He's not a hooker!"

"Hey, I just said he was a professional. I never implied he's a whore. But, oh, man, this is going to be fun. So. Much. Innuendo. Can we also take a moment to appreciate that you have a sex guy? Like some people have a weed guy, a nightclub guy, numerous guys who can hook you up with whatever you need. We have a sex guy."

"*We?*" Anders asks, his expression too stoic to tell if that makes him uncomfortable.

I clear my throat. "Uh, you."

"No, no, I like the we comment. I didn't know if there would be a 'we' after I told you ... everything."

"And have you?"

"Have I what?"

"Told me everything?" I'm fishing, so sue me. But I still can't help thinking there's something bigger Anders isn't telling me.

I know anxiety and all his issues present differently in different people, but I'm struggling to find the connection between a mugging and sex unless there was some form of sexual assault involved. I'm not going to pressure him into telling me, but I want so badly for him to trust me with it.

"I've told you everything you need to know."

Nice non-answer, Anders.

"So, the safe-word thing," I say, steering the topic back to the important part, because I know I can't push.

I understand a safe word is the right thing to do. Undertaking this type of relationship with anyone would need rules. Doing it with Anders, we probably need even more rules.

"Can we make it something easy and simple like 'stop'?" I ask. "Because if it's *tosswinkle* or something, I don't know if I'll be able to keep it serious."

"Tosswinkle it is," Anders declares.

Dammit. Definitely shouldn't have suggested that.

"But nah, seriously," Anders says, "I'm good with simple. We can do the basic red, yellow, green. Red for stop, yellow for slow down, and green is all good to go."

"Simple enough."

We stare at each other over the dining table, our plates still half-full.

Anders' mouth turns up. "Negotiating a sexual relationship is weird."

"Yup." I enunciate the *p* with a pop.

"Let's finish eating before we …"

"Break out the ropes and chains?"

"Maybe we can go chain shopping next week. I … uh, kinda made a stop at that place near the motorway on my way home."

"The all-black glass building with the huge red *X* on it? That place?" The place that looks like a hardcore BDSM sex club.

Oh, wow, I never realised until this very second that I might be a bit of a prude. I mean, I'm no stranger to sex, obviously, but this … this is a whole new thing for me. Maybe prude isn't the right word.

Vanilla, maybe?

I have no sex toys. Like, at all. Not that I hadn't thought

about possibly ordering something, but I didn't think I'd use it. I'm vers but prefer topping. Bottoming to me is just the thing you do occasionally for your partner. It feels nice, but it's not the best sex I've ever had, so given a choice, I'll always choose to top. Or even blowjobs. And my hand has always been satisfying enough for me to not have the need to look for something else.

"You look terrified," Anders says with a nervous laugh.

I try to smile. "Not at all. Just realising I've lived a pretty sheltered life, and I can't wait for you to broaden my horizons."

"I ..." He looks away as he continues. "I haven't exactly done this sort of thing either."

"So, we'll figure it out together?"

His eyes meet mine across the dinner table. "I'm not hungry anymore."

My groin stirs, and I'm out of my seat before Anders can even blink. "Neither."

Anders meets me halfway, our bodies colliding, mouths crashing together, hands exploring, and my cock goes from interested to *oh fuck, I need it*.

While Anders' mouth is enthusiastic and eager, I still sense the hesitance in him. He's holding back. I'm trying to rein in my desire to take control. I don't *need* it, but at the same time, I've only ever been the guy who takes control, so this is new to me also.

Anders breaks our kiss, staring into my eyes with a look I can't decipher.

"What were you thinking for tonight?" I ask.

This whole communication thing throughout is new to me too, but Anders seems to be the only person I can't get a clear read on. I've mistaken pain and hurt for flirting, for fuck's sake.

"I was thinking I want to finish what I started the other night, but I want you to come in my mouth."

I kiss him again, because how can I not with an offer like that. Every ounce of strength I have is used to hold me back and not overpower him. Maybe this bondage thing will be good for both of us.

"Where do you want me?" I whisper against his mouth.

"Naked." Anders walks away, leaving me to wonder if I should be undressing right here.

He doesn't go far. Pulling out a dining room chair, he brings it into the living room. "Strip. I'll be right back."

Nerves or unease settle in my stomach but not because I don't want to do this. It's because I'm so out of my element.

I undress slowly, lifting my shirt over my head and dumping it on the floor. My jeans go next.

The cat jumps up on the backrest of the couch beside me and stares at me in the way only a cat could. It's as if she's saying, "I know what you're about to do, and hey, I'm not really into kink shaming, but you should be ashamed."

Anders interrupts my stare down with her. "What's wrong?"

"Luck—I mean, *Meatball* is judging us."

Anders laughs and dumps a plastic bag on the couch. Then he picks up the cat and snuggles into her. That shouldn't be a turn-on, but it is. He's been so sweet to her since the night of the spaghetti incident, and it's adorable.

"I think it's your bedtime, young lady." Anders' cooing voice warms me, and so does the sight of his retreating backside as he deposits the cat in his room.

He really has adopted her.

In a flash, he's back at my side. "You still have clothes on." Anders' fingers dip into the waistband of my boxers and tug them down my legs.

"So do you."

He smiles up at me. "Need to even the playing field?"

"Isn't that was this is all about?" I wave a hand towards the bag. I'm dying to see what's inside, but I'm also a little apprehensive about it.

While Anders catches up by stripping down, I shuck off the boxers around my ankles, leaving us both naked.

It's the first time we've been completely naked together.

We're both breathing heavily already, only I know mine is from anticipation. I can't tell what Anders is thinking.

"How you doing? You going okay?" I try to force myself to not take in the beauty that is this naked man in front of me.

All tanned skin and toned muscles, and piercings.

I try to keep my eyes on the top half of him but totally fail.

My gaze drops to his cock. His hard, perfectly shaped cock.

Stop looking.

I shake it off and meet Anders' eyes. They're a little wide, maybe panicked. He hasn't answered me, so maybe I need to take the lead for a minute.

"Yellow?"

He shakes his head. "Green."

"You going to tie me to the chair?" I ask.

Anders nods, reaching blindly for the black bag with the large red *X* on it. He pulls out leather cuffs, and apparently my cock likes the look of them. It jerks and leaks the tiniest drop of precum.

"Take a seat." Anders' voice is deep, gruff, and sexy.

I don't even hesitate a second. The suede material of the seat is warm on my skin as I sit.

"Hands behind your back." Anders' raspy tone makes me bite my lip and practically whimper.

Anders descends to his knees beside me and adjusts the leather cuffs to go around my wrists. They're tightened with buckles and feel rough on my skin but aren't too bad, and I can hold on to the thin, short rope connecting the two together.

"Not too tight?" Anders breathes in my ear.

"Good," I croak.

Anders stands and moves in front of me, his cock just out of reach even if I lean forward. Already, being tied up is having some interesting consequences. Normally, I'd reach for his hips and pull him close to me—take what I want.

But I can't do that. It's both thrilling and frustrating.

"I didn't realise this would look so hot," Anders murmurs.

"I always look hot," I joke, because the intensity of his eyes on mine unnerves me in the best possible way.

My cock aches, begging to be touched, and again, the inability to do anything about it only amplifies the need. I grip the rope of the cuffs tighter as my wrists wriggle and try to get free.

The chafing feels like it's on my balls instead of my hands, and Anders hasn't even touched me yet.

A soft hand runs through my hair, causing shivers down my spine. My toes dig into the carpet. Muscles I didn't even know I had tense and contract.

"Anders," I breathe.

His grip tightens in my hair, forcing my head up to look at him.

The gleam in his eye is feral and hungry, and I understand why he and the therapist were adamant on a safe word because I don't think I've ever been more vulnerable than right now.

Slight uncomfortableness washes over me but not enough to slow down or stop.

Anders leans over me, his mouth coming down on mine hot and heavy. I stretch to full height as much as having my hands behind my back lets me, but it's not enough.

A whine gets stuck in the back of my throat, and Anders laughs against my lips.

"I like you like this," Anders whispers.

I won't admit it, but so do I.

"Suddenly not so cocky." He glances down at my overeager dick. "Or still a lot cocky, I see."

There's something about not getting a say, not being able to act that's somehow restrictive but liberating at the same time.

My partner's pleasure has always been a priority for me, but not being able to do anything about it frees my mind from that concern which means all I'm focused on is the sensations coursing through my body.

Like the feel of his lips on my skin as he lowers himself to his knees, his mouth trailing down my body. The feel of his soft beard brushing against my stomach as he goes even lower. Relishing the soft, wet touch of his tongue to the tip of my cock as he licks my slit.

Fuck, Anders looks good on his knees.

Thick, dark hair, loose and crazy, hanging down to his neck.

Flushed skin.

Eager mouth.

Unlike the last time he gave me a blowjob, he doesn't hesitate. When his eyes meet mine, staring up through surprisingly long lashes, there's a playfulness that wasn't there a few weeks ago.

Anders licks, he teases, he engulfs my whole damn cock to the back of his throat.

"Holy hell, you're driving me crazy."

"Mmm," he hums around me while dragging his mouth back up to the tip and pulling off.

Anders' hand strokes me from tip to root, while his mouth explores lower.

My thighs tense and widen, and the noise that comes out of me when he licks my sac is guttural and primal and a sound I've never made before.

His hand and mouth work together.

I fight against the restraints more.

The tightness on my wrists sends pain shooting up my arms and down my back, but it's the good kind of pain. The type that makes my cock harder and my mind clearer.

I reach a level of pleasurable haze I've never experienced during sex. This experiment was supposed to get Anders out of his head, but it turns out it does something for me too.

All I can focus on is Anders' mouth and the intensity in which he works me over. Wet slurps join my heavy breaths, and when he takes me to the back of his throat again, my cock pulses.

There isn't even the chance to warn him before I'm spilling over and grunting my release.

"Fuck, fuck, *fuck*!" I throw my head back.

Anders takes it all, no hesitation, no jittery reactions, just pure confidence in the way he swallows me down.

Completely wrung-out and spent, I take a good minute to recover. Anders' hands run up and down my thighs until my cock softens in his mouth. I squirm when it becomes oversensitive.

He releases me and stands, the satisfied smirk on his face catching my eye.

A hand runs through my hair again, while his other one reaches for his hard dick and strokes.

"Can I?" I rasp.

Anders grips his cock tighter. "You want this?"

I want to suck him off more than I want my next breath. And cocky Anders might be my most favourite Anders of all.

It goes twitchy Anders, relaxed Anders, and then this guy

in front of me, staring down at me with power in his eyes and happiness in his smile.

"Please," I beg.

Anders smiles wider and guides his cock to my lips.

I barely get a chance to enjoy and savour the heady flavour when it disappears.

My gaze flicks up to his. "What's wrong."

His eyes are wide. "I just realised you can't use a safe word if you have your mouth full."

"I don't care."

"No, we have to—"

"I'll kick you really hard if I want you to stop." There's no doubt in my mind; I won't need to kick him.

Anders moves closer, his cock teasing my lips. When I open, he slides in between them slowly. Hesitantly.

Noooo. He's gone back to overthinking. He's too much in his head.

I take it back. I will have to kick him.

One swift nudge with my foot has him pulling back out.

"See?" I say. "It works. So get out of your head and fuck my mouth, because if I'm not allowed to touch you, I at least want to be the one to make you come."

A shiver runs through him, and I worry I crossed a line, but it must've been the right line, because a second later, his grip in my hair tightens and his cock pushes past my lips more aggressively.

I usually have hands involved in giving blowjobs. Caressing, teasing, stroking ... it's a bit of pressure to rely solely on my deep-throating skills.

He thrusts in and out, using my mouth to get himself off, and every grunt, every push puts me in the same state of mind as when he was going down on me. My brain shuts off, and everything is automatic.

My arms have begun to ache from being tied and straining to fight the cuffs that bind me, but I don't want to slow down or stop.

So I take it and love every minute of it.

"Brody," Anders croaks.

Come, I chant in my head.

As if hearing me, warm cum fills my mouth, and Anders lets out a loud moan.

In the time it takes Anders to pull out, the haze of our orgasms fade and reality sets in. I'm in a lot more pain than I thought.

My wrists protest something fierce.

A second later, Anders is there, on his knees, loosening the cuffs and freeing me. He stands and pulls me up, holding me against him.

The kiss with the mixed heady taste of our cum is soft, his gentle hands moving over my tired muscles.

"Can I stay with you tonight?" he whispers against my mouth.

I should say no. I need to say no. But after that experience, there's no way I'm strong enough to say no.

Instead, we put our underwear back on and make our way to my bed, where I let him embrace me while I try to fall asleep.

His arms are warm and caring, and it's hard to believe this guy is the one who has issues with intimacy.

17

ANDERSON

"I'm going to kick you out if you keep refusing to sleep when you're next to me," Brody mumbles as he slowly wakes to the sound of his alarm.

It's the second time I've spent the night in his bed wrapped around him without actually sleeping.

"I'll sleep when I'm tired."

"Pass out, you mean." Closing the gap between our horrible breaths, Brody kisses me softly. "Go sleep for a few hours before you have to get up to go work. I'll be out of here in ten minutes." He climbs out of bed, and I take a minute to admire his long, lean legs and narrow waist with his bigger upper body. He's almost like one of those funny memes about the guys who forget leg day, but he's not quite *that* disproportionate.

His firm bubble butt is perfect though, framed awesomely by his tight boxer briefs.

I sigh ... and maybe drool a little bit.

Brody turns to me as he slips his suit pants on and tightens his belt. "Good view?"

"The best." I grin.

It actually feels like we're a real couple with no issues.

There's no panic, no therapist's voice in my head, and it's the closest thing to normal I've felt in a really long time.

Which is sad, sure, but also fucking amazing.

Brody moves towards his closet and pulls out a pristine white shirt.

He may hate his suits, but he looks good in them. No, not just good—mouth-wateringly hot.

"Big day at work again?" I ask, because this normal thing is kinda addictive.

"Yeah. I've been summoned." Brody's tone is ominous.

"Summoned? Like to court?"

"Worse. To my father's office."

"Someone's in trouble," I sing.

Brody laughs. "Probably, but you want to hear something interesting?"

"Interesting how?"

"Yesterday when he told me he wants to speak to me first thing today, I panicked. I spent most of the evening making sure I had all my outstanding work completed so he couldn't ream me for it, but there wasn't much there. I still don't know what he wants to talk to me about."

My lips twitch. "Oh, honey, if you think that's interesting, we need to get you out more."

Brody ignores my snark. "That's not the interesting part."

"Then what is?"

He climbs on the bed and leans over me. "Now? After last night ... after a mind-blowing experience where I wasn't in control of what was happening and I couldn't gain control no matter how hard I fought, I feel free. I don't think I've been this relaxed going into work in a long time."

"So it's safe to say you enjoyed it and wouldn't mind a repeat?" I bite my lip.

"Anytime. Anywhere." Brody leans forward and kisses my

forehead. "Not gonna lie, though, one day I'll want to touch you during sex. I know we have to work our way up to that."

"My therapist—"

"Which one?"

"The Grammy Award–winning one."

"Ah, the sexy guy."

"You haven't seen him. How do you know he's sexy?"

Brody shrugs. "Don't disrupt my fantasy. I'm picturing you and him shopping for silk rope together."

The laughter flies out of me. "And you'd be okay with that?"

He leans in, his mouth going next to my ear. "As long as I'm the only one you're using it with."

A moan gets stuck in the back of my throat. "Anyway, he says that it might be beneficial if I can get you to come to an appointment sometime."

Brody's eyes widen.

"I said no," I say quickly. "Said we weren't really there yet, but in the future. If we need it, the offer's there. He might be able to help us get through the whole no-touching thing."

He looks hesitant.

"You don't have to though."

"No. I can do that. I *want* to do that. It'll be a pain to arrange something around work, but I can make it happen."

"Are you sure? It's like ... a very couply thing to do, so I understand if you don't want to go."

Brody cups my face. "I have some really bad news for you, Anders."

I stare expectantly.

"Pretty sure we're a couple."

I pull back. "What?"

"No way am I seeing anyone else while we try to work through this."

"Me neither." I laugh. "Although, that's kinda a given. I just don't know if exclusivity really means couple. Like, calling you my boyfriend would be weird."

"We don't have to be 'boyfriends' if that's too much for you. We're ... seeing each other?" Brody's eyes travel down my body. "I mean, it's true. We're seeing a whole lot of each other."

"Of course, you make it sound dirty."

"Yup."

"Going with me to sex therapy is huge though. And soon. And it's not like I can—"

Brody presses a finger to my lips. "I know you can't promise me anything big, and I'm not asking you to. Basically, all I'm asking is for you to give this an actual try—to see past the sex stuff because I'm the only guy you've felt comfortable enough to go there with. I want more than just sex from you, however small."

"It's not like it's a lot of fun," I warn. "Talking about sex is surprisingly boring and clinical."

"You're really selling me on it."

"Not to mention the whole embarrassing thing," I continue. "You probably would've loved seeing me fumble over telling Ed Shearon how much I want to bottom for you."

Brody's head lands on my chest. "You're officially mean, and I hate you, and now while my dad yells at me for God knows what, all I'm going to be thinking about is your ass."

"Hmm, that'll be super inconvenient for you. Your dad will probably think you're a freak—getting turned on talking through judicial law."

"Do you know what judicial law means?" Brody chuckles.

"Nope. Judges ... and things."

"You're cute." Lips land on my cheek. "But I have to go get

yelled at about judges and things." Brody stands again and moves to his sock drawer. I go back to watching him.

"What have you got planned for the day other than work?" he asks.

"I have a self-defence lesson with Law during my lunch break. I've been blowing him off lately, and he's finally called me on it, so I need to make an effort."

Brody freezes. "You going to tell him about us?"

"No fucking way."

"Okay." He relaxes, and I tell myself not to read into why. I have my reasons for not wanting Law to know. He'd worry, he'd play the big-brother act, even though I'm ten minutes older, and he'd most likely come and talk to Brody about how fragile I am and that we shouldn't be together.

Maybe Brody knows this and doesn't want Law to know as much as I don't, but I also can't help wondering if Reed has anything to do with him not wanting them to know.

"How about I bring dinner home tonight? Save you cooking." He holds up his hand before I can protest. "I know you like it, but one night off won't hurt, and I want to bring you something nice."

"Are you saying my cooking isn't nice?" I shriek.

He hesitates. "It's definitely getting better?"

Brody's been such a good sport being my guinea pig, but that doesn't mean I'm not gonna pretend to be offended. "You've been too spoiled with your connection at Videre. You need to eat real-people food. And by real, I mean cheap. Because I have no money."

Brody pauses. "About that. Like, tell me if I'm overstepping, but you're an accountant, right?"

"Yeah, yeah, Law always gets on me about being shit with money when money is my profession, but it's kinda hard to have money when you spend outside your means." I shrug. "It's easy to do living in Brisbane. Everything is so damn expensive." Especially therapy and my late-night shopping channel habit, but I won't get into that.

"I already told you I don't need rent from you. Even if it's just until you get on your feet and pay off some debt."

I'm thankful he doesn't ask what has me going into debt, but I still can't take his money. "Mixing money with what we're doing is too much, I think."

"Fair enough. Offer's there though. I really have to go."

"So go already."

He groans. "I don't want to."

"Scared of your dad?"

"No. I want to stay in bed with you."

"But then I won't sleep, and you'll be mad at yourself."

"True. Okay, I'm going. I'll see you tonight."

"Can't wait." No sleep or not, I can't wait to do it again.

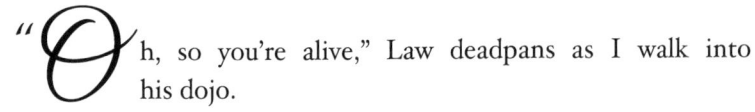

"Oh, so you're alive," Law deadpans as I walk into his dojo.

"Still passive aggressive, I see. I've been busy."

"Busy doing what?"

Your boyfriend's ex. *Yeah, don't say that.*

"Therapy," I say instead.

"Karen's got you going to more appointments?"

"Ah ..." To lie even more or ...

Telling Law the truth about seeing a sex therapist will either result in pure mockery or concern, but it's getting to a point where I'm going to forget who I'm lying to and about what. I don't *like* lying, but it's as if that part of me that can't let go of control also wants to protect me from everything—even from positive things like the love my brother has for me.

Though in my defence, he can be overbearing like Mum sometimes.

"I'm seeing a new therapist," I admit.

Law frowns. "What happened to Karen?"

"I'm still seeing her too. But this other guy specializes in … uh, why I'm a dick to men and how to get me to date for real."

"There's a special field of psychology just to get you to stop being a dick? Did all your ex-fuck buddies decide to fund a scientific study or something?"

I laugh and flip him off. I'm glad he went the mockery route, because I don't know if I can handle him being all Law-like.

Doesn't last long though, and Law turns serious. "For real, though, I think it'll be good for you. You need to learn how to have healthy relationships again."

"I know."

"And just think, soon you'll be able to break up with all the guys you want."

I force a smile, but deep down I'm hoping doing this will mean I'll never have to break up with someone again. Especially if that someone is Brody.

"How's Reed?" I ask because I need a new topic. Stat.

But maybe I should've picked something else to talk about, because my brother makes that face—the one that says *I'm so in love I can't help looking like a goofball.*

I wait for the usual pang of envy to hit, but it doesn't come. It's the first time since Law and Reed got together that I can say I'm happy for my brother and actually mean it. Well, I meant it before, but it would always come with a side of bitterness.

"We're, umm, we're talking, like, marriage and stuff. Maybe fostering some kids?"

I can tell how hard it is for Law to get that out, not

because he doesn't want it—I knew from the minute I saw the two of them together that Reed was special to Law. He was never like that with any of the women he'd been with. But it's hard for him to talk about being happy with me, because he's always felt it was rubbing his happy life in the face of my tortured one. And I wish I could say he didn't have to feel that way, but the truth is, we both know it affects me.

There's a difference this time though. Brody and I might be new, we have no idea what we're doing, we need the help of two different therapists, and we're still feeling our way, but what Brody and I have? It's so much better than sex, than dating, than anything else I've ever experienced.

What we have is hope.

And until today, I've never realised how much impact one tiny little emotion could have.

"I can totally see that with you and Reed. You'd make the most perfect parents ever."

Me, on the other hand, would worry every time the kid made a weird noise. I'd probably think it was choking or something. I'd also do stupid stuff like refer to it as an *it*.

"It'll make Reed happy," Law says. "I think he was born a dad."

I snort. "He's so a dad. I can imagine all the dad jokes now."

"You'll get there one day."

"I'll start brushing up on my dad jokes now," I say dryly. "But nah, I think I need realistic goals, and being in an actual long-term relationship should be the only one on my list."

The idea of telling Law that I'm dating Brody crosses my mind, and I begin to wonder why I've been so against the idea. Yeah, he'll worry, but this thing with Brody is something that should be celebrated.

In the short time I've been living with him, I've broken down more barriers than I have in the last five years.

"Law ..."

My brother levels me with that look—the one where he tries to hide his concern for me—and the nerves get the better of me.

"I'm going to kick your ass in training today. Just so you know."

He breaks into a smile. "Bring. It."

18

BRODY

Dad cocks a grey eyebrow at me. For a guy in his mid-fifties, he looks a lot older. *Stress of the job* he always used to tell me. But even though he seems older, he still has a distinguished charm to his looks, so he doesn't look ragged.

Still, if I'm determined to go down the same path as my father—which, for some reason I have my heart set on—I'm probably staring at my future.

Angry lines across his forehead. Mouth permanently tugged downwards.

The minute I walked into his office, he was on me about Rachel.

"So, this has nothing to do with a case or my work or anything to do with the firm?" I clarify.

"Didn't you hear me? I haven't heard from your sister in over two months."

"When you told her to *come the fuck home now*? I know."

"You're in contact with her? I've been worried sick about her over in ... whatever run-down hell on earth she fled to."

"Guatemala," I supply helpfully. He might want to know

that in case she ever did go missing. "She calls me every other week. I asked her to call me every week, but she's Rachel."

Dad shakes his head. "When is she going to learn she can't go galivanting across the world and into dangerous situations?"

For a quick second, I see a father worried about his daughter. Considering all the jokes Parker and Rachel have about that never being possible, I almost want to take out my phone and record it so they can see he does have a heart.

It's easy to see where they're coming from though. The only reason I have much of a relationship with him is because I followed in his footsteps. I remember Parker once said he'd never sell out and become some stooge just to spend time with a guy who clearly doesn't want to spend time with him.

I do believe he loves us, in his own way. Otherwise, why would I be killing myself in this job I don't even like?

"She's fine, Dad, and if that's all, I need to get back to work." I stand.

"If she calls you again—"

"I'll tell her you said to get her reckless ass home."

"Thank you. Oh, and how's it working out with Annabelle Fields? Is she taking the case in the right direction, do you think?"

I'm not sure if Dad is playing a game—making me think this meeting isn't about work and then flipping a switch so casually I'm not supposed to pick up on it—or if we're actually doing the idle chitchat thing.

"She's taking the direction you would have."

Dad purses his lips. "But not the direction you would."

"I wouldn't be taking it to trial. I'd be trying to get a plea deal."

Dad looks surprised. "Why? Plea deals are for the uncertain or repeat offenders. This is an easy case to be dismissed.

First offence, classic *he said, she said*, with no signs of forcible rape, and a girl with a reputation."

I grit my teeth. There'd be no point telling my father that society as a whole has to stop with that mentality. The statistics are on her side, but rape is one of the hardest things to prove in cases like this, and it's the exact reason why so many victims don't come forward.

That, and when they do, they're scrutinized more than the perp.

It's a messed-up system that us lawyers have perpetuated for decades.

"The kid did it, and the victim deserves justice. You know how these cases go. He takes a plea, he'll be out in a few months, which is a lot less than he deserves, but it's something."

"It's not a matter of guilt or innocence, and you know that. It's about the law and what can be *proved*. That's rule number one. What are they teaching in law school these days?"

Basically, that the justice system is flawed and sucks, but I know better than to say that to a name partner even if he is my dad.

"I know what the law is, but ..." I give up because I know there'll never be a point in trying to explain things to my dad. "Never mind. I don't think someone like you could understand."

"Someone like me?"

"You've been doing this a long time, so I guess it's easy for you to turn off your moral compass and only focus on the law, but sometimes it feels like we're just putting horrible guys back out on the streets and causing more crime."

Dad approaches and leans against his desk in front of me with his arms folded.

Here comes the *I'm not cut out for this* lecture.

"You think I didn't go through the same thing when I started out? You have to look at the law as a black-and-white thing. If you don't, you'll only drive yourself crazy with guilt."

"I know."

"It's not easy, and that's why I had reservations about you practicing this type of law."

"Yeah, I'd be more suited to environmental law," I say bitterly.

"I never said that to be condescending."

Bullshit.

"The truth is, this line of work is hard. Especially in cases like the one you've got. This will be a good test for you."

"To see if I can hack it?"

"To see if it's the right field for you. You know I could get you a job doing corporate or family or any type of law you want."

"You already think I can't do it," I accuse.

God, I can't handle this today.

I cut him off before he can try to backtrack ... or worse, confirm it's true. "I need to get to work."

"Okay." He nods. Before I reach the door, he says, "Keep me updated on your sister."

"Will do."

As I leave Dad's office and take the elevator down to my floor, all I can think about is how little confidence he has in me.

No different than any other day, I remind myself, but it doesn't work this time.

I spend the rest of my day throwing myself into my work and sensing every single time when my heart revolts.

By the time the sun sets, I don't think I can stay any longer. I generally don't leave before eight thirty, but it's only six and I'm dead on my feet. My head hurts, and I want to quit, but I don't want to give my dad the satisfaction of giving up.

So instead, I think of the one person who might be able to pull me out of this funk and then head home to him two hours early.

―――

As promised, I come home with a bag of Videre goodness for Anders.

The shower's running in his bathroom when I step through the door, so I head for the kitchen to have the meals plated by the time he gets out.

I'm greeted with a gorgeous, wet, and practically naked man, who smiles wide when he sees me.

"You're home early."

"I am. And I brought deliciousness. Although, not quite as delicious as what you're serving right now." My gaze rakes over him again.

Anders laughs. "Lame."

"Your fault for wearing nothing but a towel. Again. I swear you're doing this on purpose."

"I would say it's payback for when I first moved in and you walked around half-naked, but I truly didn't know you'd be home." Something flashes in Anders' eyes. Hesitance maybe. He grips his towel tight, and I realise he's probably antsy about the no-clothes situation.

"Why don't you go get some clothes on, and I'll get dinner ready." I don't want him to put on clothes, but it's probably for the best or dinner won't get eaten at all.

It only takes a minute for him to come back wearing jeans and a T-shirt. "Why are you home early? Did the meeting with your father not go well?"

"Oh, that was fine. It was about my sister, not work. But he said something that made me push hard all day which resulted in burning out this afternoon, and I'm all wound tight. Was hoping maybe someone knew how to relax me."

Anders steps towards me slowly. "Wonder who that could be?"

"No idea," I whisper.

His feet hit the kitchen tile, mere metres away. Then steps. Then he's right there, pressed against me lightly but not closing the gap fully.

I lower my head as he lifts his chin. The anticipation of his lips on mine is gone when at the last second, something catches his eye on the bench.

"Is that the macadamia-encrusted beef with mash and that sauce I would literally sell my firstborn for?"

"All I can say is it's lucky you don't have children. But yes. I can still remember the moan you let out when you had it last time, and I wanted to hear it again."

When his eyes meet mine again, and he leans in, my breath gets caught in my throat.

I still don't know what it is about Anders, but he makes my head foggy and clear at the same time.

He puts my life into perspective while turning it into chaos.

He makes me want things I never thought I'd want again. Not since Reed.

I want more of him. All of him.

And I want this to be our life—coming home to him, eating dinner, and going to bed.

"Kiss me already," I beg.

His mouth meets mine, hungry but soft, demanding yet full of gentleness, and I know deep down that I'm falling for this guy, even though I know the chances of him being there to catch me are slim to none.

I'm grateful he wants to work through his issues so we can have a chance at this thing, but I can't help thinking he's still keeping something from me and that his problems cut deeper than he lets on.

But I'm in too deep now. I think I was before all the sex started. Now I'm just holding on, hoping it'll be me standing beside him in the end without his anxiety trying to push me out of the way to take my place.

Anders pulls back and asks, "Dinner or orgasms first?"

I laugh. "Well, I was thinking ..."

"Mmm?"

"If what you did to me last night was amazing, that maybe ... more would be good."

"More?" Anders mocks.

"I want you to tie me down and fuck me," I blurt.

"And the beef can wait." Anders takes my hand and leads me to my bedroom.

He spins on me, bringing me against him. It's all mouth, tongue, and wandering hands as he explores me, but there's a control to his assault. It feels amazing to have any part of him on my skin, but it's mechanical.

I want the guy I had last night—the one who gave himself over to me even if I couldn't run my hands all over him.

"How are you going to take me?" I whisper.

In an instant, Anders' warmth is gone from my body. "You go jump in the shower while I set something up."

"Why am I picturing an old torture table for some reason?"

Anders grins. "You're safe. I left that in my car."

"Funny."

"Along with the cuffs yesterday, I bought like ... bed restraint things."

"Is that the official name?"

He spins and pushes me towards the bathroom. "Just go. I'll be done by the time you get out."

"Okay, but isn't showering before sex kinda counter-intuitive?"

"Not if we want to do what I'm planning." Anders winks, giving me a glimpse of the guy I was with last night.

I want more of him.

It's hard to shower and not jerk off because the anticipation has me shuddering at the lightest touch. And that's with my own hand. Even the water beating down on my sensitive skin has me on edge. I hate to see what I'm going to be like when Anders is touching me.

After the world's shortest shower, I'm clean, hard, and ready to go. I contemplate putting on my underwear or covering up with a towel, but there's really no point when it's going to come straight off anyway.

Before I leave the bathroom, I look at myself in the mirror and give myself a pep talk.

Because this isn't just sex.

It isn't just bottoming which I haven't done in a really long time.

It's bottoming for *Anders*.

Reed's off-limits warning hits my ears as if he's right next to me. The thought that Anders could still be hiding a big part of what happened to him also tries to talk me out of going out there.

I used to think I had the willpower of a saint. Yet, I can't help but continue this thing with Anders even though, objectively, it's a bad idea.

What if I do something wrong and he gets scared? What if I don't like being tied up?

I mean, that blowjob was the best blowjob I've ever had, but maybe it'll be different with sex-sex.

Oh, shit, what if I'm the one to freak out?

I dismiss that thought as fast as it comes. I want this, and we have safe words in place for this reason.

One more deep breath and I leave the bathroom to find Anders holding up a corner of my mattress over his head.

"What are you doing?" I laugh.

"Sooo, this is harder than I thought it was gonna be." He's already sweating and breathing hard.

"It looks like you started without me with how out of breath you are."

"Shut up. Can you grab the black straps from underneath and pull them through?"

I do as he says and bring the restraints out of the way of the mattress so Anders can put it down. When he picks up the straps and puts them on the bed, I realise the setup is pretty simple.

Two cuffs at the top for my wrists and two for my ankles at the bottom, connected underneath the mattress.

I eye the bed nervously. "Do we really need the ones for my feet?" That might be too much for me.

"Not if you're uncomfortable with them."

"Are you okay with just my hands?"

Anders nods. "I think so."

We stay standing a few feet apart, neither of us ready to make the first move.

Act confident. Fake it until you make it.

I fake a smile and climb onto the bed, spread-eagle, and lift my hands above my head so he can tie me down.

Anders appears to appreciate me taking the lead. He might need to be in control, but I get the feeling he might need a little push. His confidence seems to grow with mine, so I tell myself to try to stop trembling from the mix of emotions filling the small distance between us.

Nerves, a heightened sense of awareness, and a whole lot of want swirls in my gut.

Anders is still fully clothed, adding to the power dynamic I'm yet to get used to. And when he fastens the cuffs to my wrists—similar in feel to the ones he used on me last night—the shift between us is even bigger.

All I can do is watch as he moves to the front of the bed and stares down at me.

My skin heats from my face to my toes.

"Okay, I'm gonna go grab something to eat. You good here?"

I know he's joking, but I still fight against the cuffs. "Super funny."

Anders laughs and removes his shirt instead.

My cock twitches, bouncing off my stomach.

Anders' gaze goes right there, and the arrogant fucker smiles. "You're really into being tied up, huh?"

I shake my head. "I'm really into you."

Anders drops trou, taking his boxers off at the same time, and climbs on top of me before I get the chance to trace over him with my gaze like he did to me.

With a thigh either side of my hips, he sits so our cocks rest against each other, and his long torso is on display. His nipple piercings catch my eye, and I want so desperately to reach for them. Pinch them. I want to tell him to do it for me so I can watch, but he's hesitating. It's written all over his face that he doesn't quite know where to go from here or perhaps he's not ready.

"What do you want?" Anders asks, surprising me.

"Isn't this about what you want?"

"I want you to tell me. I want you to talk because your voice is ... your voice."

I don't mean to laugh, but it slips out. "My voice is my voice?"

"It's a sexy voice."

I'm not exactly great at the dirty-talk thing, but I get the feeling this isn't about that.

"In that case ... I was just thinking if I had the use of my hands, I'd tweak your nipples."

"Like this?" He moans and plays with his pecs, rolling a barbell between his fingers.

"Yes," I breathe.

"What else?"

"I'd take you in my hand and stroke you until you were begging for more."

Anders' warm eyes shine down at me, and he does as I say.

No more hesitance.

I realise that even though he needs control, he doesn't want it. He gets off on *not* being in control.

It breaks my heart that he has to deal with that, but it also urges me to give him as much as he can take.

I watch him, and I imagine as if it's my hands on him. That I'm doing the touching.

His eyes roll back in his head, and he starts moving on top of me but only small movements. I don't know where to look —the blissed-out expression that makes him so goddamn beautiful or the sight of him fucking into his own hand.

With each move, he brushes against my cock, but it's not giving nearly the amount of action I want.

"I think you should kiss me," I say.

Anders leans over me, taking my mouth with his and giving me what I ask for.

"Rut against me," I murmur against his lips.

He picks up his pace, our bodies grinding and frotting. His mouth breaks from mine, trailing over my skin and down my neck.

"Keep kissing me," I order.

Anders obeys immediately.

"I like this new trick."

He pulls back, hovering over me with a furrowed brow. "Huh?"

"Turns out if I'm tied up, I can basically get you to do anything."

He smiles. "Wanna test that theory?"

"I want you inside me," I challenge.

"Dammit. I was gonna defy whatever you wanted just to prove who's really the one in charge, but I can't say no to that."

"So, I win."

"By default. Roll over and show me that hole of yours, because I can't wait to be inside you."

"Okay." I stare up at my restraints. "Umm, how?"

He pulls on one of the straps. "They have a bit of give in them."

It's a bit awkward, but I manage to turn over, the straps crossing and bringing my wrists together above my head. There's not quite enough slack to rest my elbows on the mattress, so I can see my arms tiring easily.

"Butt up," Anders demands and gives me a small smack.

I wriggle my knees underneath me, putting my ass in the air.

Anders groans. "You look hot tied up."

"I look hot all the time. It's like you keep forgetting that."

"Right. Sorry. How do you feel about rimming?" He reaches for supplies.

"Love giving. Don't have much experience with receiving."

"Then you're in for a treat. And remember your safe words."

"Green all the way. Like, I'm pretty sure I could get a tramp stamp of that word. I'm that confident in your abilities."

"Mmm, pressure."

I don't want to spook Anders because this is the most relaxed and confident he's been around me, just like last night while I was tied to the chair.

With me unable to use my hands, he becomes this whole other person. I wonder if this is the Anders he used to be before his attack.

There's no time to think about that, because the first touch of a finger to my hole has me tensing, but when Anders' tongue joins it, I relax enough to let him in.

He works me open with his mouth and fingers, going slow.

My arms ache already, my biceps bunching and contracting.

When his fingers inch their way in and press against my prostate, there's a small sting of pain, a burst of pleasure, frustration from being restrained, and freedom from not being able to do anything to change it. I experience it all.

If he can get me to this level with only his fingers, I can't wait for his cock.

This is already by far the best anal I've ever had, because I can tell Anders cares about me.

Not that the other guys I've done this with didn't, but this part has always felt like a necessity to get to where we need to be than something to *enjoy*.

Anders takes his time. It's not rushed, and the need builds with every second that passes.

As Anders pushes his fingers back in faster and harder, bringing me closer and closer, I come way to close to the edge.

"Wait, wait ..." Fuck, safe word. "Uh, *yellow*."

He slows but doesn't stop, and I can hear his heavy breathing as he asks, "What's wrong?"

"I'm about to come."

"And there's a problem with that?"

"Yeah. I want your cock."

"If you insist." He quickly suits up, and the lube bottle makes that squidgy noise as he adds more. "Definitely ready?"

"So ready." I've never been more ready. My balls ache and my cock is hard and needy. My whole body trembles in anticipation and want.

Anders goes slow when he eases inside. The thick head of his dick stretches and fills me more than his fingers could.

My head lolls to one side, resting on my biceps as my hands cling to the straps connected to the cuffs.

I wait for the awkwardness of needing to adjust, but it's not like that with Anders. He took so much time and effort to prep me, he glides in and out smoothly, giving me the chance to open up more.

So *this* is what it's supposed to be like.

I wonder if I should've done this bondage thing sooner or if maybe it's an Anders thing.

It's weird to think that being tied up somehow relaxes me, but it does. It gets me out of my head, out of the stresses of my world, and allows me to fixate on one thing—Anders.

And right now, he's turning me out like nobody's business, and my body responds in a way it never has during sex before.

Every thrust and every touch of Anders brushing past my prostate has my cock demanding more. My hole accepts him greedily. He's so hard, I'm going to be feeling it in my ass for days to come, but I don't even care right now.

Anders picks up his pace, and all I can do is take it.

There's no wrestling, no playfulness. It goes from sex to primal fucking in the blink of an eye, and I never knew it could be so hot. I definitely never thought I'd be in a place where I'd be begging for it harder.

Anders' grunts fill my ears, and one of his hands grips my hair tight.

My cock leaks like crazy, and for a split second I think I'm going to come hands-free.

How did I not know I liked it rough until now?

"Fuck, Anders."

"Kinda ... the ... point."

I want to laugh. I really do. But all I can do is moan louder.

The fuzziness I had last night comes back and lifts me higher and higher until I don't know what's coming out my mouth, if anything.

Am I talking? Groaning? Who knows.

The only thing I know is that if Anders were to touch me right now, I'd soar.

Maybe I am speaking out loud, because fingers go to wrap around my cock, but the first jet of cum spills over before Anders can get a full grasp. He strokes me through my orgasm while he keeps fucking me at a tempo I'd barely be able to keep up with if it were me.

"I'm close," he whispers.

Good. The more he pegs my prostate, the more sensitive my ass becomes as my cock empties onto the bed and my stomach.

Anders finally stills inside me with one last hard thrust.

Apparently, he's able to recover faster than me. He pulls out, and I wince at the pain returning. Only, it's not just in my ass. It's everywhere again, especially in my arms. It's funny how I couldn't even feel it until now. Now that I'm coming down, now that I'm not blissed out on Anders' cock, my muscles ache.

Feels like I've done a full workout at the gym.

Anders' lips land on my shoulder. "Roll back over for me?"

I do as he says, and my arms get some relief.

"You okay for a sec?"

When I nod, Anders climbs out of bed and stumbles towards the bathroom, leaving me wrung out and now feeling a little vulnerable. But he's back in a few seconds, condom ditched and a wet cloth in his hands. He wipes the bed and my stomach, then leans over to kiss my chest while he cleans me off.

Thick thighs straddle me as Anders reaches for one of my wrists. Warm brown eyes meet mine, and a soft look of awe crosses Anders' face.

I squirm beneath him, loving the way he's looking at me but hating that I can't reach for him and cherish the moment the way I want to.

Anders breaks his gaze first and unties me, taking extra care to kiss the red marks on my wrists from where I fought being restrained.

Lips trail up my arm, and I use my free hand to pull Anders close. Our mouths meet, calm and relaxed, but I feel the moment Anders is no longer lost in me and fighting whatever's in his head telling him to be on guard.

"Can I stay in here tonight?" he asks. "I'll go warm up dinner. We can eat it in bed and then go to sleep?"

I want nothing more than to cuddle into his side all night, but when he says "go to sleep," he says it as if he means him too when we both know it doesn't.

"I don't think that's a good idea."

"Dinner in bed? Are you one of those 'this is how we get ants!' type of people? Law was so annoying about that."

I can totally see Law being like that. "Nope. I'm okay with dinner in bed. I'm not okay with you not sleeping again. As much as I love having you next to me while I sleep, you need to look after yourself."

"I slept this morning after you left and napped for an hour after I got home from work. I'll be fine."

I cup his face. "That's not enough sleep."

"It's enough for me."

I already know I'm going to cave, but I want to stay strong. I want to be strong for Anders when he can't be. I want to look after him when he refuses to do it for himself.

"I promise I'll sleep in my bed tomorrow night. I don't want to leave you after ..." His thumb runs over my wrist.

"I'm fine," I assure him. "More than fine."

He lowers his voice. "You're stepping out of your comfort zone for me. I want to do the same for you."

"Dammit. How am I supposed to say no to that?"

"Stay there. I'll be back with dinner." He gets up and pulls on his boxers and T-shirt, then throws me my underwear.

A night with a hot guy, eating dinner in bed, falling asleep in his arms ... it should make me deliriously happy. Instead, I'm worried how it's going to affect Anders.

I take a deep breath.

This can't be a long-term arrangement.

19

ANDERSON

Best. Sex. Ever.

That's what I've been missing all these years.

It's my two worlds colliding and making something so fucking good. I need control but to let go at the same time, and Brody gives me that.

I didn't think it was going to be possible.

I never thought I'd have this again.

But even with those things, I still can't sleep next to him.

The usual Brody-worshipping thing I've done when sharing a bed with him is happening again.

I'm not delusional; I know we can't go on like this forever. I need sleep, and Brody won't let me wear myself out, but unless we're going to be one of those couples who don't sleep in the same room, I need to work on more than the sex stuff with my therapists.

Finally, I'm at a point where I know I not only want to work on myself but need to. Otherwise I will never have the chance to have what Law has with Reed. I'll be the weird, single uncle to their kids who lives in the spare room and who sometimes breaks down at night.

I don't want to be that guy.

I want to be happy. With Brody, with someone else, I'm not sure yet.

What if I can't survive a relationship again? What if I go back to my old ways? What if this hits the one-month mark, and I give up and bail like I always do?

The need to believe that won't happen is strong because I've already done so much more with Brody than I have with anyone since Kyle. I've told him about my past and my issues, and we've worked through some of those anxieties already. I haven't scared him off with any of my panic attacks. That has to mean something.

The sound of the front door to the apartment opening echoes through the quiet night and interrupts my thoughts.

I blink away the haze and make sure Brody is still next to me, which he is.

My body goes rigid. I can't breathe, and I freeze up completely.

I could be hearing things. It could be next door.

Trying to think logically goes out the window when footsteps sound, followed by a bang and someone whispering, "Motherfucker."

It's impossible to tell if the voice is male or female, but I won't be the same guy I was five years ago. I won't freeze under pressure.

I will, however, be a big-ass chicken and wake the slightly bigger guy sleeping next to me. "Brody," I hiss, trying to be quiet.

He doesn't respond.

I say his name again and try to shake him awake. "Please wake up. Please wake up. Please wake up."

Great, now I'm chanting.

My heart pounds, and I can't stop it.

The grip I have on Brody's arm tightens. The footsteps in the living room get louder. The apartment is carpeted, so it's not a loud noise like it would be on a hardwood floor. It's more like the vibrations of heavy feet.

Now I'm imagining a T-rex like from *Jurassic Park* with water ripples in drinking cups. Although, a T-rex would be less scary than whoever could be out there right now. Because as illogical as it is, it's easy to feed into the fear that Kyle could've found me besides the fact he doesn't know where I live and is still locked up.

"Brody," I say louder, risking whoever's out there overhearing, but he needs to wake the fuck up right now. "Someone's in the apartment."

That works. Whether it's my hard tone or that he finally hears me, he's out of bed before his eyes even open properly.

"Stay here."

"Duh."

I sit up and watch Brody move shakily through the dark and close the bedroom door quietly behind him.

My hands shake.

Oh God, what if there's someone out there with a knife or a—

The crack under the door lights up.

"Fucking hell, Rachel. What is wrong with you?" Brody yells.

Rachel. His ... sister?

The relief of it not being an intruder is short-lived because now I'm freaking out for a completely different reason.

I'm in Brody's bed. He went out there in only his boxers. It'll be obvious we were in here *together*.

Brody and Rachel's murmurings fade as I calm myself from panicking about someone finding out about us.

Then something else clicks in my small brain. Meatball's

owner is back.

She's gonna take my damn cat.

As if on cue, I hear, "Aww, there's my baby girl! Whoa, you got fat."

Meatball is not fat. *Rachel's fat.*

Okay, so I haven't seen her, but she called *my* baby fat, so she deserves it.

I don't know when I became so possessive over the damn rodent, but there it is.

I want to go out there and snatch Meatball out of her arms, but you know, that involves meeting the brave woman who saves cats and builds homes for the poor in a country with the highest crime rate in South America.

"I think she's forgotten me," Rachel says, her voice closer to the bedroom door. "Come here, baby? Come on."

Meatball lets out a little meow of protest.

"Uh, yeah, we kind of bonded," Brody says. "I'll put her in my room, and then we'll—I mean, *I'll* get the couch set up for you. Not *we*. There's no we. The cat can't help." Brody's awkward rambling almost makes me laugh.

"Oh, right. You have a roommate now. When do I get to meet this random person you let live with you?"

"In the morning," Brody says. "And he's not random. He's …"

I hold my breath.

"He's Reed's boyfriend's brother."

Yeah, because that doesn't make it confusing.

"Reed Garvey? The guy you were totally obsessed with in high school and were going to marry?"

I forget I'm still holding my breath and practically choke while trying to get air into my lungs. *Marry?* Does Law know about that?

"Yes, that Reed, but it's the middle of the goddamn night.

Can we please talk more at a reasonable hour?"

"Missed you too," she sings.

"I'll get you a blanket and pillow."

Brody appears, sneaking through the tiniest possible gap in the doorway so his sister can't see me, and silently puts the cat on my lap.

He kisses the top of my head and moves to pull down a sheet, blanket, and pillow from his closet.

After he goes back into the living room, it takes what feels like forever for him to say goodnight to his sister, but they're farther away now, and I can't hear what they're saying anymore.

I stroke Meatball's fur, more to calm myself than her. She purrs loud and happy-like, and I cuddle her closer.

When Brody does finally come back, he climbs into bed next to me wordlessly and pulls both Meatball and me towards him. His arms go around me, and the cat squirms to get away, no doubt feeling trapped between us. She frees herself and lays her butt down on the end of the bed.

"I'm guessing you heard most of that."

I nod against his chest.

"We'll wait for her to go to sleep, and then you can make a break for your room."

"She won't hear me?"

"She sleeps like the dead—like me."

"Family trait?"

Brody chuckles. "Must be."

Now is not the time to bring up what I overheard, but my mouth doesn't listen. "So ... you were gonna marry Reed, huh? That's news."

We're whispering and talking low so his sister can't hear, and it makes me feel like a kid again, lying next to Law in our twin beds talking instead of sleeping.

But with Rachel's words, I suddenly understand Law's hesitance about Reed and Brody being friends. We knew they were exes, but *marriage?*

"Do you really want to have this conversation now?" Brody asks.

"Well, it's not like I'm going to sleep."

"So I don't get to sleep either?" His tone is light and teasing, despite being obviously exhausted.

"You're avoiding the subject, and that's usually my job."

Brody sighs. "Reed was the first guy to go anywhere near my dick. I thought it was true love."

I snort a little too loudly and have to bury my head to quieten my laughter.

"The furthest we went were blowjobs. To a teenage Brody, I thought it meant something. Clearly it didn't."

"If it was teenage crap, why do you hate my brother?"

More hesitance on his part. "When Reed contacted me and told me he was moving to Brisbane, I don't know, I ... I guess all those old feelings came back? I wondered if this would be our shot at a real relationship, if he was still the same guy I knew years ago, and I had all this anticipation building around him moving here. Then he went and fell for your brother within *weeks*. I don't hate Law, but I do like making him mad. Probably because his relationship with Reed threw me off kilter, so I taunt him for the fun of it."

"Hey, we have something in common—taunting Law."

"We have heaps in common," Brody argues.

"Really? Like what?"

"Okay, I can't think of anything right now, but my brain also isn't working. My sister appeared out of nowhere, it's the middle of the night, and my ass hurts."

I roll and throw my leg over his waist. "Aww, poor baby. Want me to kiss it better?"

"No, Rachel will hear us."

"And that's bad because we're not telling her about us?" I'm just double-checking. You know, to be sure. I'm not testing him to see if he wants to tell people about me. Nope, not at all.

"If you want me to, I'll go right back out there now and say 'Hey, my roommate is actually in my bed because we're testing out this bondage thing,' but I figured you're the one who didn't want to tell Law and Reed, so I assumed Rachel was a no-go as well."

Dammit. He can't even fail a stupid trick question. If he'd said no, he doesn't want to tell his sister, I would've been disappointed. If he'd suggested we tell her, I would've felt like he was pressuring me. Instead, he puts it in my hands, and now I feel guilty for not telling people.

Like everything, I'm overthinking, overanalysing, and trying to find fault in a man who keeps proving he might be my perfect guy.

"I was tempted to tell Law today," I admit. "I was close, but at the last minute chickened out, and we agreed not to, so I didn't."

Brody pulls me closer. "If you ever have the urge to tell people but are worried I won't be okay with it, don't be. I mean, Reed is going to kill me when he finds out, but I can deal with Reed."

"Why will Reed kill you?"

"He told me you were off limits."

"Oh God, why did he do that?"

"He's worried about you. He sees you like a brother, you know."

"He does?"

"Well, considering he wants a life with Law, you shouldn't be surprised."

"I ... I don't think I've been particularly nice to him. I'm not mean, but—"

"He understands your situation. He supports you. I don't know why you find it surprising when people sympathise or make exceptions for you after what you've been through."

"Anxiety and PTSD shouldn't give someone a 'be an asshole without consequences' pass."

"That's not what I mean." Brody grunts. "Babe, it's late. I need sleep. We'll talk more in the morning."

I wince and must tense because Brody senses it immediately.

"Shit, what did I do?"

"Umm, can you, like, not call me that word?" I can practically feel Brody's scrutinising stare in the dark.

"Okay?"

"Sorry. Reminds me of someone." Not a technical lie, but it still makes me feel like shit for keeping Kyle from him. And he always used to call me babe. Now the use of the pet name is like hearing nails on chalkboard.

"No problem ..." He wants more, but like needing the restraints, I need to keep my biggest obstacle, my biggest mind-fuck, locked in its cage.

I can't give him what he needs, no matter how loud the voice of rationale is yelling at me to just tell him. That voice always asks me what's the worst that could happen. And if my imagination has anything to say, it flies to worst-case scenarios like Brody telling me it's too much and walking away or even worse but more unlikely, Brody telling me I'm the weak person my psyche believes I am, and I'm not worthy of him.

Karen always tells me to challenge those thoughts.

Logically speaking, even the worst person in the world wouldn't say something like that to someone's face. The chance of Brody doing it is next to impossible. Yet, I still can't bring myself to say the words I need to.

I stayed in an emotionally abusive relationship because I ignored all the signs that it was actually abusive. Then it escalated, and I almost lost my life.

No matter how many times I'm told that's entirely Kyle's fault, I still take blame.

I could've done things differently. Protected myself more. Not forgiven him for his possessive traits or noticed them for what they were—giant red flags.

"How long do you think it'll be before your sister's asleep?" I ask.

"She probably is now. Her eyes were practically closing the minute her head hit the pillow, but maybe give it ten more minutes."

Brody untangles himself from me, lands a chaste kiss to my lips, and then rolls over to go back to sleep. I'm envious of the way he can drift off so fast.

I wait twenty minutes to be sure and then get out of bed as quietly as I can.

Meatball makes a soft thump as she jumps off the bed and follows me to the door. With a sigh, I pick her up to carry her to my room.

The living room is silent, and my breaths practically sound like Darth Vader. All I can hope is Brody's right about Rachel being a heavy sleeper.

I'm about halfway to my door when I find out that's not the case at all.

"Roommates with benefits, maybe."

"Shit," I hiss and practically drop Meatball. She jumps from my arms and scurries off somewhere.

"I'm Rachel."

A flashlight from a phone lights up the room, but I only

see a glimpse of the mysterious Rachel before the light blinds me.

I hold up my hand to block the light. "Anders."

"I was wondering how long you'd wait before making a break for it."

"So, you decided to scare the shit out of me? You're like your brother. You both need to come with bells. You're supposed to be asleep."

"*You're* supposed to be in your room." She's still kinda a dark figure with a voice, so it feels weird talking to her silhouette.

"We were ... hanging out."

"Uh-huh." She sounds unconvinced.

"Well, goodnight."

"Wait ..."

"Yeah?"

"I can't sleep."

"Is this a ruse to interrogate me?"

She chuckles. "No. I just ... don't see me getting to sleep anytime soon, and, well, you're awake."

It's not like I'm going to get much sleep either way—it's just going to be one of those nights.

I walk to the opposite side of the couch where her phone light is no longer blinding me, and I get a good look at her.

I saw a photo of her on Brody's phone once, and either she's super photogenic, it was photoshopped, or she's completely exhausted right now.

I'd say it's the latter if she just flew in from the other side of the world, but her long brown hair is scraggly, her blue eyes dull, and she has a sad, weary look on her face.

Rachel lifts her feet, so I can join her on the couch, and the second I sit down, Meatball jumps on my lap. She kneads my stomach and purrs loudly.

"Ah. So you're the reason my cat didn't want anything to do with me."

I pat the soft grey fur on Meatball's head. "She kinda adopted me."

"Not the other way around?"

"Not at all. I don't like cats. Or ... I didn't until this one came along."

Rachel smiles. "That's how cats work. They choose their owners."

Out of the corner of my eye, I glance at her as I ask, "You're not going to try to take her from me?"

"I don't even know what I'm doing with my life, so I don't exactly have the means to look after a cat right now." She stares at Meatball. "Though I'm a little sad she forgot I saved her."

"I bet she hasn't. If what you said is true, she probably knows I need her more than you do."

"Why do you need her?"

"I don't know. She's a cat. Maybe her instincts are dumb."

Rachel smiles again. "Fine, don't tell me."

"So why can't you sleep? Jet lag? Brody said you sleep like the dead."

She throws her head back on the headrest of the couch. "It's kind of just hitting me now that I'm home and have no direction. The plan was to stay over there longer, but in the last few days, we ran into some trouble and had to get out of there fast."

I frown. "What kind of trouble?"

"Oh God, please don't tell my stupidly overprotective brother."

That sounds like something I would say.

"It really is safe over there as long as you use common sense. We were going into Guatemala City for more supplies, which we'd done so many times before, but we'd had trouble with a flat tyre on one of the trucks, which meant we'd gotten into the city late. There's known gang activity there, and it was a wrong place wrong time situation, but it was bad. Like leave now with your lives or we'll hunt you down type bad. So yeah, we basically dropped everything and went straight to the airport."

"Shit. That must've been scary."

"No scarier than facing a group of teenage boys hurting a cat."

"Yeah, your brother told me how insane you are."

"You guys use the word insane. I use the word brave."

"If only you could give me some of that bravery." Shit, did that come out loud?

"Why do you … Oh shit, are you like closeted or something? Is that why you were sneaking out of Brody's room?"

"No, not closeted. Just … a little messed up." It gets easier and easier to admit that.

"Well, I like messed up, and God knows Brody needs a bit of messy in his pristine existence."

"You'll be happy to know I bring a lot of messy to his life."

"Good. Then I approve."

I laugh. "Thank you?"

"You're welcome."

"So much for not interrogating me."

In response, she grins wide.

I think Rachel and I are a lot alike, even though we're opposites. She's brave, impulsive, and strong. She's everything I used to be and everything I wish to be again.

With any hope, hanging out with her will have her positive energy rubbing off on me, because I want to be more for Brody. No, actually, I want to be more for myself.

20

BRODY

Coffee. Need brain fuel to make thoughts go.

Five thirty. Never an okay time to wake up but a necessity.

The thought of calling in sick crosses my mind so I can catch up with Rachel, but one, she'll hate that anyway, and two, if I call in sick, I'd better be dying, or Dad will send someone to double-check.

So I get up quietly and dress for work, figuring I'll need to get takeaway coffee on the way to work because both Anders and Rachel should be asleep.

Should being the operative word, because when I make my way into the living room, they're both smiling and laughing on the couch.

"There's Sleeping Beauty," Rachel taunts.

"Mmm," I mumble.

Anders laughs.

When I glance at him, the big bags under his eyes are a dead giveaway.

"You didn't sleep?" I ask.

"My fault," Rachel says. "Sorry. Your boyfriend is good company."

Anders and I stare wide-eyed at each other.

"We're not ..." Anders says at the same time I say, "He's not ..."

"Ah. Label problems? Fine. Your *roommate* is good company. Though, I'm tellin' ya, you're putting the gay rights movement back like fifty years. You know, the whole 'this is my roommate' shtick."

"Do you think maybe we should be the ones to decide our label? We *are* roommates."

Anders stands. "On that note, if I go to sleep now, I'll get at least two hours before I need to get to work."

"That's not enough," I argue.

"It's enough for me."

Surprising me, Anders approaches and kisses me good morning. Now I'm even more confused.

He lifts a finger to flatten the crease in my brow. "She caught me sneaking out of your room. She *knows*."

"Oh."

Anders goes to his room with a wave, and I go back to the coffee machine.

"Can I have one?" Rachel asks behind me.

"It'll suck compared to the stuff you get in Guatemala."

She scoffs. "Doubt that. Guatemalan coffee tastes like mud."

I cock my head.

"They export all the good stuff."

"Ah."

The whirring of the machine probably keeps Anders awake, but it only takes a few minutes to make the two cups.

"Dad will be happy you're back."

Rachel rolls her eyes. "Yay."

"He actually asked about you yesterday, so can you please call him and tell him you're fine?"

"Can you tell him when you go to work?"

"Mature."

"All he's going to do is ask what my plan is now, and considering I wasn't planning on being home at all, I don't have one."

"Fine." I drink down my coffee fast, because I should already be at work, but before I go, I pull Rachel in for a hug. "I'm happy you're back."

She holds me tight. "Thank you. But I guess asking Anders to share your room so I can have a bed is a bit too much? Just until I figure out where to go from here?"

Shit. I can't ask Anders to move into my room, but I can't tell Rachel why.

"Anders needs his own bed. He hates mine."

"You could share his?" She looks so hopeful, but I can't …

"I … I …" I don't know how to answer this.

This is a complication of dating Anders I didn't even think about. Not that it's something I could predict coming up. And normal people don't ask about couples' sleeping arrangements.

"Can't you ask Mum?"

Rachel slumps. "On the Sunny Coast? I was hoping to stay in Brisbane."

I let out a loud breath. "Okay, I'll see what we can do."

"You don't want me here?"

I don't have the power to say no to my little sister. "It's not that. At all. We just don't … we don't have a lot of room. Take the couch again tonight, and I'll talk to Anders when I get home, okay?"

"Thank you!" She throws her arms around me again. "And by the way, you did good. I like him."

"I like him too, which is why I'm scared about pushing for

more than he's ready for. We're really new, Rach. Not sure where it's going."

Understanding dawns on her face. "Oh. I thought ..." She shakes her head. "I thought, like, you were dating and then he moved in."

"No, he moved in as my roommate first."

"And you call me stupid."

"Hey, I've never called you stupid. Impulsive, maybe."

"I'm the impulsive one? You're hooking up with your roommate. That's bad. Even I know that."

I laugh. "I know, but I couldn't help it. I mean, you did see him, right?"

"He's ... interesting. The complete opposite of Reed."

"About that. Can you maybe not mention Reed to him? Reed is with Anders' brother, and Law already hates me enough as it is."

She puts her hands up. "Fine. But I cannot wait to see you all together. That's gotta be weird, right?"

"They don't know about Anders and me yet."

"Why not?"

"Did I happen to mention Anders is Law's identical twin? It's weird."

She bursts out laughing. "Anders was so right. He does make your life messy. In the best possible way."

"How so?"

"It sounds all so very twisted. You're usually so straightforward and uncomplicated."

I shrug. "I am not."

She gives me her *I don't believe you* face.

"Okay, fine, maybe that's true, but being with Anders? It makes more sense than anything else in my life right now."

"Then don't let him get away."

I kiss her on the cheek on my way out. "I don't plan to."

Only, I fear Anders has other plans.

I knew getting away from work early would be easy as soon as I told my father that Rachel was home and in my apartment.

She asked me to tell him, and I did. It's her fault for thinking Dad wouldn't invite himself over so he could lecture her.

The thought of giving Anders a heads-up crosses my mind, but if I tell Anders and he tells Rachel, she'll leave and say she had no idea Dad was coming.

Besides, this isn't like a meet-the-parents thing. I'll introduce Anders as my roommate, and that's all.

I probably won't hear the end of that either. Dad doesn't know I have a roommate, and I had planned on keeping it that way.

"I'll call ahead and order takeaway from Videre for all of us," Dad says.

"Uh, yeah, might need enough food for four. I, umm, well, I haven't told you, but I have a new roommate."

"You didn't tell me you had a ... male friend." Ah, good ol' Dad, dancing around the subject of my love life.

"He's just a friend staying with me for a while until he gets on his feet."

I almost say "it's not what you think," but I don't want to flat-out lie.

Rule number one of being a lawyer: omitting the truth isn't the same as lying.

Dad scrutinises me the way he did when I was a kid but doesn't push.

With him getting dinner, I have a chance to get home

before him and at least warn Anders but keep my sister from escaping.

I find them where they were this morning—laughing on the couch at who knows what. Though it looks like Anders hasn't been home long. He's in his business shirt and pants. It must be the first time I've seen him in his professional clothes, because the difference is insane. He's more corporate-looking and less hipster-like.

Anders stands when he sees me, and we meet halfway. His lips ghost my cheek, his soft beard tickling my skin.

"My father's on his way," I blurt.

His eyes widen.

"It's okay. I told him you were my roommate, but he wanted to see Rach, and—"

"You sold me out?" my sister yells from her spot on the couch.

"Uh, no, you told me to tell him you were home."

"I didn't tell you to say where. Australia is a big enough place to generalise."

Anders laughs.

Rachel narrows her eyes. "You're lucky I like Anders more than you right now, because I'd have no trouble selling you two out to Dad as 'naked roommates.' Payback, Brody. It's a thing."

Anders blinks innocently. "But you won't, right? Because you like me."

She grunts. "Fine, but you owe me. Like, I'm thinking free rent and a bed until I get a job."

Beside me, Anders tenses, no doubt realising that means he'll need to share my bed. I've already told her that won't be happening, but he doesn't know that.

"Haven't had a chance to bring that up with Anders yet, Rach."

Before we can straighten any of that out, the door to the apartment clicks open and my dad steps through.

He bypasses Anders and me though and goes straight for Rachel.

They hug, because even though she doesn't like our dad, she knows arguing with him is futile.

While Dad starts his lecture, I turn to Anders.

He stares at my dad wide-eyed, his skin pale and bottom lip trembling.

"Hey," I say softly.

No response.

"Anders?"

His head slowly turns to meet my gaze. "Huh?"

"Are you okay?"

Anders glances at my dad again and then back at me. The fake smile makes its return. "Uh, yeah. Yeah, fine. Good. Uh ... yeah, good."

I want to find it cute that he's nervous about meeting my dad, but something tells me this isn't just parental nerves.

"He doesn't know about us," I say, my voice low.

The nod he gives is subtle.

I eye him closer and notice his chest heaving, his hands fisted into balls, and his mouth moving ever so slightly.

"You need a minute?" I ask.

His eyes stare through me, as if my Anders isn't there. All that's in front of me is the blank face of someone I don't know.

"I'm staying here," Rachel says, her voice cutting through the apartment like a siren.

I'm forced to turn away from Anders. "We're still discussing that."

My sister glares at me.

"Anders lives here too. He gets a say."

Anders sucks in a sharp breath as Dad turns his attention to him. I want to reach for Anders' hand, give him support, but that would be too suspicious. Dad approaches, tall and domineering, but his face is the relaxed calm it always is. Cool under pressure, he's known for his stoic demeanour during court. He's firm but approachable, intimidating but can put on the nice act.

"John Davenport." He holds out his hand for Anders.

Anders doesn't move. He doesn't blink.

Dad looks at me with a furrowed brow and then back to Anders.

I nudge Anders with my elbow, and he snaps out of whatever trance he's in.

He shakes hands with my dad but remains silent. A shudder runs through him, and I'm two seconds away from blowing our secret.

"A-Anderson Steele." There's a tremble in Anders' voice.

Dad cocks his head. "Have we met?"

"I ... I ..."

I grab Anders' arm gently, and he flinches. I'm brought back to the first few months after I met him where he was too scared to be even near me.

What the fuck is going on?

"Dad, can you give us a minute? We need to have a chat."

I don't give my father a chance to respond before I push Anders in the direction of his room.

Once behind the closed door, Anders stumbles and reaches for the bed to steady himself. It doesn't work. He sinks to the floor, his back resting against the side of the bed with his head up, eyes closed, and a pained expression that breaks my heart.

I don't even know what's going on, but it's like I already know whatever it is, it's too much for him to handle. I've seen him in the middle of panic before, but I've never seen the start.

"Anders?"

His eyes fly open, and he stands. "I have to go. I have to go right now."

I expect him to walk out, but instead, he pulls a duffle bag from out of his closet.

"Wait, you mean go as in for a few days or ..."

"No. As in move out. I can't ... I can't be here. Your sister needs a place to crash, so it's all good. It'll be fine. It's fine."

He throws random things into his bag. Clothes, his phone charger, a mouse toy he bought for the cat.

I step closer. "Just tell me what's going on? Can I get you something? A Valium? A joint? You're panicking. I think you're having an attack."

His eyes are dead and cold when they pierce mine. "No fucking shit."

"Why?"

Tears flow freely down Anders' face as he knocks the breath from my lungs. "Your father? He's the reason I am the way I am. One of them, anyway."

"What?"

"Your father was Kyle's lawyer."

21

ANDERSON

Honestly, I don't remember leaving Brody's apartment. I barely remember dialling Law's number and begging him to come get me.

I do remember stalking away from Brody while he yelled questions at me.

"Who's Kyle?"
"Where are you going?"
"Can't we talk about this?"

Nope, we can't talk. Because I have no words.

I don't have a voice. That *man*, Brody's father, took it away from me.

He's the reason Kyle got a plea deal. He's the reason my psychotic boyfriend only got six fucking years.

And he's Brody's dad—the guy Brody strives to live up to. Brody sat across the dining table from me and spoke of needing this man's approval.

The panicky voice in my head screams to run, so I do it.

Streetlights cast an orange hue across the empty road and the path beneath my bare feet, leaving me to wonder if I'm in some fucked-up dream.

I keep running until my lungs burn, but even then, I push my legs harder.

Twenty minutes pass, maybe half an hour, I don't know. I only know I'm running along the same road Law will take to come pick me up. Though I don't even know if he'll be able to stop me.

My phone vibrates in my pocket, and it's probably him, but I ignore it.

Keep going, keep running.

The minute I stop, I know I'm going to fall and not get back up.

A horn blasts from a car driving by at a snail's pace, and it takes a second to realise it's Law.

I keep going anyway.

He pulls over ahead of me and gets out, blocking me off and forcing my legs to give out.

"Anders." Law reaches for me, and I lose it.

I lose everything.

My feet trip over themselves, my arms go around my brother, and I break down into sobbing tears.

"What happened?" Law asks.

I can't do anything but hold him tighter.

"Where's your stuff? You said you needed a place to stay."

Shit, my bag. "I left it," I blubber. I don't even know where I left it. I swear I had it back at the apartment, but now I'm thinking I walked out without it.

I had to get out of there. Away from that much toxicity.

"Come on." Law steers me towards his car, and I mindlessly follow.

The leather seats in his old car squeak under my weight, and I throw my head back on the headrest.

My brother knows how to read me, knows when to push and when to let me be. Right now, I need to break down.

There's a certain point I reach when having an episode—one I can't pull myself back from—and I'm so far past that point right now I can't even see where the line is anymore.

Law doesn't try to talk to me on the twenty-minute drive to his house. Nothing as we climb the porch either. Or when I throw myself face-first onto their couch.

It's Reed who asks what happened.

"They don't have the same last name," I murmur.

"What?" they ask in unison like they have one brain or something.

"Brody."

"Brody doesn't have the same last name as who?" Law asks.

I roll over onto my back. "Do you guys have any alcohol?"

Reed goes to get me some, but Law stops him.

"No. He's not drinking when he's like this. It's a slippery slope into self-medication."

I want to throw him the middle finger, but I don't have the ability to lift my arms right now. I'm heavy, physically and mentally, and I don't want to move. Now or ever. I live on this couch now. "You'll get me meds if I asked."

"Alcohol isn't meds. Tell me what happened."

"Brody's father is John Davenport."

"John Davenport ... John Davenport." Law's brow furrows as he tries to remember who that is.

"As in Mahoney, Perry, and *Davenport*. When Brody told me his father was a name partner at his firm, I assumed he worked for a firm with the name Wallace in it."

"Brody has his mother's last name. It was a nasty divorce," Reed says.

"Oh, fuck. Brody's dad was Kyle's lawyer?" Law asks.

I cover my eyes with my arm as more tears come.

Law lands beside me, kneeling on the floor. "Did you see him?"

I nod.

"Do you need me to call Karen?"

Oh yeah, I need an appointment, but not right now. I don't want to leave this space.

"Kyle," Reed says. "As in your ..."

"Yeah," Law says. "As in *the guy*."

I sit up, almost knocking my brother over, who's still by my side. "You know the worst part? He didn't even recognise me. He did the head tilt with the 'Have we met?' shit, but the man who helped ruin my life didn't immediately recognise me. How fucked up is that?"

"How did he help other than represent Kyle?" Reed asks, and my brother and I stare at him as if he's insane.

"Like representing the guy who tried to kill me wasn't enough?" I retort.

Reed becomes flustered, trying to get words out. "I didn't mean ... but ... and ... I ..."

Law stands. "Their defence was that Anders started the fight. They painted Anders to be the controlling one, intimidated him in depositions, and made it so hard on him he couldn't testify at Kyle's trial because the idea of it would send him into panic. That's when the attacks started. Not right afterwards, but having to relive it over and over again for the lawyers. It meant Kyle got a reduced charge and sentence."

"Oh," Reed says.

I stay on the couch, my head down, eyes cast at their coffee table, because once again, I'm back in *that place*. I'm the guy who froze, the guy who couldn't defend myself, and the guy who choked when it counted.

It's easy to blame Brody's dad for Kyle getting off light, but the truth is, I'm the one who let him get away with it, because I wasn't strong enough to face him in a trial.

I'm weak.

I've always been weak.

I'm worthless.

These thoughts are dangerous, I know that, but they won't stop taunting me, reminding me of who I really am.

I'm not the guy who gets to have sex with his roommate without consequences. I'm not deserving of the happily ever after my brother gets.

It's not my life.

"On second thought, I do need Karen," I say before I have the chance to believe the voices.

It's taken me a long time to get to this point—where I know I need help—but the voices are trying to drag me down, and it won't be long before they take over completely if I don't do something about them.

I should be proud that I'm able to recognise the signs and that I'm strong enough to ask for the help I need, but the truth is all it does is remind me I need help in the first place.

Then the voices start all over again.

It's a vicious cycle.

Law stands. "I'll take you."

It's happening again. My soul's splitting in half.

This will be the day I realised Brody and I could never work out.

I can't be with him knowing I'd have to see his father.

I can't be with him knowing he does to his clients' victims what his dad did to me.

Kyle's conviction broke me in more ways than the actual assault.

And nothing in my life is safe from the repercussions of that.

22

BRODY

"Care to tell me why my roommate is having a panic attack?" I ask Dad.

"Should I know?"

He and my sister stare at me, probably wondering the same thing I am. What the fuck just happened?

I'd basically chased Anders to the elevator and only stopped because I saw the horror in his eyes as I tried to get on there with him. I've gone back to being the guy who scares him.

"He said you were Kyle's lawyer. I'm assuming that's the guy who attacked him."

"Anders was attacked?" Rachel asks.

Dad's brow scrunches. "He looked familiar, and the name rings a bell, but Kyle … It's not coming to me."

I move to where I dropped my bag on the way in and pull out my work laptop. So far I've respected Anders' wishes to keep the details of his assault to himself, but I can't not know anymore.

Taking it to the dining table, I open the lid and bring up the firm's log-in portal for their network. "Look it up."

"You know I can't let you see what's on there."

"I don't care right now. Look it up. I need to know."

Maybe it's the way I demand it, the crack in my voice, or my erratic behaviour by chasing Anders out the door, but Dad eyes me suspiciously.

"He's not just your roommate, is he?"

Frustration bubbles in my chest, but it doesn't feel anywhere near as painful as Anders walking out on me.

"Would it make a difference if he was more?"

Dad takes a seat at the table. "I'm not going to give you the case files. Attorney-client privilege—"

"Yeah, thanks, I did learn something in law school. I want to jog your memory so you can tell me what you're able to."

He fills in his log-in details and then does a search for Anderson Steel.

"There's an *E* on the end," I say over his shoulder.

Dad fixes it, and something pops up on screen immediately. "Here. Public court records."

Dad stands, giving me the chance to cross a line I know I probably shouldn't.

Shit.

Now that the opportunity's here, I'm not sure if I should take it. It's an invasion of privacy.

To get straight answers for once or to keep waiting for Anders to tell me. It's a tough choice to make.

"Maybe you should talk to Anders," Rachel says.

My heart leaps into my throat.

Dad leans over the table and scrolls through the document for me, because I can't bring myself to do it.

I also can't bring myself to stop him from talking.

"Domestic situation that escalated into violence. Defendant claimed to be high and the victim hit him first in anger over his drug problem."

Domestic abuse.

There it is. There's the missing piece.

It wasn't a sex issue at all. He didn't lie about that. He lied about *who* hurt him, and now that it's been pointed out, I can't believe it didn't cross my mind.

A weight lifts off me as the truth hits.

Anders' issues with intimacy have nothing to do with the physical side of things.

He can't trust that I won't hurt him because the one person who wasn't supposed to, did.

And then my dad defended him.

I slump into the closest chair and run my hands through my hair, gripping the roots tight.

I'm a lawyer. I find loopholes and ways to get around the rules to get what I want. But there are no loopholes here, only broken hearts, and I think I'm about to add mine to the list.

"Brody, did you hear me?" Dad says.

I lift my head. "What?"

"It was a heated argument that got out of hand. Your boyfriend attacked first."

"There's no way that happened."

It doesn't sound right. That can't have happened. I pull the laptop closer to me.

The words are there in black and white. The prosecutor's case against the defence.

Dad painted Anders in a light that would make a jury sympathetic to his assailant if it had gotten that far, which it didn't. After depositions, the prosecutor offered up a plea deal.

The Anders in these papers is nothing like the guy I live with.

The Anders I know makes sure a sauce-covered cat doesn't have a PTSD episode while trying to bathe her.

He's sweet, a little sarcastic, and a lot self-deprecating. It's damn near impossible for him to trust, but he pushed himself to try with me.

He's not the type of guy to hit his boyfriend in a rage.

Then again, Reed swears Anders' brother isn't the type of guy to punch out a random guy, but Law did that. A drunk, bigoted guy, but he still lost his head.

Maybe the Steele brothers have anger management issues. Though, I still can't wrap my head around Anders being violent towards anyone. Not on purpose like these papers claim.

What happened might've changed him. He's easily spooked now, and his whole life revolves around his anxiety and therapy. PTSD has the ability to change someone. Perhaps the Anders I know is someone new—someone who didn't exist until five years ago.

Police reports for the case made note of Kyle's bloodwork. He had crystal meth in his system after he turned himself in a few hours after the fact. The evidence supports Kyle's story, and with Anders withdrawing his desire to testify, it was easy for my father to get the charges reduced.

Attempted murder downplayed to aggravated assault.

"You don't remember the case?" I ask my father.

"Barely. It was an easy case to plead out, so there's not much to remember."

I have no doubt that Anders knows every tiny little detail of the case. This only reiterates what I've been thinking ever since I've been trying the rape case at work. To be in this field, you need to be able to let shit go.

Dad doesn't remember Anders, but Anders knew who he was the minute he stepped through the door.

Kyle was sentenced to six years.

Anders has been suffering for five and a half of them.

Shit, Kyle's set to get out in a few months.

Now knowing the truth and everything that went down, I want to go to Anders. I want to hold him close and tell him in person what I've silently vowed all along. He's mine to protect, and I will do it with every fibre of my being.

This is just another puzzle piece that makes up the raw beauty that is Anders, and I'm not giving up that easily.

No matter what he throws at me.

"I have to go." I check my pocket to make sure I still have my keys and then head for the door before my father or sister can stop me.

If I know Anders as well as I think I do, there's only one place he'd be going.

Law's.

Reed answers the door with a knowing look on his face. His usual boy-next-door charm is missing, only to be replaced with anger on behalf of Anders. I can't really blame him.

His blue eyes appear stormy, and if I didn't know him any better, I'd be inclined to back away from him because he looks scary. Reed might be shorter than me, but he's stocky.

"I didn't know," I say.

The angry line in Reed's forehead eases a tiny bit but doesn't go away completely. "Didn't know what?"

"Anders told me he was assaulted, but he didn't tell me by who or much of anything to do with it. I didn't know until ..."

"Until?"

"Tonight. I looked up the court files."

"Brody—"

"Can I please see him? I need to tell him this doesn't change anything."

Reed's lips form into a thin line. "Your dad defended the guy who tried to kill him. You really think you can be roommates after that?"

"That was my dad, not me. And I don't want to be just roommates—" My mouth slams shut.

Reed switches from anger to disappointment. "What did you do?"

"Nothing!"

He doesn't believe me.

"Okay, not nothing."

"What part of off limits don't you understand?"

"The part where it came from you, not Anders. It's not like we meant for something to happen. It just ... did."

"Law's going to kill you."

"Good for him. I look forward to it. Right now I only care about talking to Anders. Can I please come in?"

Reed steps aside. "You can come in." He closes the door behind me and blocks my exit. "But Anders isn't here."

"Where is he?"

"Out with Law."

"Where?"

Reed averts his gaze.

"Please? I have to talk to him. I have to let him know I don't care he lied or why he lied or any of that. I need to make sure he's okay."

"Brody ..." Sympathy shines in Reed's eyes. "You fell for him, didn't you?"

"No. Yes? I'm in the middle of falling for him, and I don't want this to come between us."

"That's a lot of pressure to put on Anders. His anxiety, his PTSD? It's all connected to that one incident that happened to him. How do you think he'll feel if you two started dating and he had to sit across from your dad at the dinner table?"

Okay, so that presents a problem I didn't consider, but I don't care because I'll work around it. I have to make this work.

"So, we don't have dinner with my dad. It's pretty simple. He rarely has anything to do with my personal life anyway."

Reed frowns. "You're willing to disown your own father for him?"

"Well, no, but I mean, I see Dad at work and have Anders at home. They don't have to see each other."

"And if you get married? Have kids?"

"Whoa, jumping the gun there. We're just spending time together. That's all." And I want more of that.

"For now. You must know relationships have a progression. I don't see Anders marrying anyone who will remind him of his old life."

"What would you know? You barely know him."

"I practically lived with him for six months before Law and I moved in here. You're both like family to me, so this isn't picking sides. You need to back off, Brody. If Anders can't handle whatever you two have going on, you need to be the one to step back."

"I don't want to," I say softly.

"Brod—"

"You don't understand. Anders and I have ..." Okay, I don't know what we have. "Something inexplicable. I'm the first guy in five years he's come close to trusting. I'm the only one he's told about what happened to him—"

"Yet, he didn't tell you *everything*. Look, I'm not speaking for Anders—he needs to learn how to do that for himself—but all I'm saying is if you push him when he's not ready, you'll lose him."

"So I'm supposed to leave? Do nothing and let him come to me?"

I can't do that. It's not in my nature. I go for what I want, and Anders is definitely something I want. Even the thought of losing what we have has a need to make everything okay rise up inside me.

"If you want any chance with him, yes. Let him come back to you."

"Can you at least tell me if he's okay?"

Reed shakes his head. "I honestly don't know. I've seen him after a panic attack but have never seen him in the middle of one. I didn't know how to handle him. He looked distant and nothing like the Anders I know."

"Where is he?" I ask again.

"Emergency therapy session."

A wave of defeat crashes over me, dumping a bucket of cold water on my head.

I can't walk away because I don't want to lose him, but I can't stay or I will.

This is a lose-lose situation.

23

ANDERSON

"So what's the real reason behind your panic?"

"If I knew that, I wouldn't need you, would I?" My usual snappy tone is absent, replaced by some angry guy I don't know.

When I started seeing Karen, I thought it was pointless. I thought she couldn't help me, and I'd often fight her on everything she said. I mean, I still do that, but it's in more of a sarcastic fun way instead of this, where I'm too upset to play nice with anyone.

I'll apologise later, but right now I need to be a twat.

Because I'm past sad. I'm past emotional. I'm so far past angry, I don't know how to get back.

I've worked for months on trying to get myself to act like a normal human being around Brody, and in a thirty-second window of meeting his father, my walls are back up, my breathing stilted, and just the memory of kissing Brody is tainted by the memories of being accused of being the instigator in my assault.

Brody's dad deposed me before the trial. He asked questions that would make anyone sound like a liar and emphasised incidents to make it appear like I was the aggressor in my relationship with Kyle. Like bringing up the time Kyle put a tracking app on my phone and I threw it against the fucking wall.

Kyle was the one keeping tabs on me, but I'm the aggressor here because I threw my phone? Sure.

"Were you upset at seeing Kyle's lawyer again? Did you have an episode where you relived the court case, or were you focused on Brody and what it means for your relationship?"

"What relationship? We've fooled around a couple of times and fucked once. That doesn't make a relationship."

"And now you're belittling the progress you've made with him because you're scared."

"Of course, I'm fucking scared." I thought I was on the path to getting everything I thought I'd never have again, and now I'm reminded that I've always been right. I don't have the strength to fight for what I want.

I'm undeserving because I can't get past this.

"Brody's father was only doing his job, and that has nothing to do with Brody himself," Karen says.

"No, but they're related. Brody does the same job as his father. How can I be with someone who treats another human being like that? Job or not."

"Lawyers need to be able to compartmentalise between their personal lives and professional ones. Everyone has the right to legal representation, and those lawyers vow to represent their clients to the best of their ability."

"I know," I mumble.

"I think this is going to be a good test for you. An exercise in being able to face aspects of your past without having a panic attack. You've been doing really well and facing a lot of things you refused to those first few years of therapy. I don't think this is a bad thing."

"No, no, it's definitely a bad thing."

"Because you're going to shut Brody out and not deal with it?"

Exactly.

But I don't answer her.

Karen writes that down. "What do you need from me this session?"

"For you to tell me it's understandable to run away."

"It is. It's one hundred percent understandable, and a lot of people in your situation would do it. But you're better than that, Anders."

"Am I? I don't think I am. I don't think my track record of having my twin brother break up with guys for me really indicates I'm the best person I can be."

"Then answer me this. Are you going to send Lawson to break up with Brody for you?"

I squeeze my eyes shut. The thing between Brody and me is nowhere near done. I want to explore it more, but I don't think I'm strong enough.

I'm never strong enough.

The drive back to Law's place is silent between my brother and me. The sound of the wind passes through the open window, the low hum of the engine lulling me into peacefulness for the first time tonight.

Law taps his thumb to the beat of some music I'm tuning out, and I stare out the window as suburbs blur into each other as we whip through them.

Here I am again. The pressure of life sitting on my chest. The urge to wrap myself in a blanket cocoon and live there forever outweighs the need to be a functional adult.

When we're about five minutes away from the house, Law finally speaks, giving up on waiting for me to do it first.

"So, how long have you and Brody been a thing?"

I try to school my reaction by biting the inside of my cheek. "Who says we're a thing?"

"Twin intuition," Law says.

"I call bullshit."

"Honestly, I've suspected it for a while. Reed was telling me about a guy who kept rejecting Brody. Now, apart from me, I'm pretty sure the only guy in a fifty-kilometre radius to turn down Brody would be someone who *couldn't* go out with him. Add that to the fact Brody wouldn't tell Reed who he was chasing, that made me think it was someone we know. And Reed literally only knows you, me, and Brody."

I snort. "Yeah, your boyfriend is a bit of a loser."

Law laughs, knowing I'm not being serious but trying to push the focus from me and Brody.

"How long?"

"We first kissed about a month ago."

"Hmm, a month. How different for you."

I ignore his snark, because this is not the same as all those other guys. This isn't a one-month freak-out. It's a Brody freak-out. It's a "I thought I finally had something that could work, only to be proven otherwise" freak-out.

"I fought pretty hard to keep my distance," I say. I should've fought harder. Then I wouldn't be here feeling this way again.

Helpless.

Pathetic.

A lost cause.

"Mmhmm. And he's the reason you started seeing the other therapist?"

"Yup." God, I went to sex therapy for this guy. That's how

delusional I was that I could have some semblance of a normal life. I shake my head. "It was a sex therapist ... you know, in case you didn't get that from my vague description."

"Oh, it was about as vague as an anvil dropping on my head. Thanks."

"You're welcome."

"Did you think we'd be mad?" he asks.

"No. I knew you'd go all overprotective brother on Brody, and you guys already have enough bad blood because he used to have a thing for Reed."

Law side-eyes me. "Used to?"

"Yeah. Turns out he doesn't have a thing for who Reed is now but for the guy he was obsessed with as a teenager. First love and all that other bullshit. I can honestly say he does not have a thing for your boyfriend."

"Well, good, because using you while having feelings for someone else would be a shitty thing to do."

"Ooh, look at that, the overprotectiveness is already beginning, but you're too late. Won't be needing it."

"That's not being overprotective. That's me pointing out what a douche he'd be if he hurt you like that."

"Yeah, well, he's not the one who's going to be doing the hurting."

"Then who is?" Law asks, and I give him my best pleading eyes. "No. No way. I am not breaking up with Brody for you."

"You don't have to do it *as me*. And it's not really a break-up. Can't be a break-up when we're not really together."

Law looks unimpressed. "Tell that to all your little fuck buddies who threw drinks on me when I did your dirty work."

"Please, Law? I can't face him. I just can't."

"Why not?"

"Because I'm scared if I see him, it will ruin any chance of a future with him. I'm terrified that when I look at his face, all

I'll be able to see is my past. I need ... I don't know exactly what I need, but it has to be without him. It's too fresh, too raw, and I'm fucking exhausted."

"So talk to him about that," Law emphasises, and I don't care if he makes a point.

When it feels like my world is imploding, there's no telling my brain that it's as simple as talking about it.

Brody has taken all my quirks in stride. He's supported me and challenged me, but I've always known something would swoop in and take it all away. Because happy feelings never last.

Who would sign on for a lifetime of this shit? Of me breaking at any moment. Of not being able to even have sex without restraints.

It's not doable.

Karen says not to use the word impossible, but that's exactly what this feels like.

When Law pulls into his driveway, I tense at the sight of Brody's fancy-ass car.

"And here's your chance," Law says. "Explain what happened. Tell him everything. I doubt he'll run away."

"Maybe he should."

Law sighs. "Nothing good will happen when you're like this, and I'm not going to baby you into thinking this behaviour is okay. I'm also not going to go in there and tell him it's over between you two."

"Where the hell did tough-love Law come from? Fine, don't go in there and tell him it's over, but can you at least tell him to leave? There's no way I can face him right now."

"When will you be able to?"

"I dunno. Ten years?" I quip.

My brother's unimpressed. His jaw tightens, and I can tell he doesn't want to do as I say, but he will.

"You gonna wait in the car?" he asks.

"Nope. I'm gonna take your car for a drive."

"You've had Valium. Are you right to drive?"

"I'm literally going around the block so I don't have to watch Brody walk out on my life."

Law laughs. "Oh, if you think me telling Brody to leave is gonna make him walk away, you're deluded."

"We'll see."

24

BRODY

No matter how many times Reed tells me to leave, it's only when Law comes home by himself that I admit defeat.

Great, I'm giving Law another reason to hate me.

"I didn't know about my father, I promise."

Law shakes his head. "It's not a matter of you lying to him. From what I can gather, your connection to his past was a bit of a wake-up call that he'll never be able to outrun his issues, because they always come back."

Fuck.

"I don't want him to see me that way."

"Neither do I," Law says, and Reed and I look at each other like maybe his boyfriend has lost his damn mind.

"You don't?" I ask.

Law assesses me for a second, and I try to remain stoic so I don't give anything away.

He breaks first. "I'm trying really hard not to torture you like I normally would, but it's difficult."

"Umm, thanks?"

"I know you and Anders are ... umm ... together?"

"Dating. I guess. Technically." Our rock-climbing day classes as a date, right?

"Right. That."

"How did you know?" Reed asks.

"Anders told me on the way home."

I narrow my eyes. "And I'm still standing? Why? You hate me."

Law laughs. "I don't hate you, and I think ... I actually think you're good for Anders. He has pushed himself out of so many comfort zones with you, and while this is a setback, I still think you're good for him."

"Where is he?" I ask, knowing I don't actually want to know the answer.

"He asked ... if ..." Law lets out a loud breath.

"He doesn't want to see me."

"Maybe he just needs time," Law says.

"What's time going to change anything? I can't change who my father is or a case he had five years ago."

"No, but it might give Anders time to rationalise and think it through. Right now, his brain is in flight mode, and there's no getting through to him when he thinks that way."

"So, I'm supposed to sit back and wait for him to come to me? Do you know how hard that will be for me?"

"Well, it's that or lose him. Because he physically can't bring himself to fight when he gets like this. He can stay here until he starts to feel somewhat normal again."

My stubborn side that I get from my father wants me to stay right where I am. Anders has to come home soon, but if I do that and he does tell me to get out of his life forever, then I won't have any cards left to play.

I need to give in.

For now.

I last two days before I cave.

If time is what Anders needs, then I'll give him that, but that doesn't stop me from messaging him and telling him I'm thinking of him. As suspected, I don't get a reply.

I think my sister's ready to move out already with how much I'm annoying her by whining about him.

"So, go see him," Rachel says. "Maybe take over a pile of his things seeing as he hasn't come by for anything. He has to be running out of clothes."

"He's staying with Law. I assume he's borrowing his clothes."

"Damn. I wish I had a twin. I could steal all her expensive designer things."

"I'm pretty sure the Steele brothers own nothing designer."

"Not my point. But taking him some stuff could be an excuse to go see him."

"Yeah, true. Though from what Reed told me, his ex would turn up out of the blue, and I don't want to remind Anders of any more of his ex's bullshit."

"What do you mean?"

I shouldn't tell her this, but … "I might have gotten his prison file under the proviso of being his lawyer?"

Her eyes widen. "You fucking what?"

"I know. I know. I could be fired and my law license revoked if it gets out, but—"

"It's not the morality of it. It's that it was *you* who did it! You never break any rules. Ever." She wipes away a fake tear. "I'm so proud."

"Shut up."

But she's right. I'm not this guy. I should feel guilty or worried, but if I'm honest with myself, this is the first time in my life that I couldn't care less about my career.

In fact, Anders has made me realise my drive has been misplaced. I haven't wanted to chase the law. I have no interest in lining my pockets.

I've always been jealous of Rachel for following her dream. She doesn't give a shit about money or impressing our parents. She just wants to help people.

I can't do either of those things in my current career choice.

"What did you find?" Rachel asks.

I debate whether I should get into it with her, but I need advice. "So, this guy—Anders' ex—he claimed to the police and to his lawyers that he was a hardcore drug addict, right? But Anders claimed to have not noticed the signs or even have an inkling of it."

"That doesn't mean anything. There are high-functioning addicts everywhere."

"Yeah, I know that, but what's surprising is a guy like that gets locked up and becomes clean."

"Isn't that the point of incarceration?"

"Yes, and no. Seriously, it's practically easier to get your hands on drugs behind bars than it is on the street. Someone who was as addicted to ice as this guy claimed he was, there'd be about an eighty percent chance of relapsing in prison. But his record shows nothing. No paraphernalia, no drug busts. Only one weapon discovery during a random cell search which cost him his chance at early parole."

Thankfully. I wondered about that when I saw he'd been given a six-year sentence. He's been eligible for parole for three.

"It's not impossible that he turned it around," Rachel says.

"I know it's not. It's just ... unlikely."

"Maybe he has had drugs but has been lucky enough not to get caught. What's your point?"

"It's only a hunch, but I think Kyle was never a drug addict. I think he's an angry, possessive asshole who mentally groomed Anders for years to be his pet, and when Anders refused to take his shit anymore and broke up with him, Kyle lost his head and attacked him. He fled the scene, called his lawyer—who according to work files wasn't Dad but another lawyer at first—and then went and got high."

"Why though?"

"To push for a lighter charge. Turning up to Anders' apartment with the intent to hurt him would've been premeditated attempted murder. A crime of passion? One that occurs because of intoxication? The charge becomes reduced to aggravated assault. Instead of twenty-five years or more, he got six. Six years, Rach."

"I'm not saying I don't believe you, but you're basing a lot of this on gut instinct. A gut instinct that's highly infatuated with the victim."

"I know, but the whole case doesn't sit right with me. Something doesn't ring true."

"Maybe this is why lawyers don't try cases of loved ones. Even if the case was fucked up, there's nothing you can do now, right?"

I slump in defeat. "No, there isn't. He's been convicted for that crime. He can't be charged for it again. I don't know why I'm obsessing over it."

My sister's arms wrap around me. "Because the guy you love is going through a difficult time and you feel helpless. I get it."

"I don't ... it's not ..." But I can't really say it's not love, can I?

I haven't felt this way about anyone, maybe not even Reed. I thought I loved him, and even though he gave me the same gut feelings and swarming butterflies and a need to be close to him, it was nowhere near as intense as what it's like with Anders.

The front door to the apartment opening has my heart stuttering, and when Anders appears, it stops completely.

Then it plummets into my stomach. Because the guy standing in the entryway isn't Anders at all.

Even if Anders had cut his longish hair, shaved, and regrew scruff in the few days it's been since I've seen him, this guy has something else about him that's uniquely ... not Anders.

Holy shit, I'm under the same dick spell Reed's under.

"Hey," Law says.

"I'm guessing Anders isn't with you."

"Holy shit!" Rachel exclaims. "This is the brother?"

Law stands awkwardly, shuffling from one foot to the other. "I'm the brother. And I'm, umm, here to get some of Anders' things."

"Some?" I ask.

Law looks away from me as he says, "All."

I stand from the kitchen table, my laptop still open on the documents I technically shouldn't have, so I quickly shut the lid before facing off with Law. "You can't. He can't end it like this."

"I told him that, but he's not in a good place."

"Is it because I messaged him? I'll back off more, I'll—"

"It's not. Or maybe it is, I don't know. He's slipping into old habits. He's not sleeping, not eating, and he's barely leaving his room. He ..."

"He what?"

"He isn't going into work."

"Fuck. What the hell am I supposed to do?" I ask. "I need

to fix it. Make him better. I need to ... I don't know. I need to—"

"Let him go."

"No," Rachel says for me. "No, he can't do that. Anders makes Brody better. More human and less robotic. He can't walk away." She turns to me. "Tell him your theory. The ex-boyfriend was a lying dickface."

Did she not hear the part of losing my law license?

Law looks pensive. "He is a lying dickface, yes. I agree with that statement. But you have a theory?"

"Umm, yeah, just from the court records."

"And he contacted the prison pretending to be Kyle's lawyer so he could have the prison records sent over—"

"Rachel," I scold.

Law folds his arms, but I can't tell if he's pissed or not. His face is neutral. "Why did you do that?"

"Because something about his case didn't sit right with me."

"How so?" He's still giving me nothing, so I try to explain.

"The defence painted Anders as the aggressor and poor Kyle as a drug addict. I think Kyle was full of shit."

Finally, Law breaks into a smile.

"He thinks Kyle faked being high to get a lighter sentence," Rachel says.

Something weird crosses Law's face. I have to be wrong but it looks like ... appreciation?

Appears Anders isn't the only person I can't get a read on.

I've almost convinced myself that I can't be seeing awe on Law's face when he takes me off guard and approaches me.

I recoil, not sure what to expect, but then his arms are round me, taking me into a hug.

What the fuck?

"That's what we always thought," he whispers. "Anders'

lawyers never believed us, and the prosecutor kept telling Anders the evidence suggests otherwise, so they couldn't prove it." He pulls back. "I was right when I said you're good for him. He needs someone in his corner like you. Give him some space. Try again in maybe a week or two."

"A week?" I exclaim. "Do you not understand that I like shit to be in order? I need to know where we stand."

Law gives me a sympathetic stare. "If you push him before he's ready, you'll definitely lose him."

"What about Meatball?" I ask. "Does he want his cat? She misses him. The first two days, she waited by the door, and today she's gone back to her cranky old demon cat ways— hissing at me anytime I go near her."

Rachel rolls her eyes. "She's probably bouncing off your shitty attitude."

I look at Law. "You can take her with you now if he wants her."

"He hasn't mentioned the cat, but he's Anders. He won't ask for her."

As much as I'd love to make Anders come and get her himself so I get to see him, Meatball being by his side is more important. They seem to calm each other.

I go pull the cat carrier Rachel bought when she rescued her out of the hallway closet, while Rachel goes to get the cat food for me.

Getting Meatball into the damn thing is a mission, but between Rachel and me, we manage.

Law looks on with a concerned scrunch in his brow. "She's not, like, going to scratch me to death in my sleep or anything, is she?"

Rachel and I glance at each other with knowing smirks. I try to keep a straight face as I say, "Not at all."

Law takes the carrier off me. "Give me a week to work on Anders."

I watch him leave, feeling completely helpless. A week. I can do a week. I don't want to, but I can.

25

ANDERSON

I hate my body.
 I hate my mind.
I hate my life.
It's the anxiety. Don't let it win.

KISS plays through my iPhone, filtering through the still-unfamiliar bedroom even if I've seen practically nothing but the inside of these walls in the last three days. It's become my very own self-inflicted prison, but I feel safe here. Even with the unfamiliarity.

If you've never broken down in front of your brother's boyfriend, you haven't lived.

"Can I get you anything?" Reed asks from the doorway. Every day he asks me what I need and how he can help. It's impossible to yell at the guy because he's doing it as a favour to Law. "Water?"

I don't even bother rolling over in the spare bed in his and Law's house to face him as I shake my head.

"Call out if you need something. I'm out here grading assignments."

I say, "Okay," but can still sense him hanging in the doorway.

"Need me to make an appointment?" Reed asks.

I shake my head again.

"I'm sorry you're going through this," he whispers, and then his footsteps fade away.

Then I remember Ed Shearon. I sit up. "Reed?"

He turns back. "Yeah?"

"Can you cancel an appointment for me? I have one set for tomorrow with my other therapist."

"Sure. Just give me the details."

"Thank you."

He takes out his phone, and I look up the number on mine. Law comes home halfway through giving Reed the digits. The noise of him dumping my stuff out in the living room is followed by him appearing in my doorway.

"What's happening?" he asks.

"Reed's cancelling the sex therapist for me."

Reed almost drops his phone, and he scrambles to catch it before it hits the floor. When he's upright again, he stares at me wide-eyed. "I'm cancelling who?"

I smirk. "Okay, that was fun and cheered me up a little." I turn to Law. "Though I'm surprised you didn't already tell him."

"Interestingly enough, your sex life doesn't come up a whole lot when I talk to my partner. Weird, I know."

Yes. This is what I need—a sense of normalcy. Snarky, crazy normalcy.

"But you shouldn't cancel the appointment," Law says.

"Why not? I'm single and don't need lessons on jerking off. Have that down to an art."

Law screws up his face, but Reed appears even more intrigued.

"They have therapists who teach you how to have sex?"

"He's not a hooker." I laugh at the reminder of Brody's first reaction.

"I didn't think he was," Reed says. "Who would think a sex therapist is a hook—oh. Yeah, I can see Brody saying that."

That makes the sad creep back in.

The normalcy might've only lasted twenty seconds, but having been in this dark place before, I know any joking around or lightness is a good sign. Makes it seem like not all is completely lost, even if it's only for a brief time.

I force a smile. "He was actually pretty good about the whole thing."

Really good. Brody understood me and was patient. So fucking patient.

But the fear came back anyway. The dark part of my soul that I battle with daily won out. And now I'm too scared to see where we truly stand.

If his name is enough to bring me down, I don't know what seeing his face will do.

"You're keeping that appointment," Law says again.

"Why?"

"Because ..."

I know that look on my brother. He's trying to come up with a lie.

"Even if it's over between you and Brody, the therapy was helping. Maybe he can help you in your next relationship."

The scoff flies out of me. "No. No more relationships. Ever."

"And we're back at square one. If you're gonna sit in here and wallow, then fine, do it. But if you want to cancel that appointment, you're doing it yourself. And just because I'm disappointed in you, that doesn't mean you get out of going for a run with me in the morning. You haven't left the house in days, and I can't—won't—sit by and watch you fade away this time."

I mock salute him while silently appreciating the push.

Reed gets all starry-eyed at Law. "You're so hot when you're bossy."

They stare at each other hungrily, and I'm quick to put a stop to whatever they're thinking right now.

"Okay, time for you two to leave my room. Maybe I'll talk to my sex therapist about that tomorrow—how my brother and his boyfriend like to rub their normal sex lives in my face."

"Go see your therapist," Law says. "Keep pushing your routine."

He's right even though I have no idea what to talk about with Ed Shearon, considering I'm not having sex.

Routine. Stick to what I know, what I need, and fight my way out of this haze.

I want to be strong for Brody. I don't think I've ever wanted anything more.

But that's where the problem lies: no matter what I *want* and how confident I am in wanting it, it doesn't make the burden of being me easier to carry. It doesn't take away years of internalized torment.

Law turns to leave but looks over his shoulder at me. "Oh, by the way, there's a surprise for you in the living room. Brody insisted it'd help."

I frown, but my legs are eager to get me into the living room.

When my eyes land on a pet carrier with my baby looking mega pissed off, I choke back a sob. She lets out a little kitty wail, and I rush over to her.

As soon as she's out and in my arms, something good clicks into place for the first time in days.

And I will not cry about that.

I won't.
Then Meatball purrs.
Dammit.

---

*E*very day for six days, Law drags me out to go running at the butt crack of dawn. I want to hate him for it, but apart from me being grumbly before coffee, it is helping.

Getting back into any routine has been helpful in keeping my head on right, but any thoughts or mentions of Brody makes the darkness seep in, even if it's only around the edges.

I can't let it take over again. I just can't. Right now, I don't want to even risk giving it more leeway than I can control.

So I ignore Karen's and Ed's words like *avoidance* and *projecting* and all the other bullshit where they try to tell me how I can get over this roadblock with Brody, because I honestly don't believe I can.

I don't know if I want to at this point.

Working through my shit with Brody has been more than I could've imagined. I never thought I'd get to where I was with him. I didn't think it was possible for me to have any kind of real relationship again.

Then comes this massive force, as if the universe itself wants to rip us apart, and I realise I'm not that guy. I'm not the guy who gets a happily ever after. I'm the guy who has to struggle every day of my life just to get a glimpse of happiness.

When is it too much work to be worth it?

I'm teetering on the edge of a cliff, and all I can focus on is making sure I land on the right side of things. I want to be firmly in the safe area, wrapped in comfort and out of danger, but to get back there, I have to step out of my comfort zone and hope I don't fall into the abyss below me.

That's where I'm at right now. I could run away and be relatively happy living a lonely but straightforward existence where I don't have to feel. I don't have to think.

Or, I could keep fighting.

I push my legs harder and faster on my morning run because when I get in this thought loop, all I can do is try to make my brain shut up by confusing it with running like someone's chasing me.

Which, technically, they are, because Law is struggling to keep time with me.

"Bad night?" he asks, his voice breathy from exertion.

It's not that he's unfit—he's a martial arts instructor—it's that we've been at this for over an hour already this morning, and I'm only going faster and faster even if my legs are threatening to fall out from beneath me.

I shrug. "It was fine."

"I heard you up and about around three, so don't lie."

"That was Meatball. It's her favourite time of the day."

"Lie. Well, no, I'm learning that's true, but I wasn't hearing cat noises."

"If you knew it was bad, why even ask?"

"To try to get you to talk about it?"

"Less talking. More running."

"Anders!" Law's tone makes me stop, because it's his *I'm not going to put up with your shit* tone.

"What?"

Our chests heave, our scowls match, and I don't want to hear what he has to say just as much as he doesn't want to say it.

"Brody's dad is not Brody."

"Don't you think I know that?" I yell. "Don't you think I've been telling myself that for the past ten days, twelve hours, and thirty-six minutes? Don't you think if it was that simple, I wouldn't be trying to exert all my nervous energy and heartbreak by running until my legs don't work anymore?"

"So go and talk to him."

"I can't!"

"Why not?"

"Because he's the reminder my life is never going to be easy. It can be great one minute and falling apart the next, and how am I supposed to look at him knowing who his father is? You say they're separate and different and one doesn't correlate to the other, but it does. Brody is exactly like his dad. He'll come home every night, tired from a case, and all I will be able to wonder is who his client is this time. Someone like Kyle? Someone worse?"

"You didn't have a problem with that before you knew who his dad was."

"Because I tried to separate lawyer Brody from my Brody. Now they're all muddled, and I can't … I just … can't." My legs finally give out, and I fall to my knees.

My back muscles ache, and my chest constricts as I fight tears.

Of course, my brother is by my side in an instant, helping me off the middle of the path so other runners can go by us. He gets me to the grass so I can sit and take a breath.

"I do understand where you're coming from," Law says gently. "I really do. But—"

"No. No buts. If you truly understood, you wouldn't be butting me right now."

Law bites his lip to try to stop himself from laughing. I glare at him, and he throws his arms up. "It's not my fault you said *butting* in a serious conversation."

"Real mature."

"Here's the but: you haven't even seen Brody since. How do

you know that's how you're going to feel when you're around him?"

"Because it's how I feel when I so much as *think* about him. Which is all the fucking time."

"You love him?"

"How can I love someone when I'm incapable of it?"

Law's hand lands on my shoulder. "You're not incapable of it. You're under the impression you're incapable of letting go. There's a big difference there."

Deep down, I know he's right, but my unwillingness to accept it is stronger right now. "If I was ever going to fall in love with someone again, it'd be Brody."

"Then you owe it to both of you to try. Just see him."

I shake my head. "If I see him, and I do have a panic attack, then that's it. It's definitely over. If I stay away and avoid seeing him, I'm able to hold on to the tiny bit of hope that's still niggling at me. I don't want to lose that."

Law rubs his temples. "Let me get this straight. You would rather be miserable with a tiny bit of hope than take your one chance at happiness."

"Yes. Because losing him completely would destroy me."

Law mumbles something under his breath. I think it's "Not in love with him my ass."

No way I'm not going to call him out. "What was that?"

He does that Law thing where he lies. Badly. "I said that's some seriously fucked-up Schrodinger crap." It's not what he said, but it's still accurate.

"Welcome to my brain."

Law sighs in resignation. I've won this round, but I know he won't give up.

I'm both thankful for and resentful of it.

26

BRODY

*I*f I were built like Dwayne Johnson, I'm pretty sure the pen in my hand would be snapped in half.

The kid hasn't looked up from his phone since we sat him in our conference room, and his dad is doing all the talking.

"The case has taken a turn in the prosecutor's favour," Annabelle says.

"How?" Mr. Steinfeld booms.

"An eyewitness has come forward from the party. Says they saw your son dragging an almost-passed-out victim upstairs. It proves she wasn't capable of giving consent."

The punk-ass kid finally looks up from his phone. "That's bullshit."

"No, that's the law," I bite and am quickly shut up by a glare from Annabelle.

"How do we fix it?" Mr. Steinfeld asks. "Pay the witness off, or—"

I hold in a groan and throw my head in my hand.

"You cannot tamper with a witness," Annabelle says firmly. "You definitely can't tell us about it or the plan to do it or imply to the point we suspect you might execute the plan."

"Then what are we supposed to do?" he asks.

"We're going to try to negotiate a plea deal," Annabelle says.

"No. He has his whole future ahead of him. I'm not going to let some stupid little slu—"

Before I know what I'm doing, I stand and bang my hands down on the desk. "Finish that sentence. I dare you."

"Wallace," Annabelle scolds, but I'm on a roll.

"Your son is a rapist, he knows it, we know it, and the courts are going to know it. You'll be lucky to get a plea deal. Knowing the screwed-up legal system, he'll probably only get probation, a few months at the most. Maybe if he wasn't such a spoiled shithead, he'd know the meaning of the word *no*."

Fucking up my career wasn't on today's agenda, and now the ball's rolling, I should be regretful or worried. Instead, all I want to do is march into my father's office and tell him I can't do it.

I'm ready to admit that I was wrong and he was right because as I sit across from this arrogant tool and his idiotic son, all I can think about is this kid's victim. How she'd stare at me the same way Anders stared at my father, and I don't want anyone to ever look at me that way.

Annabelle touches my arm and speaks low. "How about you step out for a bit?"

"Gladly."

With adrenaline still pumping, I march straight for the elevator to go to my father's office instead of my own.

He must sense something's up, because he stands as soon as he sees me. "What's wrong?"

"I quit. I quit, I quit, I quit. I can't ... I just—"

"Whoa, slow down."

"You were right, Dad. I shouldn't have come to work for you."

He screws up his face. "What do you mean?"

"I'm not cut out for it."

"That's not true. You have the potential to be a great lawyer."

"I don't have what it takes. Not on big cases like this."

"Take a seat. We'll talk it through."

I pace back and forth, still full of energy, but then I throw myself into the chair opposite him. "I can't. I'm done."

"Don't piss everything you've worked for away for a ..."

"A what? Can you even say the word *boyfriend*? I'm not doing it for Anders. And he's not my boyfriend." Thanks to my dad.

Dad leans back in his seat. "But you're doing it because of him."

"I'm doing it because I can't handle it."

"After you pay your dues, you can pick and choose which cases to take."

"That's true, but how much work am I going to get if I only want to represent good people?"

"Good people get into trouble all the time," Dad points out.

My mind goes to when Law was arrested for assaulting an abusive parent. Those are the kinds of cases I could do.

But to get there, I have to sell my soul for the next few years, and that's something I'm not willing to do.

"I can't. I'm sorry. You were right."

"About what?"

"You're always telling me I should've gone for a different type of law. You pass it off as a joke, but I know it's not."

Dad's face falls. "Brody ... I ..." His mouth opens and closes a few times. "You know why I say those things? It's not because I don't think you can make it. I say them because you don't seem to have the drive for this. You're not passionate about it. I ... I ..."

"Just say whatever you're thinking. I can handle it."

"I don't talk about this ... stuff," he grumbles.

Yeah, so I've heard from Mum over the years.

"It's called *emotion*, Dad."

He takes a deep breath. "Sometimes it comes across like you only went into law because of me and you don't actually like it. It makes me feel ..." He swallows hard, and I swear I see sweat forming on his forehead. "Guilty."

Whoa. I may need to ask him to say that again and put it in an official record to prove to my mum and siblings that he's not a robot. He expressed an emotion! One, singular. But still.

"I like the job," I say, but it's weak. "Well, I like the law. I *hate* working here. I hate this job. And of course, I did this for you. When I told you in high school that I was contemplating going into law, you were the most excited I'd seen in ... probably my whole childhood. You said you always thought Parker would've gone down that route, and you're always on Rachel's case about getting a good job."

"You know why I was excited when you chose law? Because I could at least talk to one of my kids about *something*. I don't know my own bloody children, because I ... I don't know much outside of the law. I don't know how to be a husband or a father. I can't understand Rachel's need for danger or Parker's need to travel and not lay down roots. I don't need to tell you I don't understand the gay thing, but that doesn't mean I don't support you. Any of you. I may not understand your brother and sister, but I support all of you."

If Rachel and Parker were here, they'd probably think he's full of shit. They don't believe anything out his mouth. With me, I have the same problem I've always had with this man. I want to believe him so bad I ignore the simplest of things.

Like, why can't he just tell us what he's thinking? Why push and be mad if we don't follow his advice? Why be a cold asshole?

"It wouldn't hurt for you to let us know that every now and then," I say. "Both Parker and Rachel think you have absolutely no interest in their lives unless it's to tell them what to do. They see you as some rich guy who believes money fixes everything. You act like you're the one with the money, so you think you can dictate our lives. And honestly? I sometimes see their point. Like, with my apartment. Did you really buy that for me as a graduation present, or was it because I'd done exactly as you suggested and was coming to work for you?"

"I did that because you deserved it."

"You didn't buy Parker anything when he graduated with his BA in engineering."

"He didn't even tell me he was graduating. I got a call the week before he left for overseas. I asked to see him, and he rejected me. He said he didn't have time with all the packing and planning."

"There are ways you can learn to understand," I say. "You can talk to us. Talk to Rachel about her need to be a hero. Call Parker and ask about his life. Ask me about my life as a gay man."

"You're the only one who's willing to talk to me about anything."

"But that's the problem, Dad. When the others don't talk about what you want to talk about, you write them off, and it makes them think you don't care."

"Of course, I care. You're my children."

That might be the first time I've ever heard him say he cares. I want to scream *Then act like it!* But I don't.

"How about this: You make a dinner reservation at Videre next week. I'll drag Rachel out, and you can ask us about the stuff you don't understand. If you truly care, you'll make the effort to get to know who we are, not who you want us to be. All we've ever wanted from you is to *try*."

Dad breaks into a small, weary smile. "That, I can do."

"Good." I stand. "And now that's settled, I need to leave. I would give you two weeks' notice, but I'm no doubt going to be fired after I just called my client a rapist and a spoiled shithead to his face. So, uh, have fun cleaning that one up for me." I try to escape, but his authoritative voice stops me.

"Brody."

I freeze and brace myself for yelling.

When I turn my head and look at him over my shoulder, he says, "I'm proud of you. Even if you called your client a rapist to his face. I'm proud of what you've accomplished and how established you are already. If you want help finding a new job, I have endless connections."

Totally not what I was expecting, but I'll take it. "Thanks, but I'm thinking something along the lines of pro bono work or Legal Aid."

Dad shudders. "Good luck to you."

I huff a laugh. "Thought so."

"Guess you and Rachel have the same save-the-world attitude."

I smile proudly. "Guess so."

27

ANDERSON

Law knocks on my bedroom door, and I can't help thinking *Here comes round four hundred and fifty-two of why I should give Brody a chance.*

How my brother went from hating the guy to trying to convince me how great he is, I'll never know.

Instead of another lecture, he asks, "What are your plans for dinner?"

"Eat whatever Reed cooks me." I grin.

"SOL, brother. Reed's not here, and you know you don't want to eat my cooking."

"Understatement. I can make us something." I climb out of bed, but Law blocks my path to the kitchen.

"Want to go out? We haven't been to dinner just you and me for a while."

"I'm good with takeaway."

"No, you're not." He turns on his heel. "Let's go."

Ugh. Little brother playing big brother again. "We went for a run this morning. Isn't that enough of a field trip out of my bubble?"

"Nope."

I give in, because there's no point in fighting it. And I'm hungry.

"The pub?" I ask on our way.

"Hmm, nah. I know where to go."

Okaaay, now I'm thinking he's up to something. I just don't know what it is yet.

But when he pulls into the parking lot of a restaurant we know well, I have to hold back my eye roll.

"Really, Law? Bringing me to the place I always made you go to break up with guys for me?"

"I figured you could do with some perspective. Look at how far you've come from being that guy who can't even break up with someone without panicking."

"I haven't come that far. I'm still avoiding Brody."

"Maybe you'll feel differently once we eat."

I doubt it, and I don't exactly understand what he's trying to prove here.

We take a booth in the back, which is where I normally hide while Law does the breaking-up part.

We don't need to look at the menu because we've eaten here a million times, so we order drinks and food as soon as we're seated.

"Not feeling anything yet?" Law asks.

"Other than the awkward creepiness of you trying to psychoanalyse me? I don't understand what I'm supposed to be feeling."

"A sense of accomplishment. A shift in your shitty behaviour? I don't know. Pick one."

His plan is severely backfiring because all I have is a sense of dread and failure hanging over my head. I tried so fucking hard and I'm still *here*.

I've pushed myself and pushed myself, struggled and got

back up and pushed through again, only to be knocked off kilter and sent back to the bottom where I started.

And it all comes down to wondering *what's the fucking point?*

"I'm back where I began. Yay me." I wave imaginary flags.

Law sighs.

Our drinks arrive and the waitress eyes us in the same way everyone who isn't around twins does. Like we're so fascinating for sharing identical DNA. We don't get it, but whatever.

Law's phone goes off, and after he checks it, he stares at me with a guilty expression.

"Aww, shit. Here we go. What'd you do—" My gaze catches on two people entering the restaurant. They're hard to miss, because they're both wide and intimidating, which is funny considering they're the nicest guys I know. Hell, the nicest *people* I know. That doesn't stop the anger from rising up. "I fucking hate you, Law. I really fucking hate you." I go to stand, but he reaches out and grabs my arm to stop me.

"Brody doesn't know you're here. Storming out will only draw his attention, so sit down, shut up, and listen to me."

Reed and Brody are ushered to a table in the middle of the room, not exactly shielding us from them, but they're not gonna see us unless they're really looking.

I sit back down and scoot towards the wall, hoping to conceal myself better. "Can't believe you fuckin' parent trapped me."

"That's not what this is."

I glare at him, because he's a lying liar who lies.

"Okay, it's a little bit that, but we're not forcing you to talk to him or even approach him. Just look at him. I'm making you check Schrodinger's box and putting you out of your misery."

"I like living in misery."

"Bullshit. You hate it. You claim to be full of darkness and act all broody, but we both know if it hadn't been for Kyle, you'd already be married and doing the happy thing, and I'd be the bitter twin."

I take a sip of my beer and resist the urge to look in Brody's direction. "Yeah, well, life happens, and it clearly isn't on my side."

"You're not even looking at him."

Because I'm scared of what I'll see.

"Need me to hold your hand?"

I don't know if Law's being serious or taunting me, but it grates on me all the same.

"Fuck you." I glance at Brody and Reed to spite Law and prove I can do it, but then my eyes get stuck.

Brody is the most beautiful man I've ever seen even with his scruffy, unshaven face and the bags under his eyes.

He looks as if he's had as much sleep as I have since I ran out of the apartment.

"What do you see?" Law asks softly.

Someone hurting. "Someone who doesn't deserve to put up with my shit."

"You're probably right about that. He doesn't deserve to put up with your shit, but he's volunteering anyway."

"Don't you feel guilty about dragging Reed into our issues? You're half as fucked up as me, and I know you do."

"I won't lie. I did in the beginning. Especially because it was our issues that led me to lie to him when we met. But that all changed when Reed decided to choose me in spite of all those complications. Just like Brody wants to choose you if you let him."

"It's too hard."

"If you honestly think it'll be too hard, then yes, you should walk away because no one deserves to be hurt that way, but you're thinking it's too hard for all the wrong reasons."

"How so?" I hope Law can explain it to me, because I can't make sense of anything right now—only my need to stay away.

"When I asked you just now what you see, you didn't even mention Kyle, Brody's father, the trial, or your assault. You're worried about how he's dealing."

Law's right. As I continue to stare at Brody across the restaurant, those bitter feelings that have been brewing every time I even think of him aren't there. The thought of him coming home and telling me how he has to represent a murderer doesn't fill me with worry about how I'm going to react to that.

All I care about is that Brody is hurting, and I'm the one who caused it.

I can be the one to stop it too.

Some things are able to be overcome. Some things aren't.

I was terrified my brain had found a deal-breaker. An easy escape. An excuse to put all the work I've done since meeting him to waste.

Instead, it's formed an unspoken vow—that no matter how big my desire to protect my heart is, the need to protect and love Brody is bigger.

In an instant, I'm out of my seat and approaching their table.

The adrenaline pumping through my veins makes my heart race and my mouth dry.

When Brody sees me, his eyes widen.

I can already see the assessing gaze over my body and back up to my face.

"Oh, Anders," Reed says, his eyes comically wide in what I guess is supposed to be shock. "What a surprise."

I stare down at him. "You're an even worse liar than my brother." I tilt my head in the direction of our table. "Go. I need to talk to Brody."

Reed is out of his seat and by Law's side faster than possible.

Brody keeps staring as I take the vacated seat, his expression stoic and totally intimidating.

Where do I start?

I take a deep breath. "I can't promise much."

He doesn't say anything, so I keep going.

"But I miss you."

Nothing.

"When I found out who your dad was, it wasn't just you and me anymore. It was people, and well, I hate people."

Brody finally loses the blank expression, though he's trying desperately not to smile.

"Shit, no, I mean … Fuck, I don't know what I mean. I was scared. Scared of your dad, scared of my ex … Oh, umm, I lied. My attack wasn't random. It was actually my ex?" I don't know why my voice goes up at the end like I'm unsure if that's a question or a statement. "And I realise I should've told you sooner, but I couldn't, and then—"

"Anders, I know everything." His voice is the usual smooth tone that has the ability to calm me even when his words should elicit panic.

"Oh."

"I know it's a total violation of privacy, but you scared me too. I … I looked up your legal file. And then Kyle's. Are … are you mad?"

I shake my head. "I wanted to tell you, but I couldn't say the words. I still can't say them properly."

"I'm not either of them. Your ex or my dad."

God, I hate my brain. My elbows go to the tabletop as I put my head in my hands. "I know. But you're a lawyer like your dad. You represent people like Kyle. I've known that all along but have somehow been able to compartmentalise the two. When your dad walked in ..."

"If I'd known—"

My gaze snaps to his. "How could you though when I never said anything? I came over here to tell you I was wrong to run away and even more wrong to avoid you. But when those two worlds collided, I thought there wouldn't be any more separating them. I couldn't ignore what you do or who you are and thought I wouldn't be able to look at you the same. When I thought of you, I always pictured your dad or Kyle."

"I never wanted to hurt you like that. Ever."

"It's not your fault. Rationally, I know I can't hold it against you, but as you're aware, my anxiety doesn't care what's fair."

Brody leans back in his seat. "You said you can't promise much. What can you promise?"

"I *want* to promise you everything, but I can't. Hurting you would kill me. I want us to work."

An air of defeat surrounds him. "But you don't know how to make that happen."

This is harder than I thought it would be. I want to try, I want to go slow, but at the same time, I'm amazed I've been able to stay on this side of the table for this long.

"Sitting here, right now, all I can think about is reaching for your hand, or hell, getting up and walking the two small steps between us and kissing you until we forget that I ever freaked out."

My heart is now beating in my ears, and I'm terrified of what he might say to that. Starting again might not be an option. No matter how much I want it to be.

"We both know you can't do that."

I lower my head, unable to keep eye contact with his blue, piercing eyes. "I know this is a setback, but—"

Brody's commanding presence by my side catches me off guard, because I'm too distracted by my stupid mouth trying to make words. I don't realise he's beside me until it's too late.

The surprising thing? I don't recoil. Whatever progress we made together has stuck.

I was worried I'd go back to the edgy, unsure guy I always was around him when we first met.

Brody kneels beside me. "We can't forget it because if we did that, we wouldn't be able to learn from it. This isn't a permanent step back. It's one lesson in about a million we'll learn together."

"Together ..." I croak.

A warm hand lands on my cheek. "You're adorable if you think I'm letting you go. Do you forget how persistent I can be?"

"There's persistent, and then there's stupid. I'm still trying to figure out which one you are."

"I'm stupidly persistent about being with you."

"I think that speaks volumes about your intellectual level."

"Dude, I'm the smartest person you know."

I laugh because he's not wrong.

"I'm going to kiss you now, in front of everyone in this crowded restaurant, because I've missed your lips. Almost as much as I've missed you."

I can't find my voice to say *Fuck yes*, but my mouth has it under control.

I've missed Brody. There's no denying that. But once he closes the small gap, leaning up on his knees to kiss me, I feel the true extent of that longing in my bones. I miss him more even though his lips are on mine, his hand is caressing my cheek, and his body heat is so close I'm warm all over, like being covered by a thick blanket when I've been out in the cold for days.

My heart beats rapidly, and for the first time it's not because I'm scared or triggered or nervous. It's because my brain is finally catching up. It's because my heart knows what it wants and what it has wanted all along, only now the darkness inside me is accepting it.

Brody's not someone to fear.

Other things may challenge us and challenge my treatment, but Brody's a constant. If it weren't for his dad, I might not have ever realised that for myself.

I still hate his father. I don't know how this could work without me having to see him. But he's not Brody. Maybe if I repeat that over and over, one day I won't need to remind myself of it.

I try to push all thoughts from my head and focus on the man in front of me.

My man.

Strong lips, demanding tongue, confidently claiming me.

Before I'm ready, though, it all disappears.

Brody pulls away. "Eventually, there'll come a time when I won't have to warn you I'm going to do that."

I almost choke on the pressure he just dumped on me. "And if there isn't?"

Instead of feeding me a dismissive lie of hope or playing it off like it might not be a possibility, he smiles. "Then we keep working at it. We'll get through it all."

"You say that as if it's going to be easy."

"I know it won't be easy."

"This isn't the only freak-out I'm going to have."

"I know that too."

"Then what the fuck is wrong with you?"

Brody laughs. "Why are you being so argumentative?"

"No sane person voluntarily signs on for this shit." I gesture to myself.

I'm in the middle of embracing this, fighting it, and believing it's too good to be true.

"Well, you know what they say: sanity doesn't have anything to do with love."

Cue run-away sequence.

Brody holds me in place. "Before you start panicking again, you need to know I care about you. A lot. I might even love you, but we're going to take this at your pace. I'll go to therapy with you, I'll stand by you, and I'll do anything you need me to do."

Aww, fuck. We're both so screwed.

My heart steadies, and the fog slowly lifts.

He'll give me whatever I need. What I need is Brody.

"I need you to kiss me again," I whisper.

He leans in, everything I want moving closer, painfully slow inch by torturous inch, and then, right when I think his lips are going to be back on mine, he moves away and stands, holding out his hand for me. "I will. At home."

"Home?"

"I want you to keep living with me. In your room. Until the day you're able to fall asleep in mine."

"But if I eventually take your bed, where will you sleep?" I joke.

Brody ignores it and drags me towards the exit.

"Wait. I need to tell Law and Reed we're going." I change our direction.

"Was this a set-up?"

"Yeah, and I'm sure they'll be all smug about knowing it worked." I pull up short when we reach the table, and my brother's eating my meal. "That's not my dinner or anything."

Law shrugs. "I ordered Reed's favourite knowing you two wouldn't be eating."

Cocky son of a bitch.

"You knew I'd go talk to him?"

Law puts his cutlery down and stands. "Faith, brother. I had faith you'd do the right thing."

I'm engulfed in his arms before I can ask him where the punchline is. There's a very good chance I'm about to get emotional and shit, so I push Law away and play it off like our usual roughhousing.

"You sure you two don't want to join us for dinner?" Reed asks.

Brody and I say, "No," at the same time and then laugh, because it's pretty obvious what our emphatic rejection means.

Reed stutters and says, "Uh … umm, have fun with that."

I have no doubt. Because as Brody leads me out of the restaurant and to his car, I realise I'm not nervous. There are no trigger symptoms firing, and there's no dread in the pit of my stomach. All I have is anticipation and need, and they're propelling my feet forward faster than normal.

Brody opens the passenger door for me, and I can't help myself. I steal a kiss, soft and quick.

When I pull back, I stare him dead in the eyes. "Drive fast."

"No."

My eyebrows shoot up to my forehead. "No?"

"I made a promise to myself when I found out what happened to you that I'd protect you with every fibre of my being. And that includes taking care of you on our death-trap roads."

My chest burns. With longing, with love … with everything that is essentially Brody.

"You're kinda perfect."

He dramatically opens his arms wide and laughs. "He finally gets it."

Yeah. Finally.

28

BRODY

The anticipation on the way home from the restaurant might literally kill me. My heart is worried Anders could change his mind at any moment and take it all back.

I can't change who my father is, and I do understand where he's coming from.

To him, I'm just like my dad.

I want to tell him I quit my job, but at the same time, I need him to push through this obstacle. As hard as it will be for him to support my career as a defence attorney, I need him to promise to keep trying with me.

I quit because it was the wrong career choice for me, not to win him back, and I want him to understand that first before I tell him what I did.

My hand is on his thigh, his hand on top of mine. Anytime his grip loosens the tiniest bit, I expect his hand to leave completely and I hold my breath. Then he smiles and holds tighter as if he knows what he's doing.

While I want to get Anders home as fast as possible, I'm wary about pushing too fast or that he'll change his mind or have another panic attack. I need to make sure to take this slow so I don't lose him for good.

I can't let that happen.

I'm in this, hook, line, and sinker.

"Are you hungry?" I ask. "We did leave before food."

"You got anything at home we can cook after?"

"After? After what, Anders?" I ask as innocently as possible.

"If you weren't so adamant about road rules, I'd lean over there and give you a preview."

Suddenly, the speed limit is more of a suggestion than a law. My reservations are drowned out by the need to get home as soon as possible.

The second I pull into our underground garage and park in our designated spot, Anders' seatbelt is off. He comes across the centre console, and his lips land on my cheek and then my neck.

A moan escapes and I throw my head back on my headrest. I want to reach for him. Touch him. But I know our problems haven't disappeared. If anything, they're only more complex.

And they are *our* problems. Not just Anders' anymore.

I want to work through them with him.

I want to be the guy to bring him out of his darkness and give him light until he can shine on his own.

Though the way Anders' hand reaches for my cock and rubs me through my jeans, my self-restraint might protest holding back.

His mouth explores my exposed skin and works its way up to my lips.

Even when he kisses me deep, his tongue searching out mine, I don't move anything but my mouth.

An anguished groan comes from him. "Touch me, Brody. Please."

He doesn't have to tell me twice, but I don't dive right in. I take it slow, cupping his face right over his scar.

"This okay?" I whisper.

His brown eyes bore into mine and get shiny as he says, "Yes. Really yes. Like, I'm surprised by how much I need you to touch me right this second."

"Do you think we can take it upstairs, or will that be pushing our luck?"

Anders looks around the small confines of my Lexus IS. "We can totally do this."

It becomes evident that as soon as I put my seat all the way back and Anders tries to climb into my lap that we totally can't do this.

Anders' back hits the steering wheel and the sound of the horn echoes through the quiet garage while laughter fills the car.

"Fine," he relents. "Upstairs."

It's practically a race to the elevator, and as soon as the doors close to take us up to our floor, Anders is on me again, backing me against the wall and taking my mouth more aggressively than he ever has before.

I take that as a good sign.

When the elevator dings, we stumble our way to our front door, where I fumble with the keys until I *have* to pull away from Anders.

Hand in hand, we enter the apartment all smiles and anticipation.

All of which almost disappear when Anders' gaze darts across the room.

"Hi, Rach."

I drag him through the apartment without even looking at her. "Bye, Rach."

"Am I going to need noise-cancelling headphones?" she calls after us.

"If you're gonna keep staying here, yeah." I slam the door behind us.

"I'm glad you made up!" she yells. "I'm going out for dinner. A long one."

"Well, that takes care of her." I shuck off my T-shirt.

"Bring us back some food," Anders yells. "And that takes care of dinner."

"Brilliant."

Anders steps closer to me and eyes the bed. "I see you didn't get rid of the restraints."

"You can call it being cocky if you like, but honestly, it's been out of pure hope. I didn't want this to be the end of us."

Anders takes a deep breath. "Me either. I don't want anything to come between us."

It means so much to me for him to say that. "I know that might not be possible, but as long as you promise to try and keep trying to come back to me. To trust me. Trust that no matter what, I'm here for you."

"I'll try. Now, get on the bed." He shoves me until I fall onto my back on the bed.

"Nngh." I love confident Anders.

Actually, I love quirky Anders too.

I love every aspect of him, even the ugly, dark sides of his past.

Now to prove it to him.

29

ANDERSON

I climb on top of Brody's large body. "I want to try something."

"If it's shibari, I'm gonna have to say no. I mean, it looks hot, but I can see it now. You'll forget how to untie me, and then there'll be scissors way too close to my junk for my liking."

The laugh is on the tip of my tongue, but it's the realisation he even knows what shibari is that stops me short. "You researched bondage?"

Brody looks uncomfortable and glances away. "I researched a lot. And not just the bondage stuff."

"What other stuff?"

"PTSD, domestic abuse ... drug addiction."

I swallow hard.

"Intimacy issues for survivors, local psychologists so I could meet with someone ..." he continues.

"Umm, why?"

"I've had a lot of time since ..."

"Since?"

Brody stares up at me, his brown hair falling across his

forehead and sincerity shining in his eyes. "Since you walked out. I wanted to do everything I possibly could to try to understand what you've been through and to learn to be the kind of guy you need going forwards. If there was a *going forwards*."

"Fuck, Brody," I whine.

"What?"

"I don't know where you and Reed came from, but it has to be like some sort of angel exchange program for broken-ass guys like my brother and me."

He chuckles. "What we're about to do is anything but angelic. Actually, it's probably downright sinful."

"About that. It's what I want to try. I was talking to Ed, and—"

"You were still going to him?"

"I was going to cancel my last appointment, but it was too late, and I would've had to pay anyway, so I figured I may as well see if I could get anything out of it. I went and explained our situation, and he kinda gave me tips on hooking up comfortably without bringing out the restraints right away."

"Hook-ups. Like, with other people?"

"It wasn't like I was going to go out and test it out anytime soon ... or at all. It was something to fill the session seeing as I thought you weren't going to be an option anymore. But one thing he mentioned I thought might've worked for us."

"What's that?"

"It's the power dynamics that messes with my head, right? So, Ed suggested I even the playing field in other ways."

"How?"

I begin unbuttoning Brody's shirt. "Using logic. If someone's naked, for instance, they're less likely to get violent with a person who's fully clothed."

"I guess?"

"If I'm completely dressed and I begin getting upset, it'll be a lot easier for me to run away."

"True. Though, I don't want you to run away."

I shake my head. "I wouldn't with you, but it's the mindset that counts. The power balance."

Brody's hands run up and down my torso, from my chest to my stomach and back again. "That sounds like something I'd be willing to explore …"

"But? Sounds like there's a but coming."

"I've missed your skin on mine, and I like—no, I *love* being tied up. It gives me something I didn't even know I was missing. Tonight, I want all of you."

"Quite demanding, aren't we? Who's the one in charge here?" I joke, because we both know it's him.

I like it when he takes charge. So long as I have the control, he can pretty much tell me to do anything, and I'll do it.

Never, not once in the last five years did I think I'd be able to feel this way about someone again.

I want to give myself over to him. I want to give him everything.

Reaching behind me, I pull my shirt over my head.

This part is the easy part. I've learned I have a certain level of comfort with Brody until the clothes start coming off and I get lost in him.

I can enjoy this. Leaning down and kissing him. Running my hands over his impressive chest. Grinding against his hard cock.

"Anders? We're still wearing too many clothes."

When I scramble off him and stand, we shed our clothes and Brody reaches for the cuffs.

I want to make a joke about him being a good boy, but

honestly, the view of him cuffing himself is too hot to form any words at all.

He reaches for the second but can't quite get it right. "Going to need help with this one."

It reminds me how far this guy is going for me to be comfortable, for us to be together, and so I decide something.

I fasten the buckles on Brody's other wrist and then reach for supplies in the bedside drawer.

Brody widens his thighs and places his feet on the bed to give me access to that ass of his, but I have no plans on taking it.

Instead, I lean over him and lick from the base of his cock to the tip and then engulf him completely. He's only half-hard, so I coax him to full mast.

He moans, and I savour the sound I didn't know I'd missed so much.

When he's gasping for air, I pull off him and open a condom. Instead of putting it on me though, I roll it down his hard shaft.

"What are you—"

"I want this."

"Are you sure? Because you know I'm okay with—"

"I'm one hundred percent sure. Been thinking about it since the moment I met you, and now I'm ready."

Brody smiles, lighting me up inside.

"I love—" He clears his throat. "I love topping from the bottom."

I snort. Cocky Brody. *My* cocky Brody.

Seeing as he's tied up, I have to prep myself, and it's been so long that when I reach back and work a lubed finger inside me, I almost immediately want to take back this decision.

My mind is ready, but maybe my body isn't.

Taking a deep breath, I inch in a little more, close my eyes, and tell myself to breathe through it.

I can do this.

It's Brody.

I imagine how good it'll feel to have his cock splitting me apart. To ride him until I come all over his chest.

"You still with me?" he asks.

My gaze flies to his, and I get trapped in his blue orbs.

The concern in them makes me want to do better. Be better.

I get to two fingers and scissor them, trying to stretch myself enough to accommodate Brody's proportionally sized dick.

"This isn't me suggesting you should untie me, but I wish I could be the one doing that," Brody whispers.

"Me too." I want to get there one day so badly.

"I'd suck you off while I prepped you."

I smile when I realise what he's doing. His voice calms me because it's uniquely Brody. It reminds me who I'm with and what I'm working towards. "Yeah? What else would you do?"

"Lick you. Tease you. Open you up until you were begging for my cock."

Biting my lip, I close my eyes and try to imagine a day where there's nothing holding Brody and me back.

I ride my fingers while Brody murmurs encouraging words. It adds to my fantasy that one day we'll have it all. No restraints, no anxiety. Just us.

"Anders, I'm going to need you to hurry up or I'm going to come from watching you."

I tremble, because I could make myself come like this.

"Need you," Brody pleads.

That's all it takes to get me moving. I position myself on top of him and line his cock up with my hole. Then I send a prayer up to the ass gods and just hope I'm truly ready for him, because he's not small.

As if reading my hesitance, Brody says, "Take it slow."

I sink down on him, and we both let out a shuddery breath. Brody mimics my breathing as I take deep gulps, waiting for the sting to disappear.

"You got this," Brody says, his voice tight. "I might not, because holy fuck, you're so tight, but you got it."

With a little laugh, I take more of him.

"Holy hell," he mutters.

Brody's hands tighten around the straps of his restraints, something he does when he doesn't know whether to embrace them or fight against being held down. His muscles tighten, his face flushes, and lust clouds his eyes.

I move on top of him slowly, waiting for the sting of stretching around him to go away. The expression on Brody's face every time I take a little more of him inside me makes me melt just that little bit more.

It's not the first time I've tried bottoming since my attack, but it is the first time it's gotten this far.

I've forgotten what it's like to be full, stretched to the point of pain but only craving more.

With my hands next to Brody's head, I lean down and take his mouth. I like kissing him. Like leaving beard rash on his chin.

The marks I leave when we're together are accomplishments of sorts. Not that I've made him mine or that I'm marking him but that they're evidence that I'm doing this. I'm taking control of my life and living instead of hiding.

Brody's hips thrust upwards, his cock pegs my prostate, and I call out.

"Oh, fuck."

"Shit, are you okay?" Brody asks.

"Do it again."

He laughs. "I'll take that as a yes."

I move with him, meeting his thrusts and getting lost in the sensation of being on top of him, his cock inside me.

With Brody being tied up, I'm able to get lost, get out of my head, and just *feel*.

And being with Brody feels fucking amazing.

I'm able to relax completely, taking him all the way inside me until he's so far past incoherent, I don't know if his curses are even in English anymore.

I've missed being able to have sex uninhibited and free. I sit upright and ride him, not a warning sign or moment of self-consciousness in sight.

And it's so fucking beautiful I could almost cry.

But something could make it even better. The idea sends butterflies fluttering in my stomach, and a little anxiousness creeps in. To pull it off though? Nothing would make me happier.

I slow my hips and sink down on him one last time until I'm fully seated.

"What's wrong?" Brody asks breathlessly.

"Nothing." I'm just as breathless.

I run my hand down Brody's chest, feeling his erratic heartbeat. "I want to try something."

"What?"

Leaning over, I reach for one of his cuffs.

"Anders." He sounds panicked almost.

"It's okay. It's only one."

He turns his head and watches as I undo the buckles on his left wrist. "Are you sure?"

"I trust you."

Brody stares up at me warmly.

I place his hand over my heart. "Can you keep it there?"

He nods.

Slowly, I start moving again, fucking myself on his cock. His hand remains where I left it—right over my heart. It's the piece of me that might have always been his but that my head wouldn't allow me to acknowledge.

"It's beating so fast," Brody whispers.

"That's all because of you. Because of us."

It doesn't take long for the need to go faster to take over. Our grunts and the slapping of our bodies meeting are the only sounds in the room.

Where orgasms usually build and ebb and flow until we spill over, Brody's hits out of nowhere with no warning.

He shudders beneath me, calling out and emptying into the condom inside me. I reach for my cock, and it only takes three strokes for me to lose my load all over Brody's stomach.

I slump forward, burying my head in the crook of Brody's shoulder. His free hand wraps around my back and trails down my spine.

"That was—" Brody starts, but stops when I tremble and sniff loudly.

Shit, I really am crying.

"What's wrong?" Brody asks, panicked.

He struggles, and I remember one of his hands is still restrained.

"Fuck." I climb off him and reach to free him.

The second I do, he pulls me into his arms, and we lie side by side. I'm surprised I don't have the itch to get up and get dressed and be less vulnerable, but right now I need to let it all out.

Sobs rack my exhausted body, and if I'm honest, I don't even know where it's coming from.

"What did I do?"

I cut Brody off by kissing him. "These are ... I think they're happy tears? I think my body hasn't embarrassed myself enough around you and thinks being the clichéd guy who cries after sex will top it off nicely."

Brody eyes me, trying to figure out if I'm lying.

"I promise. I just ..." I wipe my eyes. "That was perfect."

A big hand cups my face. "As long as you're okay."

"I am now. Now I know how it can be."

Brody kisses me softly. "I'm going to go get cleaned up, but I'll be right back, okay?"

Reluctantly, I let him up and roll onto my back.

I watch him walk around the bed and head for the bathroom, but I'm not gonna lie to myself. As soon as he's out of sight, the vulnerability sneaks in and I have to get up and at least put my boxers back on. It's a safety precaution, because if the need to escape is there, I won't be running buck naked down the streets of Southbank.

I wish my need to protect myself again didn't come so soon after a perfect moment, but hey, at least it didn't come in the middle of sex.

My brain so badly wants to make a coming in the middle of sex joke, but I'm still trying to shake off the disappointment of the high being chased away so quickly.

Brody comes out of the bathroom and doesn't even blink at me being dressed again. He just goes and puts his own clothes back on.

Then he approaches and kisses my cheek. "We have stuff we should probably talk about."

"Like what?"

"Are you guys decent yet?" yells a voice from the living room.

Brody sighs. "She's back."

My stomach growls. "Clearly, I'm not as upset over that as you are."

"I am kind of hungry after that." Brody rubs his wrists which are all red.

I take his hands in mine and kiss the irritated skin. "I hope one day we can do this without the restraints. I don't like seeing you hurt."

"They're fine. Definitely worth it. Let's get the rest of our clothes on and pretend we didn't fuck the whole time Rachel was gone."

Yeah, that might be possible if Rachel didn't give us a knowing look as we leave the bedroom and head for the dining table where she's waiting for us.

"I thought you were going for a long, long, super-long dinner?" Brody asks.

"That was the plan, but then I felt like a loser eating by myself, so I decided to bring stuff home and just hope things were, umm, short. I figured, it's been almost two weeks, right? It'd be like opening a can of Pepsi after shaking it."

"Hey," Brody protests. "There was nothing short about— okay, you know what, maybe let's not have this conversation?"

Rachel laughs. "Good plan. Anyway, after wandering around aimlessly past a few restaurants, I settled on Thai. Hope that's okay."

"I'm starving," I say. "I will eat just about anything right now."

Rachel looks up at the roof and mutters, "You boys are making this too easy."

I snort laugh.

As I take the seat next to Rachel, who's at the head of the table and across from Brody, she gently pats my arm.

"I'm so happy you're back."

I think I'd spent a whole twenty-four hours with Rachel before I ran away from her brother. Maybe she's not as overprotective as Brody is, but I expect her to be a little mad.

"You're not angry at me for running away and hurting Brody?"

She looks me square in the eyes. "Your reasons for needing to run away are as valid as Brody's need to quit his job. Sometimes you just gotta do you." She rolls her eyes. "God, now I'm making it easy. Do you." She laughs. "That's funny."

I miss her joke completely because I get stuck on Brody quitting his job.

When I look at him, his head is in his hands.

"Didn't really get the chance to tell him that part yet, Rach."

"You quit your job," I say. "Like, your job. With your dad. As a lawyer."

Brody's lips twitch on one side. "I didn't quit being a lawyer. I'll find a new job. Something less ... morally compromising."

Guilt kicks me in the gut. "B-because of me?"

"Yes, but—"

"You can't quit because of me and my fucked-up issues. I won't let you. I'll call your dad myself if that's what it takes for you to not change your whole fucking life because of me." That's too much pressure. Too much to live up to. And they're not his issues. They're all mine.

Brody's smile gets wider, and I don't understand. "Calm the farm a little." He reaches over the top of the table to hold my hand. "I did quit because of you, but not because you ran away from me or were freaking out or because I thought you needed me to do it to get past our problems. I did it because I couldn't sit in that conference room another second trying to come up with ways to get a rapist off scot-free. I kept imagining that kid's victim staring at me the way you stared at my father. I couldn't do it to that girl, and I couldn't do it to myself. You were part of the reason I quit, but the biggest reason was because I needed to do what was right for me and my morality."

I sit back, completely awestruck by the man in front of me.

"Well, that, and he called his client a rapist to his face." Rachel laughs. "So if he didn't quit, he was probably gonna be fired."

"You what?" I exclaim.

Brody shrugs. "My emotions might have been slightly elevated?"

Rachel turns to me. "You have the ability to make my brother emotional. I want to keep you."

"Not if I keep him first," Brody taunts. "If that's all right with you?" He stares at me expectantly, and maybe I should be freaking out, but I'm not.

"It's more than all right with me."

Maybe I shouldn't be thinking long-term promises here—not that making a joke about keeping me is a binding vow or anything—but all that's inside me right now is something deep and meaningful and promising.

Hope.

30

ANDERSON

SIX MONTHS LATER

Wynnum Correctional Facility Parole Board.
My hand reaches for the stool underneath the kitchen bench so I can steady myself as I stare at the official emblem on the envelope addressed to me. We've been expecting it. Anticipating it. Brody and I have talked about it with Karen and each other. I've been preparing for this. Yet, it still doesn't soften the blow of actually seeing it.

I already know what it'll say inside.

Kyle Atkins has been released. He's done his time and has paid his debt to society, even though society isn't the one he hurt.

It was me.

I land my ass on the stool, my elbows on the counter, and I stare at the offending letter.

Trigger symptoms simmer in my veins, trying to come to a boil, but I don't let them.

I've been learning to control them better, and with the help of new medication, it's getting easier to do.

I was reluctant to try meds again because of all the other times it fucked me up. Just once I'd love to see "Caution:

causes dick growth" on the list of side effects instead of the super fun things like: "Mood swings, suicidal thoughts, insomnia, depression ..." The list goes on and on.

But when Karen told me of a new one on the market that is supposed to be really good for anxiety, I decided to try it. If it didn't work, I'd maybe struggle for a little bit, but the payoff could've meant the difference between Brody and I growing more as a couple and getting over our last few hurdles or remaining in our comfort zone.

Things with Brody couldn't be better in one sense, but if we were to compare it to a "normal" relationship, we're still behind the eight ball. We try not to measure ourselves against Law and Reed; it's better for our wellbeing to pretend they're the abnormal ones by being so damn happy all the time.

Before the new meds, I still couldn't sleep in Brody's bed. No matter how comfortable I was, no matter how tired or wiped, I couldn't make myself do it. And Brody never let me get the chance to get so tired that I'd pass out again like I did that night we fell asleep on the couch.

He's been patient and loving, and now that I've levelled out on the new meds, we've actually managed nights where I'd get a full two to three hours of sleeping next to him.

Might sound small, but that's the thing with us. We're able to appreciate the things most couples take for granted.

Like the simple act of falling asleep together.

Everything has been going so well, we've been reluctant to push too hard.

And with this envelope sitting in front of me, I'm worried this is going to force me to push more than I'm willing. This could turn into a setback, and it's been so long since I've had one of those. Almost six months to be exact. I haven't been this on edge since I found out who Brody's dad was.

I'm scared the nightmares will come back, which have been absent for months.

I'm worried the meds will stop working or will be recalled because they're so new to the market or I'll need to stop taking them for some reason. It's the one medication that has worked more than anything else, and if I have to stop taking it, I'll start having panic attacks again.

Worst of all, I'm terrified that Kyle getting out will hit a giant reset button on any of the progress I've made in the six years he's been away.

I never went to visit him while he was locked up. Not once. Karen had suggested it, and then she used the dreaded *C* word on me: closure.

I didn't need closure when it came to Kyle. My ex-boyfriend was a psycho. End of story. No closure needed.

He didn't deserve my attention.

No, just my sanity.

I hate that I've given him so much of my past six years. He doesn't deserve any more.

It's not fair he's being released while I'm still suffering—I'll be suffering to some degree for the rest of my life—but he gets to move on. He gets a life.

That's when Meatball jumps up on the counter and head-butts my hand. While pulling her to me and cuddling her, I look around at the evidence of *my* life.

I've become comfortable in the spacious and homey apartment. I'm even more comfortable here than I am at Law and Reed's place. Law has been my safety net for so long, I never thought I'd have this feeling anywhere but with him.

I have a grumpy cat who loves me, and, for some reason, is only grumpy towards everyone else. Although, she's tolerant of her servant boy, Brody.

And best of all is Brody. My man. The only person who

makes me feel safe and out of control at the same time. He drives me crazy in both good ways and bad. He's the most patient person I know, and I still don't know how he puts up with my shit half the time.

But I never question it.

He's seen me at my worst, and he only brings out the best in me.

The front door to the apartment clicks open, and the devil himself steps through wearing his business pants, collared shirt, and sweater.

His new job at Legal Aid is a lot more casual than his old job at his dad's firm, but it's still just as stressful. At least now when he comes home and complains about a case, he's on the right side of the argument.

Brody took it as a sign that when he enquired about working with them, they needed someone in their Family and Domestic Abuse department. He's helping more people like me, and while I don't like to hear details of the cases, I know he's doing a good job.

And the best thing? Working for a government department means he's home at a reasonable time every day.

The pay is half what he was getting at his dad's firm, but aside from my therapy bills, we don't have many expenses.

Brody must've had a good day because he drops his briefcase by the couch and stalks towards me and Meatball with a giant smile on his face.

His lips land on the top of my head and then the cat's. "My two favourite people."

"Since when is Meatball people?"

He waves his hand. "You know what I mean. How long do we have until we have to be at your brother's thing?"

"Half an hour."

Brody's eyebrows waggle. "Plenty of time for blowjobs, then?"

A laugh bursts from my throat.

Over the past few months, we've managed to have sex without restraints, but we've both agreed it might take a few more times for it to become *good* sex. It's kinda awkward—a lot of reassuring, too much worrying, and it's slow. All of which, Ed Shearon assures us, is healthy and understandable.

Still, it's been another small step in the right direction.

Blowjobs though, those, we've pretty much mastered. Even if Brody still has to sit on his hands. At least he doesn't need to be properly bound. Though if we're not after a quickie, he'll always ask to be restrained because he loves it even more than I need it.

I place Meatball on the counter and spin on my stool. Brody's chest is right there in front of me, begging me to run my hands all over it.

The chance to do it doesn't happen though, because Brody's gaze flicks to the envelope I haven't yet opened.

"Oh, shit." Brody reaches for it. "Need me to call Karen?"

Yes, my boyfriend and my therapist are on a first-name basis. No, it's not weird. Not weird at all.

It's a little weird.

"I thought you were giving me a blowjob." Oh, deflection, my oldest and dearest friend.

"You haven't opened it?" Brody ignores me. Damn him.

I shake my head. "It's nothing we weren't expecting."

"How do you know? He might've gotten shanked in prison and now he's not our problem. One could hope …"

"You're so cute, getting all violent-y for me." I pat the top of his head. "But I'm sure they wouldn't send me a letter saying, 'You're free!' if that were to happen. We both know it's gonna say *he's* free."

Brody stares at the envelope the same way I have been for the past half an hour. "Want me to open it for you?"

That envelope is gonna be opened one way or another, so I take it out of his hands. "I'll do it." It's my thing. Karen would insist I put my big-boy pants on.

The paper weighs a hundred kilos suddenly. Taking a deep breath, I rip it open to get it over with.

I mentally prepare for a bad reaction. To panic. Maybe break down.

Reading over the exact words we were expecting is as anti-climactic as my life ever gets. I have no reaction, good or bad. I'm numb and stoic and surprisingly neutral.

"Oh God, you've gone catatonic. I'm gonna call Law and then Karen, and then—"

"Brody," I say slowly.

His eyes meet mine.

"I'm okay." Weirdly.

"How okay?"

"I dunno. I'm just … okay. For now."

"When does he get out?"

I take a deep breath. "He actually got out two days ago."

"And they're only telling you now?" he booms and snatches the letter from me.

"It's my fault. I'd forwarded my mail for six months and forgot to renew it. I think this has been floating around trying to find me."

He narrows his eyes. "How … How are you not losing it right now? I feel like I could lose it, and I don't even know the guy. I don't understand."

I don't either. Not really. "I hate him. I hate him more than I've ever hated anything or anyone in my entire life. If I could choose between having him gone forever but being stuck with this stupid anxiety or knowing he's in my life and being fine, I would choose to be like this but never have to worry about seeing him again."

"I'll make sure you never see him again."

I don't doubt Brody's conviction. "There's something else though."

"What?"

"Knowing he's out in the world, there's a new voice inside me that seems to be louder than all the others."

"You're hearing voices? I'm calling Karen."

I chuckle. Wrapping my arms around Brody's waist, I pull him towards me. I'm still sitting, so I lay my head on his chest, because what I need to get out is going to give away the fact that I'm so in love with this man I can barely stand it.

I'm with someone who shows me daily what true love is. Not manipulated love or angry love. Not complicated love. It's not co-dependent like what I have with my brother.

Brody has given me the ability to stand on my own, but I choose to stand with him.

"The voice belongs to you," I whisper. "You make me believe I can work through anything and survive. You let me borrow your strength until I'm strong enough to carry my weight myself. And this"—I take the letter—"is just something else I won't let drag me back down." I swallow hard. "Because of you."

"Aww, Anders." Brody's voice is croaky which is not like him.

When I raise my head, Brody's eyes are wet, and I realise it's time.

"I love you," I blurt. "I'm in love with you."

His eyes widen, because yeah, even though I know it, and I've known it for a while, I haven't had the courage to say it.

Brody's hinted on his side. Said things and then taken them back.

We're still building trust and getting better every day, but this love thing with him is easy.

"I love you too." Brody's body relaxes into me, as if the weight of the world's been lifted off his chest.

"You've been holding on to that for a while, huh?" I'm only half-joking.

"You have no idea."

I grin. "I kinda do. Do you know you talk in your sleep sometimes?"

He gasps. "I do not."

"Yeah, you do."

"Fuck, I'm so sorry. I didn't want to put that pressure on you, and—"

I cut him off with my lips on his. It's brief and only to make a point, and when I pull back, Brody looks at me with a cute confusion line across his forehead.

"The reason I didn't bring it up is because I wasn't ready, but I knew they were my issues and not yours. You've never once pressured me to do anything, and I love that about you. I love everything about you."

"Mmm, someone's earning their blowjob."

I snort. "Sadly, now there's only twenty minutes until Law's expecting us, and it takes fifteen to get there. You gonna go change too?"

Stupid letter is now cockblocking me as well as delivering shitty news.

Brody huffs. "Fine. But tonight. When we get home."

"Promise."

I force a smile though. This apartment is a new safety zone for me. I've accepted Kyle's release while inside these walls, but I'm worried once I get out there, it'll be different, and a panic attack is a nice way to spoil an evening of orgasms.

Only, I'm not going to hide from whatever reaction I have. I'll fight it every step of the way.

While Brody was the catalyst that made me want to finally get better, I know all the work I've done has been me. I've gotten myself to this point. Sure, I've had a lot of help from a few different people, but it's been my journey, and this is just another obstacle for me to overcome.

I might not be sure of much, but my fight instincts are stronger than ever. No matter what the world throws at me.

The plan is to not tell Law the news on his big night, but all that's shot to shit when we arrive and Brody beelines it over to my brother and Reed immediately.

The new dojo is packed and probably close to breaking the fire safety code, but the thing about Brody is he's such a commanding presence, people part for him like they're the goddamn Red Sea.

I'm not so lucky.

I have to practically fight my way through the crowd.

"He's out," Law says as I reach them. His skin pales, and for a second I think we've switched bodies or something. "He's out." His panicked gaze turns to me. "Are you okay?"

"I'm fine. It's okay. Well, not okay, but I'm handling it. I promise."

"He could come after you." Law starts shaking, and again, I'm wondering if we're having a *Freaky Friday* moment. Is this what I look like when I have a panic attack? Because it's fucking scary.

Reed's at his side instantly, putting his arm around him.

"He's not coming for Anders," Brody says. "It's part of his parole conditions. He's still got four years of probation, and if he comes near Anders, he'll go back to prison." He lowers his voice and mumbles, "If I don't kill him first."

The probation might be the only reason I'm not freaking out like Law right now. Kyle might be out, but legally he can't come and see me. A piece of paper won't stop him if he was adamant, which is probably why my eyes keep darting to the door every few minutes, but logically and deep down, I think Kyle wouldn't risk it.

He's not dumb.

With Law breaking down at his own dojo opening, my confidence in being able to stay calm wavers, but with one squeeze of my hand from Brody, one look of assurance, I know I can do it.

We can do it.

"If I'm dealing, you're gonna be fine," I say lightly.

Law looks at me as if I'm joking about killing puppies. "Anders—"

"Stop. I know you're gonna try to pull the overprotective shit, and I get it. I do. I also know you have your own demons when it comes to Kyle, but for real. I'm okay."

"Are you sure?" Law asks.

"I don't like that he's out, and if this had happened last year, I probably would've needed to be sedated or something. But you know how far I've come in the last twelve months. I've got it covered."

It's probably the first time in six years where my twin has analysed me and wondered if I'm lying when I'm actually telling the truth.

He nods. "Okay."

I clap his shoulder. "Let's get this bitch opened."

Law backhands my chest. "Dude. There are kids here with parents who are prospective clients. So just ..."

"Don't say *bitch*. Got it."

"*Behave*," Law says and leads Reed to the front of the dojo where there's a raised platform for Law to do his demonstrations.

Brody leans in, his breath hot on my ear. "Behaving doesn't sound like fun at all."

"Right? Maybe I should get changed into a gi and pretend to be Law. Ooh, we could totally pull the switcheroo and make future clients think Law's a ninja."

Brody laughs. "You'd have to shave your beard to do that."

My face drops. "Oh. Right."

"You know I'd still think you're hot no matter what, right?" His lips land on my beard, right on top of my scar. "Battle wounds and all."

"I know," I say quietly. "I'd shave if it was only you or my family who'd see it. But when strangers ask what happened, it gets a little trigger-y."

"Fair enough. How are you really doing? You keep looking at the doors."

"I'm ..." I think about the right word to describe what's going on with me. "Hopeful."

"Hopeful?" He sounds confused.

"I thought the letter would set me off. It's kinda like when we found ourselves on that double date with Chris and Rhett. I keep waiting for the freak-out to come, and I'm glad that it's not. But I can't say with certainty that I won't flip about it all at some point."

Brody pulls me close. "As long as you keep me updated if you do flip out. We're all here for you."

He nods towards the front where my parents stand off to the side with Reed while Law takes to the stage with a microphone. He welcomes everyone and starts his speech as a little sprite in the form of Brody's sister bounds up next to us.

"Hey. I'm here. I know I'm late."

Rachel crashed on our couch for two months before she completely shocked us by taking a receptionist job at Brody's old law firm with their dad. Then she moved in with him.

She said something about wanting to get to know the father Brody knew, because it certainly wasn't the man she saw when she looked at their father.

Honestly, I think it'd be easier for Rachel and me if John Davenport was a huge asshole who didn't care. The man I met in depositions years ago was just a man doing his job and doing it well. That's all.

It's not personal, and I understand that, but it does make it harder to hate the man. Don't get me wrong, I still hate him. I just know I probably shouldn't. Not if I want a future with Brody.

Since Brody quit his job, he has weekly dinners with his father that I'm always invited to but never attend. Brody tells me his father wants to put Kyle's trial behind us, but I'm not ready. Maybe one day, but definitely not yet, and definitely not soon. They respect that and even understand it, so they're leaving it up to me to make the first move.

"You came," Brody says to his sister.

"Law is like a brother to me," Rachel says.

Both Brody and I wear confused expressions.

"You two are together, Law is Anders' brother, therefore, Law is like a brother to me." Rachel logic. "Duh. Plus, he's giving me free self-defence lessons."

Brody hangs his head. "You do realise this whole thing is basically a charity, right? He's helping queer kids learn to defend themselves."

"What's your point?"

"You have money. *Pay* him."

"You mean Dad has money. I'm broke."

"Shh." I stop their bickering, because Law's speech is getting real now.

"Growing up, I always knew I was going to be a teacher. I planned to be in a classroom, shaping the minds of the world's future generations. Instead, I'm teaching youth how to protect themselves from an unsafe world. It wasn't my first choice in career, but I can't imagine ever doing anything else. The fact I even needed more space because of the demand shows how important places like this are. It's not just somewhere to come and learn martial arts. It's a safe space. Somewhere I hope kids turn in a time of need. And it all started because of my brother, Anders."

He gestures in my direction, and everyone turns to get a glimpse of me.

Thanks, Law.

My neck heats, and I'm sure I'm turning red. Attention in public doesn't usually get to me, but this is too close to home. I'm a little too raw and exposed.

Brody leans in. "You're so cute when you blush."

"Shut up," I grumble.

"I have about a million other people to thank for helping me get this centre off the ground. My parents, my students. But most of all, my partner, Reed." He waves Reed up on stage, where they hug to a round of applause and cheers.

Reed mouths something I'm pretty sure is "Love you."

When the applause dies down, I expect Law to sign off quickly and get on with the night, but he doesn't.

No, he certainly does not.

Brody, Rach, and I watch as my boneheaded brother gets down on one knee.

"Holy shit," Brody and I say at the same time.

My brother takes Reed's hand and holds the mic in the other. "None of this would've been possible without you pushing and encouraging me every day. You support me in everything, and I want to do the same for you. Reed Garvey, will you be my hus—"

"Yes!" our mother calls out from the sidelines.

"—band." Law laughs, along with everyone else.

Note to self, if I ever go to take this step, don't invite Mum.

Reed looks down at my brother still on his knee as if Law created the world or something. "I want nothing more than to be your husband."

Law stands and kisses Reed to even louder screams and applause.

I feel Brody's body heat as he moves even closer to me, wrapping his arms around me from behind.

"Ever wonder if you'd want that one day?"

That's a heavy question. "Wonder? Sure. Think it'll happen? Probably not. I guess I find it too much like ownership, and then that has negative memories attached. But I dunno ... maybe if a handsome lawyer asked me one day, I'd have to seriously consider it."

"Mmm, I don't need it if you don't want it. I mean, after all, it's only been one hour since you first told me you love me. Marriage might be jumping a few steps."

I laugh. "Just a few. I predict we'll be trying to out-uncle each other before any wedding bells."

Brody turns serious. "Oh, it's on already. I'm going to start stocking up on gifts and candy for the kids Law and Reed don't have yet."

"What about my kids?" Rachel whines.

"Do you have kids we're unaware of?" Brody asks.

"No, but I could have one."

"You're single," I point out.

She huffs. "You two are no fun. I'm gonna go hit up the bar."

"You do that," Brody says and then lowers his head and nibbles on my neck. "Can we go home yet?"

"No."

Brody and I both snap to attention at Law's voice. He's now right in front of us with his *fiancé*, getting back pats and congratulations all round.

"Bold move, brother," I say when there's a din in the crowd.

"It's not my only bold move. I have something to show you." He tips his head towards the exit.

Brody holds my hand and mirrors my confused expression as we follow my brother and Reed outside.

Mum and Dad are already waiting out there for us.

Mum has been hesitant about Brody ever since she found out we're together. It's not that she doesn't like him—she loved him before I told her he's my new boyfriend—but she worries about me getting hurt again or losing myself worse than I already have.

That's just her worrying nature. I'm sure over time she'll come to realise how good Brody is for me.

"I was going to show everyone this and do a big reveal type thing, but I changed my mind at the last minute. I wanted to show you first." Law takes hold of a rope connected to the banner covering the sign. "I give you the Steele Brothers Dojo."

The sign is revealed, and I stare at the name. I can't stop.

"You ... you named it after us," I stutter.

"Uh, yeah, I did."

"It's ... It's ..."

"It's perfect," Brody says for me.

Law steps forward and hugs me. "Love you, brother."

This means so much. Law's doing what I don't have the strength to. I've come to talk to his students before about what I went through, but they're teenagers, so it's not like I gave them the deep and gory details.

Law's teaching queer kids how to protect themselves from more than random hate crimes. He's teaching them how to protect themselves against those who are also supposed to love us.

He's teaching self-confidence and awareness, and if it helps one person walk away from a situation like mine before it's too late, then I think my brother's a hero.

"I want to help," I blurt.

Law smiles. "I thought you might. I was thinking I could set a block of time for you to teach your own beginner's class."

"I really, *really* want to do that," I say.

Law hugs me again.

Tonight's been a bit of a whirlwind, but if it's shown me anything, it's reiterated that I've changed from the guy I was a year ago—sleeping around, not looking after myself, and thinking I was cured because I hadn't needed therapy in a long time.

The truth is I was running. I was running away from everything I should've been facing head-on.

Here I am twelve months later, surrounded by an amazing support system, the greatest partner anyone could ask for, and I have faith I won't crumble under pressure.

And when my brother lets me go, my biggest supporter takes his place.

Brody's strong arms wrap around me. There's barely a time where he's not touching me in some way these days. Now that I'm used to it, I crave his hands on me. It's not a possessive thing but a comfort thing—reassurance to let me know he's still there.

He'll always be there.

Long gone are the days of flinching and trying to get away from him.

My weakness doesn't define me when I'm with him. It doesn't claw at me and try to suffocate my soul.

"I love you," I say.

"Oh wow. Now that it's out there, you're going to be saying it all the time, huh?"

"Yep."

He holds me tighter. "Good. Because I wouldn't have it any other way."

Neither would I.

DEAR READER

Takes a deep breath

Confession time.

I usually do my Dear Readers at the beginning of a book, but I didn't want my experiences to affect your perspective before you had a chance to read Anders' story.

This book kicked my ass in ways I never expected.

Anyone in my reader group knows how long it took to write this book. I've touched on it briefly, but I've remained quiet about why it's taken so long.

Whenever asked about Anders, I'd laugh it off and say, "Oh, it'll be done when he starts cooperating!"

It's not because the characters were difficult or not talking to me, or not because I was lacking for inspiration. This book affected me because I had to face a lot of things I've been avoiding.

The funny thing about writing Anders' story was thinking it would be easy. Me, a diagnosed agoraphobe who has the same anxiety disorder as Anders should be able to write pages of this stuff, right? It should fall out of me.

No. I struggled. I struggled hard.

Anders made me face my anxiety head on, and nothing has ever been more confronting than analysing those irrational thoughts holding me back from life, from the outside world, and from dealing with my own demons.

I cried writing this book. That should've been in my trigger warnings, because I don't cry. Ever. Well, unless I'm having an anxiety attack. Or if I'm reading *The Fault in Our Stars*. Okay, okay, I cry sometimes, but the point is I don't cry *easily*. It's rare for a book of fiction to affect me that way unless it involves someone dying.

Anders' book, while heavier than my usual light and fluffy tone, isn't a sad book. I know that. I wanted to give Anders hope while also addressing real issues, but it's those real issues that had me floundering.

I connected and related to the way Anders' anxiety takes hold of his emotions. I've experienced it all personally. I just didn't realise it'd be so hard to write about.

I'm a writer. It's what I do. Some people wonder how I can write MM romance when I'm a woman, but being in the head of a gay male comes a lot easier to me than being in the head of someone who suffers the way I suffer daily. And maybe that's because I am disconnected enough to write and not overthink when it comes to MM.

I learned a lot from writing Anders' story. A lot about how self-aware I am and how I could be doing a whole lot more to help my own situation.

Anders' struggle and thought process has so much of me in it, and I wanted to be true to the ugly "irrational" side of anxiety. He pissed me off while I was writing, so no doubt he made a lot of you angry as well.

But the reason it was so important for me to keep that is because so many times I've been told: "Why can't you just let go?" "You gotta just do it and get over it." "The only way to get over it is to face your fears." I've even had someone say I use my anxiety as an excuse to get out of going out. Because, sure, having a panic attack is so much more fun than hanging out with friends.

People who don't understand think it's easy to push through the paralysing fear.

This book will always be special to me because of the connection I share with Anders, and I only hope you appreciate him as much as I do.

XOXO

BOOKS BY EDEN FINLEY

FAKE BOYFRIEND SERIES
Fake Out (M/M)

Trick Play (M/M)

Deke (M/M)

Blindsided (M/M)

STEELE BROTHERS
Unwritten Law (M/M)

Unspoken Vow (M/M)

ROYAL OBLIGATION
Unprincely (M/M/F)

THE ONE NIGHT SERIES
One Night with Hemsworth (M/F)

One Night with Calvin (M/F)

One Night with Fate (M/F)

One Night with Rhodes (M/M)

One Night with Him (M/F)

ACKNOWLEDGMENTS

I want to thank all of my betas for your valuable feedback.
Thanks to Susie Selva for development edits.
Sandra from One Love Editing for the copy-edit.
To Lori Parks for one last read through to catch ninja typos—
they come out of nowhere.
And to AngstyG for the amazing cover.
A big thanks to Linda from Foreword PR & Marketing for
helping get this book out into the world.

And lastly, a special thank you to my very own therapist,
Renee, who, a lot like Karen in Anders' life, won't let me pull
the *woe is me* crap but can still have a laugh with me.
If I can't laugh at myself, I'm only gonna cry.